I0623985

Deadly Abandon
by
Kallie Lane
Shadow Soldiers Suspense
Book 1

DEADLY ABANDON: A Shadow Soldiers Suspense Novel
COPYRIGHT © 2012 by Kathryn Donaldson
Publishing History
First edition published 2012, The Wild Rose Press, Inc.
Second edition published 2018, Kathryn Donaldson
Third edition published 2021, Kathryn Donaldson
Digital ISBN 978-1-7779233-1-0
Print ISBN 978-1-7779233-0-3
Published in the United States of America
Thank you for your support of author's rights.

Dedication

This book is dedicated to the memory of two young men who left us too soon; David Donaldson and Sean Hill. You made the world a better place and will never be forgotten.

To my readers, with heartfelt thanks. Without you, I wouldn't exist as a writer.

To the men in my life who show me the way, my sons, Chris and Dave, for your endless support and positive input.

Special thanks go to those who keep me sane when I'm writing...

Very special thanks to Steve Roberts, Lieutenant Detective of Major Crimes Division Ret., SPVM (Service de Police de la Ville de Montréal). You kept me honest with this one, Steve, although I may have ventured into "improper police procedure" territory a time or two. You're not to blame; any mistakes are entirely my own.

Jennifer Martin, friend, hockey player, and hockey mom. (We hung out in the arenas like rink rats when our kids were young.) Thanks for your invaluable help with this one.

Coreene Callahan always made me laugh, even when my villains brought me down.

To J.J. Wilhelm for reading the final draft. Thank you for putting your amazing brain to work and discovering threads to my logic that don't always make sense to anyone else.

Chapter 1

Mallard Bay, Lac St-Louis

M He followed her on the lake from a distance. There was no point in getting too close. He'd done his homework, stalked her for months, and knew her most intimate secrets.

Her hopes and dreams.

The squall raging overhead jazzed the blood flowing through his veins. Lac St-Louis was a she-devil at the best of times, famous for her mood swings and hidden perils. Tonight, she was his ally—lots of *boom, boom* noise and no one else on the water for miles.

Lightning stroked the underbelly of thunderheads and backlit his quarry. The canoe battling the waves, her muscles pumped like pistons to outrace Mother Nature's onslaught. Sniffing the air, he imagined the faint scent of her shower gel drenched in sweaty fear. Inhaling deep, he savored the imagery, tasted it on the back of his tongue.

Keying the Whaler's ignition, he idled, waiting for the right moment to strike. Her head turned in his direction. Was it female intuition or something more primal...maybe the will to survive? Recognition widened her gaze.

"Yeah, baby. I'm here."

The hunt was on.

Gunning the engine, The Shepherd closed the distance between them within a few seconds. He clipped the canoe broadside with a shuddering crunch. She flew through the air and crash-landed in the water. Quickly reversing thrust, he settled alongside her in the backwash then stretched overboard, hooking a hand at her nape to keep her afloat.

His gaze roamed the shape of her in the skin-tight training gear. He envisioned her naked where his hands ached to cruise. Wild-eyed and bloody, she fought to break his grip. He laughed, grabbed her windpipe, and squeezed. Not too much, but just enough.

It wasn't long before she writhed from lack of oxygen. Her throaty rasps almost drove him to his knees. Disgust at his own body's weakness transferred to the woman, fueling him with white, hot rage.

"You're evil...like all the others."

Scooping her paddle from the waves, he wielded it one-handed above her head, swung it again and again, until she had no more voice. No more air. No more life.

Her dead eyes slid open and stared at him as if begging to know why. He released his grip on her neck, watched her sink like a rock, and shook his head in disbelief.

You know why, Miranda.

HOMICIDE LIEUTENANT Detective Sullivan Sauvage entered the red brick cottage in time to catch his lead detective's wince as he blew past him for the door.

What the—?

Something was off.

His gaze tracked Detective Clemente as far as the foyer before it wide-angled on the cottage's interior. Local Mallard Bay police trampled the crime scene like elephants at the Big Top, guaranteeing the evidence integrity lay somewhere between royally screwed and a major dung fest. With practiced control, Sully swallowed his distaste and resigned himself to salvaging whatever was left.

"Listen up! A woman has died here, and whether it was accidental or murder still needs to be determined. Let's show her some respect by letting the experts do their jobs."

He ripped a page from the notebook he carried and passed it to the closest uniform. "Unless you're an evidence tech, I want you to beat your boots out of here. Print your name and badge number on the sheet before you leave. The rest of you start processing the scene."

He watched the Mallard Bay uniforms head for the door as Clemente pushed his way back through it. He was easy to spot in the tan suit, cream shirt, rust-colored tie and brown wingtips. A six-five, loose-limbed clotheshorse, he hissed a breath freshener spray in the direction of his chalky lips.

"Sorry, Loot. My stomach's not as cast-iron as it used to be."

"Let me guess...you scarfed down hot dogs and fries for breakfast again?"

"Nope. Pizza and a chocolate shake on the way to the scene."

"A dumb-ass move when you're about to view a corpse, Sal. You're worse than a junkyard dog."

"Yeah, well, my refined taste buds crave junk food."

Sully shot him a glare. "The next time you hurl at one of my crime scenes, I'll ship you over to Vice. A willowy guy like you...they'll pour you into a dress, slap on a wig, paint on some make-up, and then use you on the streets for stake-outs."

"Shit, Loot. You wouldn't..."

A smirk tipped the corners of Sully's mouth before widening to a grin. "Don't tempt me, hot shot."

While the criminalists started their evidence sweep in the front rooms, he motioned his detective along the hallway leading to the back of the house. He couldn't help but notice the framed photo on a built-in shelf as he passed. Three bikini-clad women splashed in a hot tub. Champagne flutes raised, they grinned for the camera. He guessed one of them was the victim, Rainey Dubé.

What a damned shame. She'd been a woman in the prime of her life. He saw a lot of cases like this one, and he gritted his teeth every time he encountered such loss. Such tragedy. Such tremendous sorrow from victims' families.

As they moved through the house, he turned the dial down on his disgust and cranked the switch on his cop instincts to pick out all the little details.

They entered a white brick kitchen with black granite counters on the left and steel appliances to the right. A chrome table in an alcove was set for one, the remains of a meal congealed on a dinner plate. The woman had eaten alone.

French doors at the far end of the room opened onto a landscaped yard. Sully followed Clemente down the steps, along a flagstone path to where the body had been found. "Tell me what you've got."

Pulling a notepad from his jacket pocket, Sal flipped through the pages. "The pool guy called it in an hour ago, after he found the victim lying at the bottom of her hot tub."

Sully recognized the redwood tub from the photo in the hallway. A Japanese portico surrounded it, trellises thick with greenery and trailing flowers. Fairy lights bobbled from the ceiling. A tinkle of wind chimes stirred in the morning breeze. A woman's place with a woman's touch. It should have been a safe haven.

A ceramic frog croaked when they entered the portico, its *ribbit* sound a clear warning to anyone in the tub if someone approached.

He glanced at Clemente. "What was the pool man doing here?"

"A follow-up visit for routine maintenance. There was a faulty timer switch on the tub and the jets wouldn't kick on. The problem was diagnosed a week ago and the part special-ordered. It arrived early this morning so he came back to do the installation. His story checks out with the pool company."

Sully nodded then steadied his nerves before peering over the side of the tub. A noxious odor hovered. Small wonder Clemente had spewed his breakfast.

The woman lay naked at the bottom, her hair caught in the drain. Sightless eyes stared up at him as if pleading for his help. He returned the stare, noticing signs of petechial hemorrhaging in the whites of her eyes. He knew in his gut she'd either been strangled, or suffocated; just as he knew there was nothing he could do for her now, except catch the monster who had murdered her.

He recognized her from the photo in the hallway. She was the blond; the redhead and brunette had book-ended her in the snapshot.

Sully frowned. "The water is filthy, hasn't been shocked with chemicals for days. She wouldn't go in there without a fight."

"I know, and it all slides downhill from there," his detective grumbled. "The first responders were a couple of patrol yahoos who decided this was an accidental drowning. To make matters worse, they invited their buddies from the precinct over to view the scene and confirm their "accident" theory—never called it in downtown. We would never have known about it, except Sergeant Millette was in the area and had his scanner turned on. Your first day off in over a month and the shit hits the fan."

"Sounds like the MBPD didn't want Homicide taking the lead on their home turf." Sully rolled his shoulders to ease the kinks out of his neck. "The first bozos on the scene will be on bike patrol by the time I'm—" A barrage of snarls and barks erupted from the house. "What the hell?"

"Uh, I was just getting to that. It's the victim's dog. He passed out for a while but I guess he's back in fighting form again. We found him locked in the laundry room and had to leave him there. The mutt is insane, Loot." Clemente hauled out his weapon and checked the load, seemed nervous as hell. "We're waiting on Animal Control to come and put him down."

"No way. Call them off, Sal." Sully retraced his steps to the kitchen and the adjacent laundry room. Easing the door open, he moved inside. The small space contained a washer, dryer, and a shelf for cleaning supplies.

A massive Rottweiler crouched in a far corner. The dog rose on its haunches, crawling toward him with gums and jowls dripping blood...his own. Jagged slivers of wood jutted from his muzzle and between his teeth. With his front paws also impaled with splinters, the animal couldn't stand.

Judging by the gouges in the hardwood floor and at the base of the door, the dog had tried to break out of the room for several hours, if not days.

The Rottweiler snarled, struggling to close the distance between them. He could imagine how the animal felt being locked up without food or water and injuring himself. Not to mention the fact his human was dead. He crouched in what he hoped was a non-threatening stance. "It's okay, boy. We're here to help you."

Like that piece of news made a difference. The dog kept on coming, growling deep, its flews curled back to display a lethal set of choppers. Catching Sully off guard with a powerful lunge, the Rottie attacked. It clamped down on his left forearm and then released it with an ear-splitting howl.

"Son of a...!" Sully flew back against the doorframe while the dog retreated to the corner, clawing at its face and whining like a banshee. "Serves you right. I'm guessing you drove splinters through the roof of your mouth with that stunt. Snagged me with a couple of them too, along with your teeth. Hurts like a bitch."

"Out of my way, Loot." Clemente drew his weapon and inched in front of him. "I'll put the beast out of its misery pretty damn quick."

"Back off, Sal." Sully dug in his back pocket and pulled out a bandanna, wrapped and knotted it over his wound. The coppery tang of blood filled his senses. "I need him alive."

"Lieutenant—"

"I mean it. Besides, it's only a scratch."

"What? You have a death wish or something?" Clemente blew out a breath and shoved his gun back in its holster. "Fine, it's your call. Got any ideas on how we'll get the mutt to play nice with us?"

"Just one. The veterinarian's phone number is on his tags. I'll read it to you...if dog breath here lets me get close enough to see the number. You can make the call and get someone over here to tranquilize him so we can examine him for trace evidence."

Sully eyed the Rottie who eyed him back, liquid brown eyes sharp with intelligence. Would they go another round before he got a take on the vet's contact information? He advanced slowly.

"You got it, big guy, I'm heading your way. I need to see those dog tags of yours." The dog watched and waited, whining as if to say 'enough is enough.' "I feel the same way, so let's just get along. Deal?"

Sully reached him, praised him, and massaged his neck while he memorized the phone number.

BREEANA MCGILL CURSED herself for not changing out of her workout gear before racing to the address dispatch gave her answering service. Only emergency situations warranted a police call. It had to be bad. She could handle it better, keep her feelings in check, if she could hide behind professional detachment which wasn't going to happen in this outfit.

Luckily, she kept a medical bag stocked in the car. No, the situation had nothing to do with luck. More like a full-blown nightmare. She'd recognized the address—*Rainey's* address—the implications of why she'd been called to tranquilize Bruiser turning her blood to ice.

Her stomach dry-heaved. Sweat broke out and chilled her skin. She knew something horrible had happened without being told. Something she couldn't face again. Not now. Not ever.

Please, let it be a cruel joke. Not a repeat of Miranda.

Police cars lined the curb in front of the house. Breeana pulled into a bordering alley, grabbed her medical bag, hauled herself out of the SUV, and slipped through the side door of the garage with her key. Stopping in the mudroom to calm herself, she heard voices coming from the front of the house. The sounds of a vacuum scraping floors and bumping into walls filled her with dread. She focused on moving down the short hallway to the kitchen, blocking everything else out.

Don't think about what's happening here. Focus on what I can do. For Bruiser.

She rounded the corner and smacked into two-hundred-plus pounds of raw power. He was a tall man—maybe six three or four—wide-shouldered, narrow-hipped, easy on the eyes and impossible to ignore. His frame lean and hard, he wore thigh-gloving jeans and a T-shirt tattooed across a rock-solid chest.

A black bandanna wrapped around an arm. *Fashion statement or injury?* Before she had time to decide, he snaked a hand out to restrain her.

"Stand still," he said, when she struggled in his grasp. Voice deep, the rich baritone rumbled through the room with quiet authority. "Who are you? How did you get in here?"

His grip eased a fraction. She drew in a breath as the heat of his strong fingers loosened around her biceps. Then she shifted back a few paces to look him in the eye. He was a man used to being obeyed. Squaring her shoulders and gritting her teeth, she flipped him a *get real* glower. She also ordered her legs to stop shaking.

"I'm Dr. Breeana McGill, the veterinarian. I was called here for a police emergency, to treat an injured dog."

His gaze missed nothing as it raked her over, apparently trying to decide if she was legit. She knew how she must look in her frou-frou gym gear, wanted to sink through the floor, and disappear from view.

A birthday gift from her son, she hadn't had the heart not to wear it for her workouts, not after he'd tried so hard to pick out the outfit. So what if it was a little too girly-girl for her taste? Cody had made the effort, and she didn't appreciate the cop's reaction.

If it wasn't for Bruiser and the gnawing, sick feeling about Rainey in the pit of her stomach, she would slap the smirk off his face right now and run hell-bent for freedom.

"You're the vet? Really?" He cocked an eyebrow, pressing his lips together as if stifling a laugh. "Get some booties on your feet before you destroy more evidence."

"What? I don't care about you and your booties. I have a sick animal to deal with. Step aside."

A full-blown smile edged his lips as he grabbed a pair of blue shoe coverings from a box on the kitchen table and waited for her to slip them over her Nikes. Only then did he reach behind her and touch the handle on the laundry room door.

"Cookie, this I gotta see."

That stopped her in her tracks. Her eyes narrowed, and for a moment, she forgot the terror churning her insides about Rainey. "Cookie? Do I look like some fluffy confection to you, as in all sugar and spice with nothing between my ears?"

He leaned toward her, his minty breath closing the distance. "You really need to ask me that question? With the glitter stripes on your shorts and the matching, miniscule halter top you're wearing? Workout fashionistas have nothing on you, waltzing in here all sweated up and smelling like coconut-lime spritzer."

The corners of his mouth curved after giving her what could only be termed as a full body scan. "Now, let's be real clear about this. The dog isn't a Pekinese named Cutsie-Poo with silk ribbons in its hair. He's a bone-crushing brute in a great deal of pain. So, if you're not up to the task, tell me now. I'll call in someone else and you can be on your pop-star way."

Arrogant ass. She wanted to throttle him, but thought better of it. She needed to focus on what was important. On Bruiser. "I know the dog, and my qualifications have nothing to do with how I'm dressed. Quit wasting time."

She pushed by him into the room and stared, goose bumps erupting across her skin. Bruiser lay on his side and whimpered. His muzzle and front paws were swollen to twice their normal size, imbedded with jagged splinters and covered in congealed blood. Her heart sank. It was worse than she had imagined. All kinds of questions echoed in her mind.

Shoving those aside for the moment, she knelt to stroke the dog's massive head, soothing him with the sound of her familiar voice. "Easy, boy. I'm here."

She turned with some surprise when the cop cleared his throat just behind her. His hands poised in the air on either side of her hips, he looked ready to toss her out of harm's way the second there was any trouble.

Puh-leeze! Save me from macho men who think I'm the defenseless little woman.

"Pass me my medical kit. I'll sedate him so I can transport him to the clinic. There's a gurney in my SUV. I'll need it and some men to carry him out of the house."

He shook his head. "No way. The dog is evidence. You will tranquilize him so the criminalists can go over him here for trace. Then Animal Control will take him to their facility and you can leave."

First the booties and now this. The man liked to have his way. Well, not today, not on her watch.

"I don't think so." Breeana jutted her chin out and gave him *the look,* hoping he would retreat a few steps. He didn't. "Bruiser goes with me now. You can follow and take whatever evidence you need at my clinic. I only care about the welfare of the dog and he needs medical attention."

"Maybe you didn't hear me, Doc." The cop blew out a breath and ran his fingers through sable dark hair, the resulting disarray standing up in short spikes. "Let`s not butt heads over this. Understand, it's a homicide investigation. I won't risk losing evidence if you drag the dog out of here. The dog stays. The decision is out of your control."

Breeana ignored his words. Even so, a morbid chill prickled her nape. *Homicide...don't think about the word,* she told herself, *or you'll only fall apart. Focus on Bruiser. Do what needs to be done.*

She grabbed a syringe from her case and mechanically administered an anesthetic before Bruiser became more agitated, counting off the seconds until his tense muscles slowly relaxed beneath her touch. Once he slipped into unconsciousness on a noisy exhale, it was time to make her move. Taking a cleansing breath, she prepared to do battle with the cop barring the doorway.

"Perhaps I forgot to mention I have a Mallard Bay judge on speed dial? Yep, her aging Cocker Spaniel is one of my pampered pooches. Actually, I called her on my way over here this morning and got a court order in the works. Bruiser goes with me."

She snapped her medical bag closed with finality and rose to her feet. "I'll need the gurney now."

He stared down at her and said nothing. His whiskey-colored gaze was unreadable and more than a little frightening. Still, she would move heaven and earth to save Bruiser from neglect and abuse, even if it meant facing off against a cop.

"Oh, don't look so glum," she said. "Think of it as protective custody. I'm the most qualified person for the job and the judge agrees with me. I don't give a damn what you say about it because it's already a done deal. Call the judge if you don't believe me."

"I intend to. The Rottie doesn't move from the room until I make the call. I won't risk the chain of evidence because of your whim, cookie."

Bruiser was wrapped in a blanket, loaded in a police-issue Tahoe, and headed for the veterinary clinic five minutes after the phone call to Judge Wells. Super cop drove and Breeana followed along behind him in her SUV, an inch off his bumper. The look on his face when he rolled to a stop at the back door of the clinic said it all. He was pissed off.

Well, tough sheep-dip.

Rainey's cell phone had gone directly to voice mail when she'd called her again. Twice. Not an unusual occurrence, since Rainey hated her cell phone and rarely answered anyway. Still, what were the chances she was safe and unaware cops crawled through her house looking for clues to a crime? Not good.

Breeana shoved the phone in her purse and walked across the parking lot on shaky legs. The tubular steel handle chilled her palm as she swung the door open and entered the clinic. The cop followed behind her with the gurney rolling and then transferred the Rottweiler to the examination table when they reached her surgery.

"Cody?" She called to her son who was usually within hearing distance. "I need help in here."

"Be there in a sec." Clearing the doorway at a trot, Cody stopped dead in his tracks and gawked at the animal on the table. His fingers trailed a path along the dog's sleek shoulder. "Jeez! What happened to Bruiser?"

"I don't know yet, but I need you to assist me. It's still early and Laura won't be in for another hour."

Breeana's gaze cut from the clock on the wall to the police officer in the doorway while her son prepared a surgical tray with instruments, antiseptic, and gauze. Panic crawled up her spine. She shoved it back. Sticking her head in the sand obviously didn't work for her. She had to know the truth. "How did the dog get hurt?"

The rhythm of her heart outraced the ticking of the clock while she waited for the cop to answer. *Tick-tock, kathump, kathump.* He hesitated as if deciding how much to tell her. She held her breath, hoping he would answer, but dreading what he would say.

Folding his arms across his chest, he seemed to be choosing his next words. "He did this to himself while attempting to chew and claw his way through a door. My guess is he'd been locked up without food, or water, for a few days."

Breeana's heart sped up again. "Where is the dog's owner?"

"I'm sorry, that's classified information."

"Classified? Come on, man. The dog's owner is one of my clients."

He leaned back against the doorframe, his gaze searching her face. Oh, damn, she could tell by his cop-face mask of indifference—he was about to drop the mother lode of all bombs squarely in her lap. She dredged up her courage and swallowed the urge to flee whatever he said next.

Pulling his badge and identification from a jean pocket, he held them up to her face. "I'm Lieutenant Detective Sullivan Sauvage of the Montreal Homicide Division. This dog is a material witness in a pending investigation."

Rainey must be dead. Otherwise, he would have told her. Any residual hope she'd clung to since answering the police summons to treat Bruiser drained from Breeana's body in a rush.

The floor shifted beneath her feet and the blood nurturing her brain left for parts unknown. She sensed Sauvage trying to reach her before she hit the floor. Fighting dizziness and nausea, she grabbed the edge of the steel operating table, barely managing to stay upright and shove his arms aside.

"I'm all right."

"Sure you are. I've noticed." The lieutenant clenched his jaw, looking like he wanted to say a whole lot more. "Your skin is as green as swamp water scuz. Maybe you should sit down."

"It's nothing, just a touch of the flu."

Breeana rubbed her hands along her arms. She was unbearably cold and feared she would never be warm again. One quick glance told her the lieutenant still had his antennae twitching in her direction.

She turned her face away from his scrutiny, hunched over Bruiser, and started removing the splinters. Pretended her world hadn't just spun out of control.

Her son's voice threaded through the ringing in her ears. "You never said you had the flu. Is it the hurl variety or the blow-your-brains-out-sneezing kind?"

"Give me a break, Cody. I'm trying to concentrate."

It was all she could do to keep focused and not slide to the floor in a grief-stricken heap. She dug deep for endurance and tried to block everything out, except for Bruiser. She couldn't face the heartache of losing Rainey. Not now. Not with Cody in the room. Not when they both still grieved for Miranda.

Sauvage hovered in her peripheral vision. She felt trapped, didn't need to see him. His piney masculine scent was a dead giveaway. Why wouldn't he leave her alone? She jumped when his fingers brushed her shoulder.

"Doc? Why not take a breather and talk to me?"

"Look, I've got to get this done. I'm fine, really."

She inched out from under his big hand, uninterested in his concern. She wanted nothing to do with the man. After all, had the local police launched an investigation into Miranda's death? No.

Had anyone on the force believed her when she had insisted Miranda was murdered? No again.

The Mallard Bay Police had labeled Miranda's death an accidental drowning and closed the book on it. A senseless tragedy, they had said, and suggested Breeana take her murder theory to the nearest crime publisher and leave the real crime solving to them. Ha!

"Cody, take the lieutenant over to the sink and pour some antiseptic on his arm, then show him to the waiting room. He's bleeding on my patient."

The lieutenant shot her a steely look. "I'm not going anywhere."

Chapter 2

Sully glanced at his forearm after the boy removed the makeshift bandage, surprised to see a gaping wound oozing blood down to his wrist and between his fingers. The sight and coppery scent caused pain receptors to flare, like they'd only just realized he'd been bitten. He gritted his teeth, counted to ten under his breath, and focused on the vet.

Mistake number one.

Her sleek body clad in workout gear was one hell of a distraction. Against his will, his gaze traveled, taking her in, assessing how long it would take to get her out of all the spandex. *Shit.* The true problem? The doc piqued his interest for many reasons, most of which had nothing to do with his case.

Mistake number two.

He'd tried to adjust when he'd first seen her at the crime scene. Hell, he'd behaved like a jerk, playing the chauvinist card, attempting to screw his head on straight while she choked on the 'cookie' comment. It hadn't worked, not after she blindsided him with frightened eyes, swayed on her feet, and almost passed out from the shock once she realized her friend was dead.

Talk about a damsel in distress.

He scrubbed a hand over his face and risked another glance in her direction. She was still there. Still trembling. Still packaged in an athlete's body with a riot of auburn hair and the face of an angel.

He tried to switch gears, to categorize her as a person of interest in his murder investigation. He couldn't. Withholding information about her relationship with the murder victim didn't mean she was involved.

Hell, who am I kidding? Her duplicity was huge. Gigantic. The cop inside him reasserted itself and regained control.

He moved back against the doorframe after stepping away from the boy and snagging a fresh towel for his arm. His gaze zoomed in on her as closely as an entomologist would study a new species of insect under a microscope. He noticed how she shifted her bottle-green gaze everywhere in the room but in his direction. A guilty conscience, maybe? Or just plain unimpressed with him and his bad cop routine?

Edging to the table, he ignored her chilling stare, extracted several baggies from his forensic kit, and got to work. Over the next half hour, he immersed himself in the job, sealing bloodied splinters and bits of fluff combed from the animal's fur into individual bags. Labeling and setting them aside for the lab. Swabs of blood taken from Bruiser's muzzle, teeth and gums were added to the evidence. Sully hoped the lab would find the killer's blood in the mix. Bruiser may have had a chance to do some damage before being locked in the laundry room.

He intentionally crowded the vet, wanting to see how far she'd take her 'I don't know anything' stance. Brushing up against her, he moved to the Rottie's hindquarters. The clatter of steel on steel resonated as tweezers tumbled from her grip, clanged against the table, and broke the silence. So did her sharp intake of breath. The woman was a bundle of nerves.

"Cody, please call someone to drive the lieutenant to the hospital. Bruiser took quite a chunk out of his arm."

"I'm staying with my witness." End of discussion as far as he was concerned.

"Hey, I'll drive the lieutenant." The kid piped up from his perch in the doorway, ignoring him as if he hadn't spoken. Sully was pretty sure he wasn't invisible. He returned his focus to Bruiser's paws, intent on probing the pads and clipping the nails.

"Nice try, kiddo," his mother said. "You're only thirteen and don't have a driver's license."

"Aw, come on, Mom. Gramps taught me in the driveway in case of emergency."

"In your dreams, pal." Sully's brain grappled with the vision of the teen behind the wheel of a vehicle. *NASCAR here we come.* "If I ever catch wind of you out on the roads without a license, I will toss your scrawny butt in jail. Are we clear?"

"Sure, Lieutenant," the boy snickered. "It was just a thought."

"Hmm, driving without a license." The doc's brows shot up. "I hope this doesn't mean you've decided on a life of crime?"

The woman bantered with her son as if the topic of homicide had not reared its ugly head. She was obviously stalling for time. His gut said she had a story to tell.

What is she hiding? Come on, come on...tell me what you know. Don't make me drag it out of you.

"Yeah, right." Cody patted his mother on the head, smooched her cheek, and slid a hand along the sleeping dog's flank. "If there's nothing else I can do, I'll go finish up those cat cages. Since it's a school holiday, I'm meeting the guys at the deli for pizza."

"Mmm, pizza sounds good."

"Sweet, Mom. Can you spot me some cash?"

The doc pulled some bills from her lab coat pocket and handed them over. Sully almost laughed at the exchange. Breakfast was barely over and the boy had already lined up his lunch. Maybe his mother paid his meal ticket just to get him out of her hair. She was still washed-out and shocky looking. So much so, he was tempted to wrap a comforting arm around her.

Whoa, where had the protective urge come from? Coddling her wouldn't give him the answers he needed.

She grabbed a cell phone off the counter and tossed it to her son. "Don't forget your paper route today. Keep your cell on and stay in touch."

"You got it." As an afterthought, Cody added as he headed for the door, "Can we take Bruiser home until Rainey comes to get him? Where is she anyway?"

The brilliant flash of tears in the vet's eyes softened Sully's initial take on her more than he wanted to admit. "We'll talk about Rainey later, but Bruiser will come home with us tonight. It's only fair he stays with people he knows."

Her son gave a two-fingered salute and sailed out the door.

Sully moved to the doctor's side and tapped her on the shoulder. "All right, cookie. He's gone, so let's have it. Tell me what you know."

Her gaze jerked to his face, her voice thick with tension. "What do you want me to say?"

"I saw a photograph of you with the deceased at the crime scene. Nice glossy by the way. Sure looked like you girls were great friends."

Bingo. She froze like a fox cornered in the chicken coop.

"I recognized you the second you walked in the house this morning. Oh, don't look so surprised. Why didn't you just tell me you were her friend from the get go?"

She recoiled as if he had just delivered a physical blow. His instinct to calm her down nearly overpowered him. Damn, he couldn't afford the luxury, not if he wanted to get at the truth.

"First off, my name is not *cookie*—so get it straight. Secondly, I didn't say anything because I needed to pull myself together. Add that to the fact I was busy treating the Rottweiler and you get the picture."

Sully wanted to believe her, but he wasn't convinced. Grieving in silence only proved she had strength of character, not a helpful nature. Instinct said she wouldn't tell him anything she didn't want him to know.

How can I get her to open up to me?

He ran a hand along the dog's smooth coat. "It's a shame what happened to Bruiser. He's a beautiful animal. I hope he recovers from his injuries and from losing his mistress."

"He will," Breeana said, conviction strengthening her voice. "I'll make sure of it."

"I believe you will." His hand moved from the dog to circle her wrist, turning her toward him. Their gazes fused. "What about Rainey Dubé? Are you willing to help her, too?"

Sweat broke out across her brow, the only indication she had even heard what he said. She shrugged, lowered her eyes, and said nothing.

"Breeana, you may know something that could help find her killer."

"I can't talk about this now." Turning her back on him, she stifled a sob with her hand and pressed a switch which lowered the hydraulic examination table to the floor. Wheeling an oversized crate over to the surgical table, she locked its wheels in place.

"Can I give you a hand?"

"I don't need your help," she whispered.

She was right. She managed to crate the dog, and then busied herself inserting an IV drip to infuse what he assumed was saline solution and antibiotics.

And never glanced in his direction. Which was all well and good, except Sully had the nose of a bloodhound and a job to do. He wouldn't be ignored for long.

"Look, there is no way I'm leaving here until you talk to me."

She spun on him without warning, so fast she tripped over his feet and almost fell. His hands shot out to make the save and she ended up pressed hard against him. Close enough for him to see tears dampening her cheeks, and her mossy eyes widen with surprise. Close enough for him to want a taste of her full mouth.

She still smelled of coconut and lime, a light scent with a touch of spice that sucked the air right out of his lungs. He dropped his hands from her shoulders and took a quick step back. Apparently, he wasn't the only one affected by their close encounter. She seemed to fight for composure as well. It was another few seconds before she found her voice.

"I will talk to you, but I need a couple of hours to get organized here first. It knocked me for a loop when I realized Rainey was dead. I didn't know how to handle it, especially in front of Cody."

"Look, I get it, but we're alone now and your son's out of earshot. Just give me a few minutes, then I'm out of your hair. I'm already peeved at you for pulling the stunt with the judge to get custody of the dog. Talk to me now and we'll call it even."

Her hand flew out and poked him in the chest. "Can't you understand why I went to the judge? Rainey doesn't have any relatives and she would want *me* to care for Bruiser."

The redhead clearly had a temper to go along with her red-hot looks. Anger was good. It worked better for him than quivering lips and eyes overflowing with despair. The tip of a fingernail scored the skin beneath his shirt. He flinched, tugged on her wrist, and edged closer before she could jab him again.

Her curves fitted his length as if she belonged there. Her woman scent shot straight from his nose to his loins. He scowled inwardly, released his hold on her while wrestling with his body's unrealistic desire to mold her harder against him.

"Easy, or I'll arrest you for assaulting a police officer."

"Go ahead. I know a great lawyer, not to mention a judge."

Sully relented, softening his stance. "Let's forget about the dog. I am sorry for your loss, but it doesn't change a thing. If the murderer isn't caught soon, chances are it will never happen."

Breeana smoothed a lock of hair away from her cheek. "Of course I want to help with the investigation. Just give me a little time."

"Fair enough, but I'll be back." His words hung in the air for a moment, before he ended their conversation on a more negative note. "Just make sure you're ready to answer my questions when I get back. You don't want to get on my bad side."

Sully didn't anticipate her bull-headed insistence on having the last word.

"You can cut the bad cop routine, Lieutenant. I said I would talk to you. At this point, I'll do whatever it takes to get you out of my life. In case you haven't noticed, I don't like you."

He leaned forward until his mouth was an inch away from hers.

"Understood. You don't have to like me. But, cookie, you'd better get used to seeing me around. Because I will keep coming back until I uncover your deepest, darkest secrets."

IT WAS TIME TO GO HOME. The day had dragged endlessly after the lieutenant left. Breeana went through the motions of her daily routine operating on automatic pilot.

Her grief mounted faster than a lava build in Mount Vesuvius. She sensed it was only a matter of time before she blew like the volcano. She was heartsick and disillusioned, wanting nothing more than to get home and have a whopping good cry.

Her cell phone rang as she opened the door to her SUV and climbed inside. She dreaded answering the call in her present state of mind. Any more bad news today and the men in white coats would bundle her off to the funny farm. Still, the call might be an emergency; it could be Cody or her father. She glanced at caller ID but the display showed Unknown Caller.

"Hello?"

Silence greeted her from the other end of the line. She was about to disconnect when she heard breathing rumble against her ear. Was someone in trouble and unable to speak? "Who is this?"

A hymn started playing, softly at first, before building in volume to an ear-splitting crescendo. It belted out of her cell phone and grated her nerves. A crank call adding to the stress of a horrible day. She disconnected and turned her phone off.

Perfect, just what I needed.

Whoever had phoned her, it was a sick thing to do. He—of course it was a man, no woman in her right mind would make the call—had better not phone her again, or she would clean his clock. She waited a few minutes until her annoyance dissipated. Then she straightened behind the wheel, started the engine, and headed for home.

Home was east along Lakeshore Drive, a well-travelled route looping the north shore of Lac St-Louis. Sunlight dappled through trees as a breeze crested blue-green waves to life. Her mind derailed by the nuisance phone call, Breeana hardly noticed her surroundings, until her gaze cut to the canoeists heading in toward shore. They reminded her of another friend lost. Miranda had loved setting out on the lake, paddling hard, enjoying the peace and quiet around her.

The dam holding Breeana's emotions broke without warning.

As she sobbed, tears tracked down her cheeks. Swiping at her eyes, she tried to reel herself back in, but the waterworks just kept coming. She wasn't some prissy Hollywood diva. When she cried it was an all-out effort, with mascara smeared clear to her chin.

She pulled off the road and went through a box of tissues while making the necessary repairs to her face. Cody and her father would pitch a fit if they saw her right now. *Damn it, Bree, pull yourself together.*

Five minutes later, she was back behind the wheel and almost to her door. She veered onto the cedar-lined drive, pulled up in front of the garage, and killed the engine. Sliding out of the Pathfinder, Cody's Golden Retriever moseyed up to greet her. She patted Bear and used her trusty bottle of Visine to disguise the fact she'd been bawling her eyes out.

Turning her key in the lock, she pasted a smile on her face and followed the sounds and aromas coming from the kitchen. The men were cooking up a storm; the kitchen rated as a disaster area with dirtied pots and cluttered counters.

"Hey, something smells good."

"It's our own special recipe," her son answered, withdrawing his head from the oven. "You'd probably call it baked macaroni and cheese with sun-dried tomatoes, but Gramps and I call it baked barf."

"Right you are," her father chuckled. He paused at the sink to wipe a smudge of tomato from the bridge of his nose. "It has the same consistency."

"Dad! Cody doesn't need any help from you in the gross-out department. He does fine on his own."

Breeana hugged her father and planted a kiss on his handsome face. He was dressed casually in chinos, a Hawaiian print shirt and sport sandals. She noted Cody had used the sculpting gel on his grandfather's hair again. Sixty-three and a widower, her dad still turned his share of female heads. "You're supposed to set an example for your grandson, not encourage him."

Her father cocked an eyebrow and harrumphed, before winking at Cody over her head. Breeana ignored both of them, surveyed the messy scene of the kitchen, and frowned.

"We're missing a major food group here. I smell garlic bread and I see the macaroni but I do not see veggies. Come on you two, set the table in the sunroom while I toss a salad and open a bottle of Merlot."

"All right!" Cody's fist pumped the air.

"Nice try. You're drinking milk, kiddo."

Dinner discussion was murder, literally, once she announced in as calm a voice as she could that Rainey was dead.

Cody put down his fork and looked from her to his grandfather and back again. "Are you sure?"

"Yes, honey. Lieutenant Sauvage told me after you left the clinic today."

"God, that's crappy. We should keep Bruiser with us then. There's no one else to take care of him."

Thank God for the simplicity of a child's thought processes. Cody insulated himself against the tragedy, breaking down the details to focus on what he could control. Rainey's death, combined with Miranda's, was a terrible blow. The fact he'd lost his father a few years earlier only compounded the grief of this newest loss.

Her son took advantage of her silence to fill his grandfather in on the day's events, including meeting Lieutenant Sauvage. She tried hard to stay in the here and now. It wasn't easy. Miranda and Rainey consumed her thoughts.

While Cody cleared away the dishes and loaded the dishwasher, her father turned his attention on her. "You're not saying much, pumpkin. I can't begin to imagine how upset you must be."

"Rainey must have died horribly, Dad."

"I hear you." He leaned forward, placed his elbows on the table, and clasped her icy fingers in his warm palms. "I know she was a close friend. Are you going to be all right?"

"Of course, I am." She held back the tears and swallowed hard. "Even if I do want to crawl in bed, hide under the covers, and cry for a week. It's hard to lose both of them. We grew up together...I loved them."

"I know, pumpkin." Breeana focused on his thumb rubbing circles on her hand.

"Bree, you should talk to the homicide lieutenant about Miranda. It seems too much of a coincidence the women died within a month of each other. I'm telling you, I don't like it."

"I plan to tell him. I just hope he believes me and doesn't listen to those jerk detectives on the Mallard Bay force. I'm sure they'll have a few choice words to say about me."

"Horse hockey. Who cares what they say? This is your chance to have the case reopened and set the record straight."

"I do want Miranda to have justice, Dad."

"That's my girl." He kissed the top of her head and tossed his napkin to the table. "I'd better get going. You know where to find me if you need me."

Cody returned from the kitchen as her father pushed away from the table. "Leaving so soon, Gramps?"

"It's been fun, folks, but I have to get to work. Laura will tan my hide if I'm not there in time for the evening appointments."

Besides being her father, Jack Forest was also her partner at the veterinary clinic. It was a family affair. Splitting the work schedule allowed her adequate time for Cody's many activities, while her father used his spare time for playing golf and 'Old Timers' hockey.

"I'll stop by with Bruiser on my way home tonight."

BREEANA'S NERVES WERE wound tighter than a Slinky by the time Cody went to bed. Her father had dropped Bruiser off hours ago and left her alone with her snarly mood.

She paced the length of the living room, her mind honed razor-sharp by a sense of foreboding she couldn't ignore. Frustrated, she gave up the pacing before she wore a hole in the carpet and headed for the shower.

A half hour later, she pulled on boxers and a T-shirt and slumped in front of the wide-screen to watch *Ghost*, a favorite DVD. Two wine coolers later, she nodded off to dream about Patrick Swayze.

Except Swayze's face soon became the police lieutenant's, and the passion of those kisses escalated into a pornographic dream fest. Breeana stirred in her sleep, her body heating with the expertise of her phantom lover.

A chiming sound broke into her dream and almost shot her off the couch. She glanced at her watch—eleven o'clock. Shoving the mop of hair out of her face, Breeana rubbed her eyes as the chime vibrated again. The doorbell? Who would drop by at this ungodly hour? She stumbled to the door, Bear and Bruiser beside her launched into a vicious guard dogs' routine. *Poor Bruiser.* While he tried hard to look the part, his limping gait was a dead giveaway.

"Not quite ready for action yet, eh buddy?" She stroked his head.

Breeana glanced out the hall window and recognized the lieutenant's Tahoe parked in the circular drive out front. *Holy smokes!* The smooth muscled male with a flirty smirk on his lips leaned against the porch rail. She stood there half naked while he signaled her to open the door.

What should I do? A futile attempt to paste straying hair into some semblance of order had little effect. She resembled Sasquatch on a bad hair day. Added to that, her emotions were in an uproar, percolating about Miranda's and Rainey's senseless deaths. And the weird phone call with no one talking and nothing but church music hadn't helped matters.

Crap, the lieutenant will think I'm a nutcase if I don't pull myself together fast.

She inhaled a steadying breath, turned the handle, and swung the door wide.

SULLY WAS USED TO A certain degree of hostility from reluctant witnesses, but Breeana seemed unreasonably put out to find him on her doorstep. As he considered why, he knelt to give his attention to the killer beasts who seemed eager to lick the aftershave from his chin.

"Hey, pups, at least someone's glad to see me. Whoa, is this Bruiser? I can't believe he's doing so well."

"His wounds were superficial; it's amazing what a lot of love and a good meal can do. He'll be fine. Speaking of which, how is your arm?"

"Almost as good as new," he lied, eyeing the bandage taped from his wrist to his elbow and feeling the ache throb beneath it. "It just needed a few stitches and some antibiotics."

"I'm glad you had it looked at." She frowned, and he tried not to notice the adorable pucker between her brows. "Is it normal for you to barge in on people in the middle of the night?"

Her voice was more of a sultry exhale. She was entirely too sexy with those emerald eyes flashing and her hair looking as if it'd been tousled for a photo shoot. The swell of her breasts filled a red T-shirt. The striped red and white boxers—hugging the contours of her butt—reflected in the hall mirror; the effect certainly wasn't lost on him. He could feel his body heat escalate. *Damn.*

"I know it's late, but it's not the middle of the night. This won't take long and it is official business. You did agree to give me some time, Dr. McGill."

She sighed and stared up at him for a moment. "Please...call me Breeana. And come inside. How do you like your coffee?"

"Black would be great."

Breeana went through to the kitchen while he dropped into an oversized chair in her living room and propped his feet on an ottoman. Ah, yes, it worked for him, the first chance he'd had to get off his feet all day. The dogs settled alongside him with their tails thumping, or stump wagging in Bruiser's case.

A few minutes later, she returned with the coffee and a robe covering her from head to toe. It even had a hoodie. He figured his grandmother had one just like it for those cold winter nights up in Labrador.

Face it, Breeana could wear a tent and still be the most provocative woman to cross his path in a very long time. He had run a security check on her this afternoon and found out she was widowed. *Double damn.*

"I see you've made yourself comfortable." She passed him a mug and sank down across from him in a matching leather chair. "The dogs will be bringing you slippers next."

"No kidding? Do they have anything in a size thirteen?"

The beginnings of a smile curved her lips, a nice touch in comparison to her green-eyed stare. He imagined she'd put in one hell of a day after learning her friend was murdered. He wanted to cut her some slack, but it was time to get down to the business of catching a killer.

"You know why I'm here. I came to check on the dog and question you about Rainey Dubé. I'm sorry it's so late, but it has taken this long to process the crime scene."

As soon as the words left his lips, Sully wanted to bite his tongue. Tears gathered on the doctor's lashes and dripped into her coffee mug as soon as he mentioned the crime scene. *Hell, I'm a first class jerk.*

"I'll be right back."

She left the room, no doubt to dry her eyes somewhere else. He started to worry when she was still missing-in-action some five minutes later. He should have gone with her. "Hey, do you need some help?"

"No, I'm okay." She returned to the chair and almost staggered into it. "I had to do a few things."

Uh-huh. He could see she'd been crying. Her eyes were red-rimmed, the lids swollen. He guessed she hadn't wanted to fall apart in front of him.

"How could it happen? Rainey didn't have an enemy in the world. I can't imagine anyone wanting to kill her."

"Was she seeing someone new recently?" He reached for the notepad in his jacket pocket and opened it to a fresh page. "Or did she have a boyfriend in her past who had threatened her? Maybe she dated over the internet?"

Breeana shook her head. "She's been with the same guy for three years. He'll be devastated when he finds out. They planned to get married when he returns from Afghanistan. Tim Matthews is a pilot with the military. He has been stationed overseas for the past several months."

Sully knew it was easy enough to check. "What about her relationships at work? Is there anyone she didn't get along with?"

"She taught first grade, Lieutenant. I don't think any of her students are capable of murder." Breeana leaned forward in the chair and hugged her arms around her waist, rocking slightly. "How did she die?"

He gauged how much he should tell her. It wasn't his practice to discuss the facts of his cases with anyone. Yet, she appeared so fragile. He could well imagine what she was thinking and didn't want her envisioning the worst. If nothing else, perhaps he could lay her nightmares to rest.

"I don't have the forensics yet. However, it appears she drowned in her hot tub."

"That can't be right. Not another drowning..."

"Breeana? Stay with me." She swayed in her chair and slid toward the floor. Sully flew to his feet and caught her before she hit the ground. He lowered her head between her knees and took a quick glance around the living room. "Do you have any liquor in the house?"

"I...in the sunroom, but I don't need anything."

Jesus, he'd seen better color than she had right now on week-old corpses. "I'll be right back."

He found the bar and poured a generous shot of brandy. Returning to her side, he leaned her head back against his arm to press the rim of the glass to her lips. Her gaze struggled to remain focused. "Easy, I've got you. You'll feel better after you drink some of this."

She coughed as the liquid slid down her throat, her eyes tearing. It was another few minutes before her color returned and he was satisfied she wouldn't keel over in a dead faint. He released her, reluctantly, and settled on the ottoman in front of her. She had felt incredible in his arms, smelled like honeysuckle after a soft summer rain; the thought blindsided him. Her lower lip still trembled. Her mouth opened as if to speak, but no sound came out.

"Don't talk. Just breathe for a few minutes. I don't want you hyperventilating."

He continued to watch her until she regained a bit more color in her cheeks. Hell, would it be so bad to postpone his questions until tomorrow? Maybe she didn't have anything useful to tell him. Then again, there was only one way to find out. He gave her another few minutes to compose herself before he continued.

"What did you mean when you said 'not another drowning'?"

Breeana's limbs still shook, but her voice seemed steady enough when she answered. "Another friend of mine, Miranda Greene, died almost a month ago. She was canoeing on Lac St-Louis, practicing for an upcoming race."

"Miranda was a professional athlete?"

Breeana wrung her hands in her lap. "A social worker, not a professional athlete, but she was competitive in just about everything. She intended to win the Ultimate Paddler's Award at the Dragon Boat races coming up in July, so she practiced in the canoe alone. The police insisted she was out too far on the lake that night, in the shipping lane of the Seaway passing along the far shore. They claimed her canoe was hit by a tanker. Her death was classified as an accident."

Sully bit back a sigh. He knew what was coming next. "You don't believe their theory?"

"No, they've got it all wrong." She dug in her pocket for a tissue and dabbed her eyes.

"You don't think the Mallard Bay Police did a proper investigation." It was a statement, not a question. He already knew the MBPD had mishandled valuable evidence at Rainey Dubé's crime scene.

"Not thorough enough," Breeana insisted. "Or they wouldn't have drawn the wrong conclusions."

She blew out a breath, her throat working several times before she added, "I know Miranda never went near the shipping channel. She told me her coach had warned her about the danger. There was also a storm on the lake that night. She would have headed *for* shore when the storm hit, *not* in the opposite direction."

If what Breeana said was true, Sully figured the Mallard Bay Police had screwed up royally on Greene's case, as well as Dubé's. "Is there anything else you can tell me?"

"Yes." Her tears flowed freely now, and he nudged a box of tissues in her direction. He was powerless when it came to a woman's grief. "M-Miranda's father came to see me shortly after he identified her remains. He had to identify her by a tattoo on her shoulder because her face was almost unrecognizable, maybe from being in the water so long. But, he saw no indications of the damage a collision with a ship would have done.

"The accident report makes no sense. There is no way she died the way the police said she did. I argued her death wasn't an accident, over and over again. The last time I went to the station, they told me not to come back. They threatened me with harassment charges unless I backed off. But I know it in my heart—Miranda was murdered, like Rainey. I can't prove it and I can't let it go. Will you help me?"

Breeana had lost two friends in a month? Both to supposed water accidents? What was the law of averages against it? Sully didn't like the odds. "I'll check into it, I promise. Did Rainey and Miranda know each other?"

"Yes, of course. We grew up together and went through grade school and high school at the same time. We were best friends, Lieutenant. Actually, Miranda was the other woman in the photo you saw at Rainey's house."

"Sullivan...call me Sully." He didn't like coincidences, and he didn't like where this was going. The cell phone chirped on his belt. He grabbed for it, glanced at caller ID, excused himself, and moved out to the hallway to take the call. It was the medical examiner. "Marie, what do you have for me?"

"I found a fresh cigar butt smashed between the flagstones near the hot tub, Loot. I've already verified it didn't belong to anyone viewing the crime scene. I'm sending it now for DNA, but it could be months before I get results. And if the perpetrator isn't already in the system, we'll need someone to compare it with."

"Well, well. Nice work, Matisse."

"Hey, I'm the best, as you already know. I also did a vaginal swab. No semen present and there are no obvious signs of vaginal tearing or bruising. The victim doesn't appear to have been raped, based on cursory examination. I won't know for sure until I do the complete post mortem tomorrow."

Sully glanced over his shoulder to make sure Breeana wasn't within earshot. "I'm thinking the guy who killed her got off on admiring his handiwork."

"Ain't that the truth? Imagine standing around smoking a stogie at the scene of the crime. The creep must have brass balls, but it wouldn't be the first time some sicko got his rocks off by killing a woman."

"You see everything in our business, Marie. Listen, I need an exhumation on a woman named Miranda Greene. I don't think her father will fight us on this one. From what I understand, the Mallard Bay squad may have botched the investigation into her death."

Marie's shrill whistle shot through the phone. "I'll start the paperwork, Loot."

"Please. She and Rainey Dubé were tight, had been friends for years. Greene died a month ago, an accidental drowning on Lac St-Louis, according to the MBPD."

"What? Another floater? You think she was helped along?"

"Damn straight, but we won't know for sure until you exhume the body, do an autopsy yourself, and run the forensics. You know what to look for."

"Okay. I'll call in some favors and get the court order ASAP. One question...are you talking serial killer here?"

"Bite your tongue, Matisse. It's possible Greene died of natural causes."

"Oh, sure, and maybe pigs fly. I've never known your instincts to stray off course."

"Let's wait for the evidence. It will tell us where we need to go from here."

"I'll be sending up a silent prayer to God and all the angels. I hope you're wrong."

Sully disconnected the call and rejoined Breeana in the living room. She still looked vulnerable and shaken. For some stupid reason, he wanted to hold her in his arms and tell her everything would be all right.

Sure, like that would happen. First off, she was a potential witness in a murder investigation. And second? Sully freely admitted to being the king of commitment phoebes. His live-on-the-edge life and dedication to the job didn't allow any time for a serious love interest. He gathered the coffee mugs and headed for the kitchen, loading them in the dishwasher. Then he continued on to the front door, before he gave in to the sappy impulse of crushing Breeana against him. He must be going soft in the head.

"I'll let you get some rest."

She followed him to the entrance and placed a restraining hand on his arm. Electricity zapped him like a Taser. She dropped her hand in one hell of a hurry. Too late, his body had already responded to her touch. He was human, after all.

"Lieutenant, do you think Miranda's and Rainey's deaths are connected?"

He wanted to lie, but he had already started thinking along those same lines. She needed to be careful. "It's too soon to tell. Just be sure to lock up behind me and don't answer the door unless you know who's standing on the other side. And the name's Sully, remember?"

He slid a business card from his jacket pocket and placed it on the entryway table. "Call me anytime, day or night, if you feel anxious for any reason, or if you think of anything you forgot to tell me."

"Lieutenant...Sully...right, I will. Thank you."

Sully left her house with his groin cramping. He climbed into his unmarked and started the engine, disgusted with himself. After all, he'd gone into the vet's house with questions about a murder and come out with a probable second murder on his hands.

He had more than enough to keep him busy without getting hot and bothered. Sure, he enjoyed his fair share of women—okay, maybe more than his fair share—but without strings attached. And he never got involved with a witness. Damn sure if he nibbled on this one, he'd be hooked by the bait.

Chapter 3

Breeana went to bed late, chewing on Sully's questions about her friends. At three a.m., the phone rang, cutting into a restless sleep. Her heavy breather was on the other end of the line, the same hymn blaring in the background. *What's the matter with this idiot?*

"Listen, you creep. It's been a lot of years since I was afraid of a man playing with himself while he breathes in my ear. Shove off!"

The line went dead.

Morning broke early. The dogs saw to it, bouncing to greet each other and the new dawn. Sun barely flushed the horizon when Breeana crawled out of bed. Sleep had eluded her since the pain-in-the-butt phone call. She felt drugged from the lack of it. With a sigh, she pulled on her running gear. Time to shake it off.

Cranking out a steady pace, she took the dogs for a brisk walk down by the lake, keeping a close eye on Bruiser's ability to keep up. He seemed to be doing better today. Sunrise held the promise of a clear day, the air crisp and clean, a faint breeze dissolving fingers of mist above the water. She tried to find comfort in the beauty around her and not dwell on thoughts of murder. She was convinced the same maniac had killed both Miranda and Rainey.

There were no signs of life as she passed neighboring houses, only the symphony of birds taking flight and an occasional boat trolling out in the bay. A flock of ducks, late heading north, rested in the reeds. The dogs charged through marsh grasses to roust them, returning to the beach dripping mud and slime.

Breeana played fetch when she arrived back on her property. The dogs dove from the dock to catch sticks; silt and debris shaking loose from their coats as they swam.

Back inside, she put on a pot of coffee before heading for the shower. It was now or never. There would be no hot water once Cody took over. Not a morning person, his daily routine was to stagger to the bathroom and brace himself against the shower stall until the water pressure pelted him back to life. A thirty minute resuscitation, she could set her watch by him.

An hour later, Cody's summer hockey team practiced on the ice while Breeana nursed a coffee in the stands. It was hard for her to believe only a day had passed since the discovery of Rainey's body. Her world would never be the same. Yet, life held a false sense of normalcy, the busy routine of day-to-day living dulling the horror and pain.

Another disturbing anomaly was her attraction to Sullivan Sauvage. The man wasn't just a cop. More like steel-edged, sexy-as-sin with a dash of choir-boy compassion thrown in.

His mouth hinted of sensuous possibilities. His scruffy, bad-boy appearance screamed *GQ* cover. Breeana knew in the depths of her soul that he was a man women chased and thought they could tame. *Nuh-uh, not me, I'm nobody's fool.*

She hadn't wanted to be touched since her husband's death, yet this man threatened her resolve. Surviving these last two years on fading memories and the love of her child; those were the things giving her strength. Not her sense of abandonment and the physical needs buried deep within the recesses of her heart.

Sully was the embodiment of an alpha male who would take full advantage of a woman like her, if she let him. No. Tom was her mate for life, the only man to ever share her bed, or her body. He was the father of her child, a very pleasant and secure memory. She wanted her life to continue to be safe and uncomplicated, like it was right now.

"LIEUTENANT, YOU GOT a minute?"

Sully glanced up from reading the Dubé file to find Sergeant Jacques Millette loitering in his doorway. Millette's short, compact body and hesitant gait suggested weakness where there was none. The bald patch spotlighting his comb-over of stringy brown hair added to the misconception.

Early forties, the man was about as lethal as an RPG sailing through an open window. An ace detective, Millette had an arrest record Sully admired and a mind as sharp as a stiletto. He had also raised the red flag on Rainey Dubé's murder, while the MBPD had passed it off as an accidental drowning.

Sully closed the folder to focus instead on the man entering his office. "Come in, Sergeant. What have you got for me?"

"You might want to take a look at these." Millette crossed the room and dropped several thick files on his desk.

Pushing his coffee mug aside, Sully cleared some space on his blotter and reached for the folders. "What are they?"

"Cold cases for the Mallard Bay area, beginning thirteen years ago. I've found four deaths raising a lot of questions. They have marked similarities to both Rainey Dubé's murder and Miranda Greene's death, although I know we're still waiting for the findings on Greene.

"These are the dossiers of four other women who died under questionable circumstances, the findings on their deaths listed by the coroner as being inconclusive. Three appeared to have drowned and the fourth died in a fire of mysterious origin. While the fire is a different type of death, I included it because there still might be a connection to the other cases."

Sully thumbed through the folders and processed their contents. This old information supported his serial killer theory. If these deaths were murders, there could be a psychopath on the loose who had been killing for the past thirteen years, at least, and getting away with it.

"How did you find these, Millette? Some of these aren't just cold cases—they're cold as ice."

The other man shrugged. "I've had them for a while. I like to review old cases whenever I have a chance between my active files. It seems a shame these women died and nothing was ever done about it."

"Nice work." Sully flipped the last folder closed and handed them back. "I want you as the primary on Dubé's investigation. Word just came down the woman was strangled. Apparently being in the water delayed the bruising pattern around her neck.

"Hand off everything else you're working on to detectives Chartrand and Brown. You're taking the lead on this, and also on Greene's suspected homicide. But, I'll be working with you every step of the way and I expect to be kept fully informed."

Millette nodded while shuffling the files in his hands. "You got it, Lieutenant."

"Good, just as long as we understand each other. Sal Clemente is working full-time on the investigation as well, and he'll report to you. Pull the evidence on these cold cases and have it run through forensics again. God knows, evidence processing has improved over the last thirteen years. Maybe we'll get lucky, or at least be able to determine if these deaths were accidental, or not. Because if these cases are connected to Dubé and Greene, we're heading into the biggest shit storm the city has ever seen, and we're going to be smack-dab in the middle of it. I need answers and I want them yesterday."

"I'll get right on it. Is it too soon to call in a profiler?"

"Probably, until we have more information." Circling a pencil on his blotter, Sully thought about his sister and came to a snap decision. "I have someone in mind; I'll give her a quick heads up. I'll tell her what we have so far and see what she has to say, off the record. We might be way off base here. I want to be sure before we sound the alarm."

"Sure, Loot, whatever you say." Millette gathered up the files and exited the office.

Sully wasn't fooled. He knew Millette hated his guts. He had been overlooked for promotion when Sully came from the outside to head up Homicide due to his extensive military background. The grapevine also buzzed Millette was doubly pissed, because Sully still hung with the military in a reserve capacity. He cursed, switched mental gears and grabbed for the phone. Joelle. Would she even talk to him?

His sister had been a behavioral sciences profiler with the Royal Canadian Mounted Police for three years before turning her formidable talents to mystery writing. After the *incident*, as she liked to refer to it, the one that almost took her life.

Now, he worried she had another incident in the making, if the hate e-mail glimpsed by her assistant was anything to go by. But he would *not* have that particular conversation with his sister. Besides, his friend Hawke was keeping an eye on her.

Joelle answered his call on the third ring. "Hey, little sister, don't hang up. I need your help, big time."

"Just as long as you aren't trying to drag me back from Houston, Sully. I'm a big girl now. I don't need any of you macho males trying to run my life."

"Hey, not me, kid. Pop told me he has already tried and it was a no go." Sully leaned back in his chair, his voice lowering a notch. "Seriously, Joelle, I may have a serial killer working the area and I need your expertise."

The line was quiet for a second. "I'll give it a shot, but I'm a little rusty. It's been a long time since I've done profiling for a living. Tell me what you've got."

He brought her up to speed on the cold cases, as well as Rainey Dubé's murder and potentially, Miranda Greene's. There was silence again on the telephone line.

"Well, that's not much to go on. Do you have any communication from the creep? Notes left at the crime scenes? Phone messages or emails? Maybe some mementos left with the bodies?"

"Nothing has turned up so far. The fire has me stymied, too," Sully admitted. "Five of the deaths simulated drowning, if I include Dubé and Greene. I'm not even sure the fire death is connected."

"Motive is important here, not the killer's methods," his sister offered. "Serials need to satisfy their sadistic fantasies. And they will play out those fantasies to achieve some kind of sexual gratification. In the cases you've described, water and fire are both symbolic cleansing rituals. If you do have a serial operating in your area, and I think it's possible, I suspect he's justifying his kills by thinking of the women as unclean. It's his reason for preying on them."

"How does he choose his victims, Joelle? None of these women were prostitutes, or had criminal records."

"Why does a serial killer choose one woman over another? Why is *she* the one? Sully, those are questions profilers have asked for years. Sadly, it can amount to very simple things. For example, it could be the color of her hair, the clothes she wears, or maybe he just has easy access to her. He stalks her for days—sometimes months—before he attacks her, because it's all part of the thrill for him, part of his fantasy.

"He learns everything there is to know about her, goes inside her home, touches her belongings, and may fondle himself in her bed. He also plans several escape routes. And when he tires of hunting her, he moves in for the kill. He probably also keeps souvenirs of each victim to help him relive his sexual highs."

"Is there anything else you can tell me?"

"A geographic profiler will tell you he usually kills near where he lives. It's his comfort zone and he won't stray too far out of his territory, which should make him easier to find. By the way, if these killings started thirteen years ago, you're searching for a male in his mid-thirties to early forties now. I think he's Caucasian, the same as his victims. He is also probably quiet and very ordinary in his private life, because he won't bring unwanted attention to himself. This is why he's been so successful, because he blends in so well. And he is highly organized. Otherwise, he would have been caught years ago."

Sully heard her suck in her breath over the line. "Watch your back, bro. You get in the guy's way and he will come after you with both barrels. He may enjoy the sudden recognition of his talents, but he doesn't want to be stopped. He's been getting away with murder for a lot of years and now he's escalating, judging from the short timeframe between Dubé's and possibly Greene's murders."

"Yes," he acknowledged, "The unsolved cases seem to be spaced much farther apart. Unless he's committed other atrocities in between we don't even know about."

"It's possible. And if there is a serial killer operating in your area, he's worked undetected under the noses of the Mallard Bay police force for a lot of years."

"Yeah, which surprises me," Sully admitted. "You'd think someone would have clued in."

"Honestly, it doesn't surprise me at all," Joelle said. "Forensic techniques and DNA collection were still in their infancy when these killings began, not to mention police databases weren't around to share information. This killer's smart—smart enough to kill in the boonies where local police had jurisdiction. None of these cases were ever brought to Montreal Homicide, were they?"

"No. Most of them appeared to be accidents, at least on the surface."

"See what I mean?" Joelle's fingernails *tap, tap, tapped* on her headset through the line and caused him to wince. "He can't stop now, Sully, even if he knows you're on to him. And he won't want you hunting him down and depriving him of his fantasies. He places absolutely no value on human life."

In other words, he is one sick son of a bitch. "Thanks, kid. I appreciate the heads up."

"Yes, well, be careful. I don't want anything to happen to you."

"Same goes. By the way, I've been reading your books. You won't believe it, but I actually caught a guy who faked his own death by following the plot of your first novel."

His sister's voice rippled with laughter. "I never thought I'd see the day you would actually read my stuff, let alone learn anything from it. Then again, a lot of what I write is loosely based on actual case files I studied while with the RCMP."

"Oh, I'm learning a lot, kid. Maybe we can talk about it when you come home for a visit? I love you, and I'm just starting to figure out what makes you tick. Take care of you, little sister."

"You take care of you. Sully? I love you too."

"I know, kid. I know." He sighed as she hung up; praying to God she would stay safe and come back home so they could work on being a family again. They had a lot of catching up to do. Wounds needing to heal had festered far too long.

BREEANA WAS EXHAUSTED when she arrived home late that evening. As co-manager of her son's hockey team, she attended every hockey meeting. The meeting tonight had turned into a free-for-all, once the kids' parents started arguing about fundraising and the team budget. The get-together had droned on for hours.

A headache throbbed behind her eyes. She needed some aspirin. The truth was, she still hadn't heard from Sully and there wasn't anything on the radio about Rainey's death. Couldn't the blasted man keep her informed? Was it too much to ask?

She sighed, recognizing the unfairness of her complaints. He had a job to do, after all, and it didn't include reporting back to her about the case. If she was really honest with herself, she would admit she wanted to hear the sound of his voice, which was ridiculous.

Plugging in the kettle, she sank to a chair while waiting for the water to boil, willing all wayward thoughts of the lieutenant out of her mind. Tea and aspirin in hand, she eventually dragged herself upstairs and along the hallway.

Opening the door to Cody's room, she peered inside. Always the mother bear, she needed to see her cub tucked in his cave, even if the cub in question was fast becoming a man, already five inches taller than her and outweighing her by fifty-five pounds.

Bruiser and Bear lay sprawled on the opposite side of the queen-size bed where Cody snored softly. The dogs lifted their heads and eyed her through heavy-lidded gazes. It was pointless to demand they get off the bed. Boys will be boys and dogs will be dogs. It was easier to turn a blind eye and save her battles for the important stuff.

After showering, Breeana tumbled into her own bed. Lying in the dark, she listened to a June squall gusting across the lake and the rain pounding the dormer roof in a staccato rhythm. She loved the smell of rain, but not tonight. She rose and cranked the windows closed, locking them, an uneasiness gripping her as she gazed across the lawn and down to the black expanse of Lac St-Louis.

The normal sounds of the house settling took on an ominous feel. She was grateful for the distraction when her phone rang; however, she did breathe a sigh of relief to hear her answering service.

"Dr. McGill, I'm sorry to bother you so late but there's been an accident. We have a report of a dog hit out on Highway 20 in the storm. The police are requesting to transport to you for surgery."

Breeana slid open the wardrobe door and hauled out some clothes. "What's the status on the dog?"

"A probable broken leg and several lacerations."

"Tell them to come ahead. I'll be at the clinic in fifteen minutes." She disconnected, tossed the phone on the bed, and dressed in sweats and a rain jacket before scribbling a fast note to Cody to leave under a magnet on the fridge.

The storm battered her SUV as she drove. Lightning cracked, illuminating the road ahead as she white-knuckled the drive along Lakeshore in record time. She swerved into the parking lot and braked to a halt. No sign of the police transport vehicle yet.

Punching her code into the security system, Breeana rushed inside, switched on lights as she jogged down the corridor, and hurried to do the surgery set-up. The walk-in buzzer sounded as she retrieved surgical instruments from the autoclave. Seconds later, the lights went out, plunging the surgery into darkness.

"Hello? Is anyone there?"

No answer.

Her eyes cut to the angled blinds where streetlights still penetrated the slats. Her brain kicked into gear, her sixth sense sounding the *D-A-N-G-E-R* alarm. This was no ordinary power failure.

Someone had cut the electricity inside the clinic, someone out in the pitch-black reception area where the breaker box was located. And she'd bet her bottom dollar...he hadn't brought in a dog with a broken leg for treatment.

Breeana berated herself for being so careless, for not verifying the emergency before heading into the night and making herself a sitting target. She knew in her soul Rainey and Miranda had been murdered. Was their killer after her now?

Stupid, stupid, stupid! The frantic slamming of her heart rang in her ears. She prayed whoever was in the outer office wouldn't hear it.

How would she escape the maniac? The windows to the surgery were sealed shut due to the heat pump installation. The phone died in the power outage. She realized she forgot her cell phone at home.

She didn't dare make a break for the hallway leading to the back and front exits of the building. In other words, she was a sitting duck in the arcade of her own clinic. Adrenaline punched her system to a whole new level of survival.

Slipping into the small stockroom off the surgery, she snicked the door shut behind her. It was so dark she could hardly see her hands in front of her face. She fumbled on the shelves for anything she could use as a weapon. A disposable scalpel was her weapon of choice, but Laura had reorganized the shelves during a cleaning spree and everything had been moved.

Her fingers touched a box of wooden matches. Those could work. If the security system overrode to battery power as it was supposed to, the matches could be her ticket out of there. Inching her way up the stockroom ladder, she lit a match under the smoke sensor located in the ceiling. The match flashed for a second and died. Breeana cursed under her breath.

A draft nudged her spine as the stockroom door flew open and smacked against the outer wall. She choked back a scream, gripped the top of the ladder, and froze.

The shaft of a penlight danced across the small space before coming to rest on the ladder. On her. With fumbling hands, she struck more matches, held them like a flare beneath the sensor, and prayed for a miracle.

As if on cue, the haunting lyrics of a hymn filled the room. Breeana couldn't believe her ears. Her obscene caller had escalated from telephone intimidation to physically assaulting her within the space of a few days. His malevolent voice behind her, the beam from his penlight blinded her when she twisted on the ladder.

"Say your prayers, Breeana. You're about to meet your maker."

The matches scorched her fingers but she held fast. She could use them as a weapon to poke out his eyes. An instant later, a piercing squeal filled her ears as the smoke sensor responded above her head. Its deafening screech rebounded off the walls.

Her attacker roared, shoved the nearest shelving unit, and sent it flying. It crashed against the ladder and toppled her to the floor. Frantic, Breeana tore at the sharp edges of metal pinning her down, slicing her hands. The twisted pieces wouldn't give an inch. It was useless.

The slamming of the stockroom door barely registered until she smelled the acrid stench of smoke. *Crap!* The sprinklers weren't working. He must have turned off the water main outside the building. Wide-eyed, terror slammed through her as she watched flames lick upward from the base of the door, a pool of burning accelerant streaming toward her from the surgery beyond.

"Help! Help me!" She beat back the flames with a blanket that fell from the shelving unit. Choking on smoke, she fought dizziness, praying for the sounds of running feet, the clamor of voices, and the swoosh of fire extinguishers. The wail of the fire detector was the only sound she heard.

Help would never arrive in time.

Chapter 4

Sully was the first to reach Breeana, flashlight in hand and gun ready as he forced the supply room door. Air filtered in, clearing the smoke. His heart lurched when he saw her, pale-faced and gasping for breath on the floor, tears streaking her cheeks.

Hell, she could have died in there. It took every ounce of willpower for him to keep his voice even. "You're okay now. We'll have you out of there in a minute."

He holstered his gun. When she didn't respond right away, he started to panic. "Talk to me, Bree. Are you hurt?"

"I'm okay." She wheezed in a gasping breath and launched into a fit of coughing. One of the paramedics leaned through the toppled shelving and fit an oxygen mask over her nose and mouth. In another moment, her breathing seemed to ease, her chest rising and falling with a natural rhythm.

Sully's concern relaxed a little, but it didn't last long. He'd screwed up. He should have anticipated the attack on her. *Jesus.* With at least one of her friends murdered—maybe two—it stood to reason she'd be on the killer's hit list.

There was no way she had done this to herself. He'd seen the remains of accelerant-soaked towels shoved against the supply room door, her assailant's parting gift before escaping out the back of the building. His mind also registered the empty bottles of Isopropyl Alcohol tossed in a corner, confirming the prick had used her own antiseptic supplies to try and burn her alive. She'd been lucky, but it didn't make him feel any better. Curse words threatened to spill out of his mouth. He clamped his teeth together and swallowed hard. Swearing wouldn't catch the psychopath. Only a full-scale police investigation would hunt the bastard down.

As soon as the power was back on, firemen helped Sully drag the mangled shelving to the side. "Be careful," he cautioned. "I have criminalists on the way to take evidence."

Breeana fell into his arms as he scooped her up and carried her to the reception area. EMTs examined her there, closing the cuts on her hands with butterfly bandages. It was a miracle she wasn't burned or suffering from serious smoke inhalation.

Sully kept a hand on her shoulder to forge a connection. He doubted she would ever think of the clinic as a safe haven again. She glanced around the room while breathing in fresh, clean air. He could see terror reflected in her gaze. "How are you doing?"

"I feel like I've been hit by a semi," she rasped. "But all things considered, I'm okay. My throat hurts but the EMTs said they're satisfied I haven't inhaled dangerous levels of smoke. At least I don't have to go to the emergency room."

He steadied her when she stood, placing an arm around her waist. "Are you sure you didn't get burned anywhere?"

"The flames never reached me." Breeana took a faltering step then straightened, visibly pulling herself together. "How did you get here so fast?"

"Cody called me." He held her against him and brushed the hair back from her face. Another few minutes and she wouldn't have made it out alive. He didn't want to think about it.

"Good thing he found my business card and has a hell of a lot more sense than you do. He heard you drive off, saw the note on the fridge, and couldn't raise you on the cell phone. With Rainey Dubé and possibly Miranda Greene murdered, he had good cause to be alarmed. I put out an APB on your vehicle, and was on my way to your place, when the fire call came through on the scanner. I recognized the address."

"I'd better call him, Sully. I can't believe I was so stupid."

"We'll call from the car. I'm taking you home. This time you're going to stay there."

The storm had tapered off when he handed Breeana into his Tahoe and buckled her seatbelt.

A second later, a sedan swerved to the curb right in front of them. Breeana held a hand in front of her face to shield her eyes from the glare of headlights, and peered at the driver. "It's my dad."

"Okay. Stay put and let me talk to him for a minute." Breeana's father angled out from behind the steering wheel. Sully crossed the grass to meet him. He'd been in such a hurry to get inside earlier, he'd parked on the lawn. Forest noticed the badge clipped on his belt. "Are you the police lieutenant my grandson called?"

"Yes, sir. The name's Sullivan Sauvage. And before you ask, your daughter is fine. A few minor scrapes, but nothing serious to worry about."

"Thank God for that." Forest heaved a sigh of relief. "What the hell happened? I got a call from the security company that the clinic was on fire."

Sully eyed him for about a nanosecond before making a decision. There was no point trying to stonewall a man like Forest with empty platitudes and bullshit. He wouldn't buy it, even if it was gift wrapped. "Someone broke into the clinic tonight and attacked Breeana. He managed to set the fire before he escaped."

"Holy frickin' cannoli!"

"She's okay, Dr. Forest." Sully angled his chin at the SUV. "You can check for yourself."

Forest crossed to the Tahoe and sprang the passenger door in an instant. "Pumpkin? Did that nutbar hurt you?"

"No, I'm perfectly fine, Dad. Even the EMTs said I'm good to go."

Right. A person would have to be blind to believe that load of BS. Sully figured Jack Forest couldn't help but notice his daughter had seen better days. A slight breeze would knock her flat if she wasn't already sitting down. Her eyes were red-rimmed, her face sooty with streaks of grime.

"You look like hell and you're a terrible liar, my girl." Jack stared her down, crossed his arms and rocked on his heels. "But I am going to call your bluff. If you think you can manage, I'll stay here tonight, and catch a few winks in the office. The animals boarding with us will be upset by the smell of smoke and so much activity going on. It's really a blessing they were in another wing of the building."

"I know, and I'm glad you're keeping them company." Breeana shot her father a ghost of a smile. "And don't worry about us. Cody and I won't be alone. We'll have the dogs."

"Sure." Forest snorted, turned in his direction, and spoke in a low voice. "You'll stay with them, Lieutenant? I don't want any harm to come to my family. Who knows what the maniac will do next, and Bruiser isn't back in fighting form yet. The Rottie needs a few more days to fully recover."

"Don't worry, sir, I'm not leaving them alone."

Forest's clear-eyed gaze studied him for a time, taking in his measure. "I'm relying on you to be professional, Lieutenant, to do the right thing."

"I understand, sir." Oh man, did he ever. *In other words, keep your grubby paws off my daughter.*

Satisfied, Jack nodded. Turned back to the SUV, and leaned through the window to kiss Breeana. "You stay home and rest for a few days. And don't worry about the mess at the clinic. I'll have a crew make the necessary repairs in the morning. From now on, I'll handle any emergency calls coming in after hours. Goodnight all."

THE SHEPHERD SMILED to himself. It felt good to be alive. Thank God, Breeana McGill couldn't say the same. He'd nailed the bitch but good.

Taking a drag from his cigar, he watched the circus—the troop of police and firemen outside the veterinary clinic—satisfaction a living thing inside him.

He couldn't wait to see them wheel her out, black body bag strapped to a gurney. Too bad he couldn't attend the autopsy too. *That would be the pièce de résistance, and—oh, shit. What's this?* The coroner's van pulled out of the parking lot without a dead body.

It didn't take a crystal ball to figure out what had happened. While he'd slipped out the back way—whistling to the hymn on his iPhone—the cop and firemen must have charged through the front door and saved her. The smoke alarm's wail inside the clinic hadn't clued him in to their approach.

Man, I was lucky to get out of there undetected.

After making his escape, he'd almost freaked when he'd seen the rescue vehicles in front of the building, strewn across the lawn like tinker toys. They must have responded in record time, quick enough to pluck Breeana from the jaws of death.

He circled the block for the third time, shot the brown sedan into a parking space, and killed the engine. Cracking his knuckles to ease the tension, he cursed the adrenaline still pumping through his veins.

The night air stirred around him, the quiet almost absolute with most of the city tucked safely in their beds.

If they only knew.

The only noise came from the crime scene on the far corner, the hustle of firemen dragging hoses and setting equipment to rights.

The collective murmur of the crowd gathered on the street. He needed a closer look.

A small bottle lay on the console. He tapped its contents into his palms, masking the smoky scent still lingering on his skin with expensive sage cologne. Next he stripped off the coveralls, stuffed them in a garbage bag, and tossed them in the trunk. He'd burn those later.

A brief glance at his golf shirt, khaki trousers and spit-shined shoes confirmed he was good to go. Locking up, he set off down the street and noticed a uniform panning the crowd with a camera zoom lens. Thanks to *CSI* and other crime shows, even dumbass local cops filmed at arson investigations now. It seemed everyone knew firebugs returned to the scene.

I'm here. Come and get me.

Images of Breeana poured through his mind and taunted him. Her perfect face. Her tight body. Her slutty woman scent. Was she badly burned and disfigured now? She had better be, considering the trouble he'd gone to. He needed to see the damage for himself, but doubted she was still inside.

Wind whipped around a corner of the brownstone, bringing with it the smoky stench pouring from a broken window. The Shepherd inhaled deep, searching for the stink of burned flesh. It wasn't happening.

An hour later, the front door opened and a man came out carrying several garbage bags. Jack Forest, the devil who had spawned her. A local television reporter rushed up to catch a few sound bytes before he dropped the trash in a dumpster and moved back inside.

"Doctor Forest, is there any news on your daughter? How is she doing?"

Forest turned to the woman and smiled. "She's doing fine, Katy. She'll be back at work in a few days."

The Shepherd clenched his fists, moved out of the crowd, and headed for his car. *We'll see how fine she is after I'm finished with her.*

Angling into his ride, he cranked the engine. He had to move. Breeana was waiting.

CODY PACED THE RAIN-soaked driveway when they rolled to a stop in front of the house.

"Mom? Are you okay?"

"I'm fine, kiddo. The smoke got to me, that's all. I just need a hot shower."

"Yeah, and a bowl of my famous chili to perk you up. It's an old family recipe. Gramps and I made it for dinner when you were at the hockey meeting."

Much later, after they'd eaten the chili—well, Bree only nibbled a few bites—and after she'd shared the details of the clinic fire with Cody for the umpteenth time, her son headed back to bed. Sully could see Breeana was shaken more than she'd wanted anyone to know. Hell, she crumpled before his eyes. While she could hide her face behind the fan of her hair, she could not control the tremors racking her body.

Unable to help himself, he sank to the leather couch beside her and drew her into his arms. Regret hit him like a sidewinder. He shouldn't be doing this—holding her, comforting her, getting too damn close for his own good.

Her hair was damp from the shower and smelled of flowery shampoo. The intoxicating scent soon combined with the rustle of black silk pajamas skimming her curves and drove him wild. Whoa. He brushed his lips against her temple and his groin twitched up a notch. She must have felt it, yet she snuggled deeper into his shoulder as she sobbed her heart out.

Lord have mercy.

He broke into a cold sweat; the significance of Jack's parting words topped the 'Keep-Your-Hands-Off' list of reasons why he could not have sex with an assault victim. And as if it wasn't enough, there was also Breeana's son sleeping upstairs, the woman's total vulnerability, and the full-scale police investigation he conducted.

Maybe he should also add she wasn't a one-night stand. This woman came with a convoy of baggage; permanency in a relationship, and one lanky teenager being the obvious parts of the equation.

And didn't *that* put a man's brakes on in one hell of a hurry? Yeah, permanency was a totally foreign concept to him. Protecting the innocent and solving homicides took too much out of him. He had nothing left to give a woman.

"Cookie? You okay now?" He needed to separate their bodies by the length of a football field. Maybe two.

"I'm fine," she said with a muffled voice. Yet, she didn't pull away from him.

It was okay. No harm—no foul. None of it was a problem because he hadn't crossed the line. He was a sucker for a damsel in distress, that's all.

He could still protect her. And when she was out of danger, he had enough willpower to walk away. The important thing was to maintain his professional distance until then, to keep his edge and keep her alive. Otherwise, she could well be the next victim of a nutcase.

Joelle may have hit the nail on the head when she said the psycho would go insane if his plans were thwarted. His plan to kill Breeana had just failed, big time. Would the killer come after her again? He'd bet his last dollar on it.

"I never cry," Breeana snuffled into his shoulder, knuckling tears from her eyes. "So don't think I'm crying now, because I'm not. It's an allergic reaction to the smoke. That's all it is."

"Hey, I believe you." Sully rubbed her back in slow, lazy circles. Hell, most people would be mainlining tranquilizers after being baptized by the fire. Not this lady. Nope. Instead, she put on a brave face and stiffened her backbone. He could not help but admire her tenacity. Who would have thought the heart of a warrior beat in such a womanly chest?

"Okay, tell me one more time. Are you sure you didn't recognize your assailant?"

She tossed him a glare that spoke volumes. "Yes, I'm sure. I've already told you. It was so dark in the storeroom I could barely make out an outline of the guy. And even when he did use his flashlight, he was shining it *at* me."

"Well, you're going to tell me again. What about height?"

Breeana shifted to study his face, her breath hitching in her lungs. "I was standing on a ladder staring down at him, Sully. I have no idea about height, or anything else, for that matter. But he seemed really tall to me, larger than life."

"What about the voice, Bree? Think hard. Was there anything familiar about it?"

"An evil hiss," she whispered. "I don't know if I would recognize it again. I could barely hear over the music."

"Music? After the power was cut? What—"

Breeana touched a finger to his lips. "Sully, *please*, I have a terrible headache. Can we finish this in the morning?"

He focused on her trembling mouth. Impossible to resist, he leaned in close and slid his lips along hers. She tasted sweet, warm, and vulnerable. He regretted the impulse because he wanted more. Like a man starving at a banquet table, he wanted Breeana as the main course. Naked.

Back the hell off and get yourself under control, asshole. "We're done for tonight."

"Yes...done." Breeana seemed dazed by his kiss, not that he blamed her. It sure wasn't standard operating procedure for him. Her eyelids lowered to half-mast, probably more from confusion than exhaustion.

He fought the urge. He really did, but still managed to pull her against him and tuck her head under his chin. Then her fingers strayed on a journey of their own, along his shoulders to the longish hair at the back of his neck. He tugged her hands down, his lips again brushing the sweetness of her mouth, alarm bells bonging inside his head.

He almost lost it when her lips parted for him, his tongue slicking their velvety interior. *Enough.* He sighed with regret while forcing his mouth away from her open invitation.

What the hell? He never got this close to women in the line of duty.

Man-oh-man, the police ethics board will have a field day if I don't stomp on the brakes with both feet. I'll be FUBARed and fried. I can see the headline — 'Death by Professional Suicide.'

He set her slightly away from him, ran his hands through the russet curls at her shoulders, and frowned into the forest depths of her eyes. "Bree, I need to back off."

"I know," she sighed.

She leaned into his side again, her breath squeaking in her throat. He kissed the top of her head, smoothed a loose strand of hair behind an ear, and gave her a gentle nudge.

"A man can only take so much, cookie. Let's get some sleep before I change my mind and we do something we'll both regret in the morning."

Sully camped on the sofa after taking a long, very cold shower. The protectiveness he felt for Breeana was out of character. Lust he understood. But, the sappy need to coddle and touch her in non-sexual ways was new to him. Maybe he had a raging fever.

All he knew for sure was he burned from the inside out. He suspected he wanted a lot more from the woman than a romp in a king-size.

THE SHEPHERD CREPT along the stone retaining wall to get a closer look at the living room—Breeana and the cop on the couch. Touching and kissing.

He spat on the ground, his mind seething with anger and disgust. The woman was a slut, a lousy whore. She was all over the police lieutenant like fleas on a dog. Even a man of strength was powerless to stop her.

The Shepherd wanted inside the house to punish her.

Too bad it couldn't happen tonight, not with super cop on the job. He'd checked the man out, knew the lieutenant was military trained, Special Ops trained, and still on the active reserve list.

Hell, the man dodged bullets for fun. He liked playing with guns and other bang, bang toys. And, oh yeah, he mixed it up with his fists like Rocky on steroids.

I won't go up against him, not yet. Especially not with the Rottweiler staring out the window as if it knows I'm here. The dog wants me dead. Another time. Another place.

He watched Breeana and the cop climb the stairs with their arms wrapped around each other—probably headed to her bedroom to sweat up the sheets.

He lowered the binoculars, checking for passers-by before dropping from the retaining wall to the well-worn path below. Keeping to the shadows, he followed the shoreline to his car parked near the marina.

Rage ate holes in his gut. Burning was too good for her, the pain too quick. It came to him then, a message from the Lord, Himself.

He needed to step up the pace. He knew the kid's schedule, only had a few days to put his plan together.

Why not? He'd use her son to draw her out.

Too bad, so sad, Breeana. Satan's got you by the throat, but not for much longer.

Chapter 5

The alarm beeped. Breeana hit the snooze button, rolled over, and covered her head with a pillow. She hadn't slept well, wanted to stay in bed. Still, Cody had an exam today. Would he get up on his own and be ready to leave on time?

The sound of someone moving around downstairs sharpened her focus. Way too early for Cody's feet to hit the floor. And she remembered. Sully. *Crap.*

Did the fire at the clinic have something to do with her restless sleep? Sure. But holy, holy cow, her grieving widow's restraint slipped big time last night, singing *Hit Me With Your Best Shot* while she crawled all over Sully on the couch. She groaned. When had her need for comfort shifted to lusting after him? Thank God he'd pushed her away and slept on the couch.

The front door opened and closed. Breeana crept to the window and peeked out. Below in the driveway, Sully spoke with the uniforms in a police cruiser parked in front of the house. He glanced up at her window, saw her standing there, nodded as he unlocked his Tahoe, started the engine, and pulled out of the driveway.

Embarrassment flooded her system. *Congratulations, Bree. Not only does he think you're a sex starved idiot, but you're a freaking voyeur as well.*

An hour later, she was showered, dressed in apple-green yoga pants with an oversize tee, and headed back upstairs with coffee in hand. Fortified after two cups, she swept her unruly hair into a tail on top of her head and applied some lip gloss. Not a bad way to start the day, considering her experiences of the night before.

She grimaced into the vanity mirror and stuck her tongue out at her reflection as her wayward actions on the couch last night came flooding back. Good grief, she had practically jumped Sully's bones when he had comforted her.

Her cheeks flamed at the memory of her reckless behavior. For some reason, she was more than attracted to Sullivan Sauvage. He'd captured her attention. And no matter how hard she fought the pull, he drew her like metal to a magnet. The mysterious hold unsettled her, making her want to run in the opposite direction.

Life after her husband's death was still unchartered territory. Uncertain how to begin again, Breeana had buried her female desires right alongside Tom's body. She had barely managed to survive his death and go through the day-to-day motions of living without him.

It had taken months for her to pull back from the raw edge of despair. Another year before she could stand on her own two feet again. These were hard won victories, ones she couldn't throw away by having an affair with any man, not even Sully, tempting as he might be.

So, why did she feel like a lovelorn spinster in some historical novel? Because Sully made her feel. He made her want things she had not felt in a very long time. But, she refused to indulge and invite pain back into her life. No, her best friend was, and would stay, her vibrator—something impersonal and without emotional ties.

The doorbell rang.

Grabbing her mug, she took a sip of coffee and headed for the front entrance. Following Sully's orders, she looked through the side window.

There he was, the object of her sexy ruminations back on her doorstep, and he wasn't alone. Taking a breath, she flipped the deadbolt and opened the door.

"Morning." Sully inclined his head toward the woman and man standing beside him, both of them carrying bulky silver cases. "May we come in?"

"Yes, of course." She stood to the side, allowing them to enter.

"I'd like you to meet Denise and Pete from the crime lab. They'll be spending some time here today searching for possible evidence."

"Evidence? Evidence of what? I was attacked at the clinic, not here. You're at the wrong address, Lieutenant."

"Maybe, but I don't think so." Sully drew her aside and motioned to the staircase. The two criminalists hoisted their cases and headed for the second floor. "Start in the master bedroom. I'll join you there after I've had a chance to explain things to Dr. McGill."

As the techs reached the upstairs landing, Breeana allowed herself to be hustled through the sunroom and into the kitchen, all the while working up a full head of steam.

As ridiculous as it felt, she worried the crime scene techs would find the vibrator tucked away in one of her bureau drawers. Her *purple* vibrator—the deluxe model with extra batteries—a joke gift from Miranda and Rainey for her last birthday.

The thought sobered. *What is the matter with me?* Her friends were dead, someone had tried to kill her last night, and all she could think about was the looming discovery of a vibrator? How ridiculous was that on a scale of one to ten?

She tugged her arm out of Sully's grasp the instant the kitchen door swung closed behind them. He must have gone home to shower. Dressed in crisp black slacks, shirt and tie, this was not a good omen in her book. The only color relief was the oatmeal jacket he wore over a gun holstered at his waist. She could see the telltale bulge of it.

"How are you feeling today?" he asked.

"I'm okay, but that's not the issue here. Do you mind telling me what those people are doing in my home? And why are they in my bedroom? I want the truth and I want it now."

Sully met her urgent plea for information without a hint of emotion on his face. Instead, he straddled a kitchen chair and pointed to the coffeemaker; the passionate, compelling man who had comforted her in his arms last night had been erased. The man was all business.

"You really want to know, cookie? Then make us a fresh pot of coffee and I'll tell you. And I wouldn't say no to a muffin to go along with the coffee. I missed breakfast this morning."

At those callous words, Breeana glared at Sully as if he were something unpleasant clinging to the bottom of her shoe. But, staring at him only flooded her with memories of the night before, the feel of his strong arms wrapped around her, the knowledge of what she'd wanted to do in those arms. Thinking about the closeness they had shared only made the moment worse. She marched to the table and sank into the chair opposite his.

"If you want coffee and a muffin so badly, you can get them yourself. This isn't a restaurant and I'm not Rachael Ray."

"Sure, turn me loose on the coffeepot," he said, his voice soft and even. He unfolded his large frame from the chair and moved to the counter to grind coffee beans.

As he set up the coffee maker, Breeana dialed Cody on his cell phone to let him know there were sleuths looking for clues in her bedroom. *Clues to what, for heaven's sake?* She didn't know. But, in spite of her growing alarm, she couldn't help noticing Sully smelled delicious. Shower gel, underlying woodsy cologne, and his own virile scent taunted and teased.

His body was as big and powerful as she remembered. She wanted to throw herself on his mercy and beg him to make love to her right there on the floor. *Ridiculous.*

Breeana girl, face it, you need major professional help. One bad scare and you're ready to tumble at the man's feet.

Why, even Tom hadn't elicited this kind of response from her hormone-frenzied self. Her pheromones were so out of whack her senses were having a field day.

While he got his snack, she satisfied herself by drilling holes in his back with a glare that could melt polar ice. Oblivious, he grabbed a couple of homemade muffins from a container on the counter and placed them on a plate. Once the coffee was ready, he poured two cups and returned to the table, setting one in front of her.

"Here. You might want to add a little brandy to yours."

Brandy? At seven o'clock in the morning? Breeana almost snorted. The cop was certifiable if he thought alcohol would help. "Will you just get on with it? Tell me what's going on."

"Have it your way." His gaze held hers from across the table, his expression unreadable. Shivers ghosted along her spine, intuition warning her she wouldn't like what he had to say.

"Here's the thing. I believe the person who attacked you last night has already been inside your house. It's why I brought Denise and Pete with me to gather evidence."

"What? You think they'll find evidence in my *bedroom*?" Breeana jumped to her feet and toppled her chair in the process. She felt her face flush a bright crimson. "Have you lost your mind? What makes you think the guy has been inside my house? Do you honestly believe I have a parade of men sliding between my sheets on any given night? Of all the filthy-minded—"

"Calm down and let me explain."

He crossed his arms over his chest and quirked an eyebrow in her direction, waiting for her anger to run its course and for her to take a seat again. She righted the chair and dropped into it.

"I think the person who attacked you has been stalking you for a while. And, okay, I'm guessing he's been inside your home. It's part of his methodology, and he's done this before."

Her eyes searched his over the rim of her mug. She understood. "You're talking about Rainey and Miranda, aren't you?"

"I'm talking about Rainey, for a fact, and possibly Miranda. Her body is with the coroner now and we should have some answers later today."

"I think I'll have that brandy now."

Without another word, Breeana stalked to the bar in the sunroom, fighting to control her emotions every step of the way. She searched desperately for a calm she could not quite capture. Moving back to the table, she placed the bottle in front of her after splashing a generous portion of liquor into her coffee mug.

Sully leaned toward her. "I want you to tell me about the music you heard last night at the clinic. Where did it come from?"

"He played it on his phone. And I've been getting weird calls from him, too. He never says anything to me when I answer. He's more like a heavy breather...with weird taste in music."

"And it's the first time you've mentioned it?" Sully snarled. "In case you haven't noticed, someone tried to *kill* you last night. Did you ever stop to think this might be important information for the investigators to have?"

She was about to argue the point when Cody pushed through the door and shuffled past them on his quest for the fridge. He grabbed a bottle of orange juice from a shelf and tossed the drink back in three smooth gulps. Then he wiped his mouth on the arm of a ratty sleeve and eyed her curiously.

"Hey, Mom, if you don't want to lose the necklace you've got stashed in your underwear drawer, you might want to get upstairs fast."

"What necklace?" Sometimes this kid of hers operated on another astral plane. Breeana had no idea where he was coming from.

"It's the one with all the fancy bead work."

"I don't know what you're talking about, because I don't own anything like that."

"Huh, thought so. It's what I told Grissom and Willows up there. Then they became all secretive and stuffed the thing into a baggie when they thought I wasn't paying attention."

She was on the move before Cody finished his last sentence. Sully pounded the stairs behind her and slid to a halt close on her heels as they reached the bedroom door.

"Doc!"

She swiveled when he grabbed the waistband of her yoga pants to hold her back and noticed his gaze glued to her backside. "Are you staring at my butt?"

"I've been admiring your very fine assets every step of the way," he whispered out of earshot of the criminalists. "How do you think you beat me to the door in the first place?"

"Dirt bag," she murmured, trying not to smile. It felt nice to be admired, even though she didn't want to be. Unfurling his grasp from her waistband, she flicked his hand away and plowed through the bedroom door. "I want to see the necklace."

Denise glanced in Sully's direction. When he nodded, she reached inside her case and pulled out a sealed evidence bag. Taking it, Breeana examined the chain of pink beads sliding against the plastic wrap and her fingers.

"This isn't mine. I've never seen it before, but I know it's a rosary. I attended mass a few times with Miranda and Rainey at their church. But I'm not Catholic, so I've never had any reason to own one."

A muscle ticked in Sully's jaw as his gaze locked on hers. He was impossible to read, but she didn't need psychic abilities to sense his mushrooming concern.

The psycho had invaded her home and left her a strange parting gift. Why did he leave her a rosary when she wasn't Catholic? And why had he tried to roast her like a wienie on a spit last night?

The space between them closed as Sully came forward to grip her upper arms. "You've had company in your bedroom, Bree, whether you were aware of it or not."

"I swear...I don't know who could have done this. No one has been inside the house, except for Cody and my father."

"That you *know* of," he stressed in a tone that scared the stuffing right out of her.

Her eyes went wide as the ugly realization dawned. She could feel the blood drain from her head. Eclipsed by a nauseating wave of dizziness, she clutched the lapels of Sully's jacket to hold herself upright. "The music he plays when he calls me—it's always the same hymn—something about a shepherd. He played it again last night when he attacked me at the clinic."

Sully's glance cut to Denise and Pete for an instant before sliding back to her. "Did Rainey, or Miranda, ever mention receiving the same type of phone calls?"

"They never said anything."

He inhaled a quick breath and she could feel the muscles tense in his hands wrapping her arms. "After I leave here, I want you to stay in the house until I get back. And lock the doors. I'll keep the patrol car outside in the driveway. If you see, or hear anything unusual, you boot it to the door and get those officers inside with you. Do you understand what I'm saying?"

"I've got it." She was sickened by the implications of the rosary tucked in her drawer and the killer tracking her down on both her cell and home phones. He not only watched her; he had come into her house. "But, I'm not staying inside forever, Sully. I won't let the creep curb my actions or control my life."

"Bree, if this guy gets a hold of you, you won't have a life."

"I'VE GOT THE INFO ON the rosary," Sal mumbled to Sully between mouthfuls as he reached for another chocolate donut. Detective Clemente was a bottomless pit with a lanky frame to fill. The man never stopped eating, but he was a talented cop. Jacques Millette and Marie Matisse were also in the conference room to compare notes on the investigation. Sully poured coffee all around before taking his seat at the table.

He spared a glance at the puke-green walls and grimy windows before flipping open his laptop and powering up. At least the electronic equipment was up to scratch in the department, if not the decor.

"In a minute, Sal. Let's start with the autopsy results on Miranda Greene first."

Marie Matisse opened the file folder in front of her and gave them the specifics. "Cause of death was difficult to determine. But, not impossible. I can tell you this; Miranda wasn't on the lake by herself that night, not when someone wrapped their hands around her throat. The bruising pattern is significant, as well as the repeated strike marks on her face and shoulders. She was hit with a wooden object for sure. It could be a paddle because I found splinters in the wounds. The official cause of death is blunt force trauma, which nullifies the accident report of the Mallard Bay squad doing the initial investigation, Loot. No way was the lady hit by a tanker."

"Do we know where the canoe and other evidence are now?"

Jacques grunted at him in obvious disgust. "The canoe was never recovered. Everything else was destroyed when the accidental death ruling came down."

Sully shook his head. He couldn't help but wonder how many other crime scenes had been botched. How many other women had lost their lives to the madman with no one being the wiser? *Jesus Christ. It ends here.*

He and his squad were on the case now, and he would nail the bastard if it was the last thing he did. "Marie, do you have forensic results on the evidence from the cold cases yet?"

"No, it's still too soon. I'm hoping for some news by late afternoon. I'll call you."

"Good." Sully zeroed in on Clemente across the table while he updated his notes in the laptop. "Sal, what did you find on the rosary left at Dr. McGill's house?"

The detective dropped his donut and wiped his hands on a napkin before reaching for his notebook. "No prints, Loot, but I do have some information on the rosary itself. The sterling silver chain is twenty inches long with pink glass beads. The crucifix and Madonna medal centerpiece are also sterling silver. You can buy it on the internet for about forty dollars and small change from several suppliers." He paused to glance at Millette across the table. "Jacques, you want to take it from here?"

Millette leaned forward, excitement flaring his expression. "Here's where it starts to get interesting, Lieutenant. I called the suppliers Sal gave me and discovered there is only one manufacturer for the design. And Dr. McGill's rosary is an older version of what is currently being manufactured. Fifteen years older to be exact.

"The rosary was hand-crafted, the silver work on the chain distinctive, whereas the newer version is assembled by machine with no obvious tool marks. I have the suppliers pouring through old records now. Maybe we'll get lucky and get a name and address for a large sale in the area."

"Hold it." Sully stopped tapping the keys to focus on Millette. "You want to explain what you mean by a *large* sale, Jacques?"

"I went back to Rainey Dubé's house and guess what I found tucked in her underwear drawer?" Millette answered his own question without waiting for a response. "She had an identical rosary. Then I visited with Miranda Greene's family and asked to see her personal effects. She was in possession of a third matching rosary. Her mother had found it in Miranda's apartment, in her lingerie drawer. The family hadn't thought anything was unusual about it because Miranda was Roman Catholic."

"So, you're thinking the killer has left an identical rosary among the personal effects of every woman he's murdered?" Sully's mind sifted through the profile Joelle had created on the unsub, or unknown subject.

"The profiler I contacted believes our serial killer thinks of his victims as unclean. She also asked if he'd left any mementos with the bodies, which we now know he does. Added to that is Dr. McGill's mystery phone caller who has a proclivity for religious music." Sully cursed under his breath, leveled his dark gaze at everyone sitting around the conference table. "It seems we're hunting for a sexual deviant who uses religion as his excuse to commit murder."

They were hunting a serial killer. The three identical rosaries confirmed it, and the public had a right to protect themselves. Sully knew this wasn't the kind of case he could keep from the media. If he did, and the killer struck again, the mayor, the city, and the police force would be held jointly responsible.

After some discussion with his captain, a press conference was scheduled for early the next morning, when police mouthpieces would announce to the world there was a serial killer hunting in the Montreal area. Sully knew the scene would be wall-to-wall news vans and talking heads. The media would work themselves into a feeding-frenzy, especially if his team tied the current cases to the unsolved ones. The killer may have gotten away with murder for the past several years.

Sully dreaded the mammoth headache the announcement would cause his task force. Newshounds would be dogging their heels from here on out, not to mention the mass hysteria and inevitable false leads which would flourish from this kind of sensationalism. Every lead would need to be checked out and followed up.

Later that afternoon, Sully rubbed his forearm, where the healing stitches from the Rottweiler's bite tugged at the skin, and reached for a coffee to go along with a migraine-relief chaser. He had just hung up from a frustrating conference call with his team. Forensics had reviewed the evidence from the earlier cases but was unable to make a connection between the first three drowning victims and the current cases they pursued. The bodies would not be exhumed. They had been buried too long to offer significant scientific evidence.

They did, however, hit pay dirt on the four-year-old, cold arson case. The charred remains of a pink-beaded, silver rosary had been discovered among the ashes of the victim's home.

It had been photographed and bagged by investigators at the scene. Forensics confirmed it was a match to the rosaries recovered from Miranda Greene, Rainey Dubé, and Breeana. Given the charring, it was impossible to fully check for fingerprints but in the few areas available, there were none to be found.

Clemente and Millette were out pounding the pavement now; contacting the families of the unsolved drowning victims to see if those women had also possessed identical rosaries at the time of their deaths. It was a long shot, but worth a try.

Sully needed to talk to Breeana before all hell broke loose in the media. He wanted her safely under wraps and in protective custody until they caught the creep—no ifs, ands, or buts about it. Too bad if she didn't like it. He would set her straight if he had to. He was the one with the badge, and she would do what he said.

He pulled up in her driveway and talked to the officers stationed out front. "How's it going?"

"It's real quiet, Lieutenant, but if you want Dr. McGill and her son, they aren't here. The kid had his hockey gear with him when they drove away, so I guess they're at the arena."

"Why the hell didn't you go with them?"

"We offered, but the lady refused," the officer answered. "She told us to watch the house until she got back."

Sully ground his teeth. Breeana had taken off with Cody and not given a thought to the maniac stalking her. The woman was a serial killer's wet dream.

He hit the siren and laid rubber to the sport's complex. She was in the stands watching the on-ice action by the time he caught up with her. He settled in the seat next to hers and handed her a coffee.

"Bree, I'd like to drop-kick you from here to the arena floor. What are you doing here without a police escort? And what part of 'stay in the house until I get back' didn't you understand?"

She shrugged, avoiding his gaze as she opened the lid on the cardboard cup and took a hit. "What part of 'I won't let the maniac curb my actions' didn't *you* understand? My son's team has a tournament starting tomorrow in Laurelville, and he has to be here for practice. We *are* going to the tournament."

"Hell, woman, do you have some sort of chemical imbalance resulting in suicidal tendencies? Or are you just plain ornery? I *do not* want you going to the hockey tournament. What are my chances of changing your mind?"

"About the same as winning the lottery," she shot back.

She was insane, all right. Short of locking her up, he was going to have to take her to the blasted hockey tournament. He tried a change of tactics to wear her down.

"Just so you know...the coroner's office won't release Rainey Dubé's body until further notice, because her fiancé insists on having her cremated. It might be necessary to exhume the body later, and the ME doesn't want to take the chance on losing evidence."

"Boy, you're just full of good cheer, aren't you?" Tears glazed her eyes, and she blinked them away. "Rainey is dead and we can't even lay her to rest?"

"Afraid not. You'll just have to wait."

Not a nice way to put it, he knew, but Sully couldn't afford to let up on the pressure. Not when their kiss last night could be a prelude to something, well...something special, although he wasn't sure what. *If* Breeana got out of this alive. And that was a mighty big *if* when he factored in how many women had already died to satisfy the sick cravings of a lunatic. A bad, bad feeling slithered up the back of his neck and left him more than a little freaking upset.

Doc Stubborn wasn't taking the threats to her life seriously enough. "I'll do whatever it takes, cookie, so long as I don't have to bury you next."

She glared at him and muttered something indecipherable under her breath. He was pretty sure it was a curse.

"From now on, I will personally handle your babysitting detail, because you can't be trusted to stay out of harm's way. So get used to it. What I say goes. And, if I hear any more potty language coming out of your mouth, I'm going to wash it out with soap."

"Really?" The grimace playing her lips morphed into a smirk. Then Breeana stood and made for the arena doors, a volley of "*shit, shit, shit*" trailing along behind her.

THE EVENING SUN GLANCED off the water as the Tahoe hummed across the bridge and took the exit ramp with Sully behind the wheel. Breeana sat beside him with a curve playing her lips. She listened to her son talking hockey from the back seat. Sully reached over and squeezed her hand as he swung the vehicle into the parking lot of the arena. He had a smile on his face too. Maybe Cody's excitement was contagious.

The three of them together in the SUV felt like they were a real family. Breeana kicked the thought to the curb in a hurry, reminding herself of her widow's status. After all, she planned to stay single for the rest of her life. *Crap.*

Sully angled out of the Tahoe and popped the hatch. "Okay, hot-shot, grab your gear. You only have an hour before game time."

Cody dragged his hockey bag to the pavement. "That's good, Lieutenant. I'm going to hustle up the rest of my team and check out the competition."

"How about finding your coach first? He may have other ideas." Sully handed him his hockey sticks and closed the hatch. "Whatever happens—you have fun out there tonight."

Her son flipped his baseball cap backward on his head and headed for the arena, loaded down with his equipment and a grin from ear-to-ear.

Breeana was quiet as she entered the arena. Her mind seemed to run in ten different directions. Sully spanned her waist with his hands, standing behind her in the queue at the ticket counter. It felt good when he touched her in a casual way. *Too good...I could get used to this.*

He whispered in her ear. "I know the stalker situation weighs on you, but we can't disappoint Cody by being preoccupied."

She turned to gaze at him, her head leaning against his chest. She gasped as his mouth brushed hers before he placed her at arm's length.

"Sorry, I shouldn't have done that. I don't know what gets into me when you're around."

Heat flooded her cheeks. "I believe I'll take that as a compliment, as long as you don't make a habit of kissing all your assault victims."

"Hey, I always pass on the ones with bushy beards and hairy chests."

"Well, that's comforting. I wouldn't want you comparing me to a biker type."

"Bite your tongue, woman." He chuckled. "I have a feeling I wouldn't find one stray hair on that female chest of yours. Although, perhaps I should check, just to be sure."

"You could try," she laughed, "if you don't mind spending the rest of your life missing your exterior equipment. I should warn you I'm handy with a scalpel."

"Ouch. Why don't we call a truce and go out for dinner after the case is solved instead?" He reached into his jacket and pulled out a wallet. "I promise to leave your body parts untouched, at least until after we've eaten."

"Why, be still my beating heart. I don't think I've ever been on the receiving end of such a romantic invitation."

"Romance? Forget it." Sully's expression sobered. "Who has time for that stuff when we could be dead within the week?"

And what kind of drivel is he spouting?

They reached the front of the line at the ticket counter. Sully paid for the tickets and escorted her into the building. Breeana tugged on his sleeve and dragged him into the nearest corner to finish their conversation in private. "What the heck was that all about?"

Sully quirked a sheepish grin, put his hands in his pockets, and studied the toes of his shit-kicker boots. "Listen, I wasn't referring to you, or your present circumstances. You'll get through this safely. I'll make sure of it."

Breeana stared at him. "Just who were you referring to then?"

"I was talking about myself. I've been in some pretty tight spots," he said, sounding like the Oracle of Reason. "It doesn't pay for me to think long-term."

Talk about a defeatist attitude. Breeana had the urge to pop him in the jaw. Her brows furrowed as she continued to watch his face. "Really? I don't agree with you. You see, my husband was in the military and died overseas. Yet, we still managed to have many wonderful years together, not be mention a child."

"Listen, I know all about military life. I'm still a weekend warrior myself, all the more reason why I *don't* get involved in personal relationships. I'm sorry to hear how your husband died, but as far as I'm concerned, he wasn't thinking clearly when he married you. Maybe he should have stayed single if he planned to engage in combat situations."

That did it. The man was certifiable. "Are you quoting from a Spec Ops manual or something? Because that is the biggest pile of shit I've ever heard. I must have missed reading that chapter when I was a military wife."

Sully leveled his gaze on her and squeezed her shoulders. "Look, it's how I feel, okay? I won't risk loving a woman and leaving her to pick up the pieces if I don't make it home to her. I don't want her to feel the loss you've suffered, and I don't want her raising our kids on her own."

"You don't understand love at all, Sully, not if you think it should come with a guarantee of happily-ever-after." Breeana huffed out a breath. "I never asked, nor wanted, Tom to leave the military. He wouldn't have been the same man if he had. Is that so hard for you to understand?"

He dropped his hands and shoved them in his pockets, rocking on his heels. "I guess it is. I believe when you defend society against the dregs of humanity, you can't afford to have relationships. The risks are too great to your loved ones, the divorce rate too high. Tell me...loving Tom...was it worth the heartbreak of losing him?"

"Damn straight." She nodded. "I only have to look at my son to remember how lucky I was. How can you believe a woman isn't strong enough to carry on if something happens to the man she loves?

"The women I know have inner strength and bravery in spades. And *those* women don't do one night stands, Sully. Not for you. Not for anyone. They would rather risk it all for love. You know nothing about a woman's love, or her strength, because you've always settled for less. I know your type. With you, it's only about sex."

She turned and strode into the arena, head held high and without a backward glance.

Chapter 6

The teams hit the ice a half-hour later. The crowd cheered as the whistle blew and the puck dropped at center ice. Breeana ignored Sully, hadn't said one word after chewing him out for criticizing her marriage. He understood. He'd been way out of line.

They focused instead on the plays as the WARRIORS moved ahead for a 2-1 lead near the end of the second period. Just before the buzzer sounded, one of their players was hit from behind, resulting in a dislocated shoulder and possible concussion. The boy was taken out on a stretcher.

Their coach overreacted when a penalty wasn't called on the play and received a game suspension. After Ben Prewitt was removed from behind the bench, the other team seized the opportunity to even the score. The buzzer sounded to end the period, the gates opening for the Zamboni to clean the ice.

Prewitt shouted up to Sully in the stands, signaling for him to meet him below.

Sully touched Breeana's shoulder as he moved past her along the row of seats and headed down to the ice. She acted as if he wasn't there. "Stay here until I get back. I won't be long."

The coach paced the corridor like a lion in a cage, huffing and puffing when Sully clamped a hand on his shoulder. "What's going on?"

"Lieutenant, we don't have much time. I need you to coach the WARRIORS for the third period."

"What? You know I can't," Sully said, eyeing him. "Even if I had the qualifications, my name isn't listed in the books as a coach for the team."

Prewitt laughed and punched him in the arm. "I recognized you straight off, last night at practice. I watched you play for the Royal Military College. You were damn good, one of the best wingers I've ever seen. I heard some of the pro teams wanted you on their roster. Why'd you pass up a hockey career?"

"I wanted a military career and where it would take me more," Sully admitted. "I still play hockey when I can. There's an organization for street kids—"

"The WARRIORS need you right now, Lieutenant. Cody called me last night after practice, told me you'd be here today. I took the liberty of signing you up as alternate coach for the team. The organizers checked your stats and your qualifications aren't in question.

"You know, my temper gets the better of me at these tournaments, especially if one of my kids gets hurt. You're my ace in the hole. My defensive coach can't handle the forward lines, or make the power play decisions, but you can. Besides, I'll bet you've already sized up the team and know what the boys are capable of. Come on, what do you say?"

It didn't take much for Sully to convince himself he could still watch over Breeana while giving the team a helping hand behind the bench. Sitting with her wasn't doing either of them any good. They were worlds apart in every way that mattered.

He had hurt her. He could see it. He just didn't know how to change things. He was a homicide cop and still a military man with his reserve unit. Even if he wanted to be Breeana's lover, and he sure as hell did, she was right about one thing. It would only be for sex. There was no room in his life—or hers—for a romantic entanglement leading nowhere.

"Okay, man, you win. Where do I sign up?"

"Here's your tourney ID, Lieutenant. Now get out there and kick some butt." The coach shrugged out of his jacket and handed it to him along with an official pass. "Come down to the locker room and I'll introduce you to the kids before we're back on the ice."

Shaking his head, Sully opened the gate and slid on the ice toward the visitor's bench. "I'm not leaving the rink, Prewitt. I'll be here when the team comes out."

Scoping out the stands behind him, Sully assured himself Breeana was where he'd left her. No way he'd let her out of his sight. With the bleachers packed and standing room only at all the exits, she'd be safe as long as she stayed planted in that spot. His stress eased a fraction when her father pushed through the crowd and dropped into the seat Sully had vacated. Laura, their assistant at the clinic, grabbed a seat on the other side of Breeana. No worries.

SULLY DIDN'T RETURN to the stands when the teams hit the ice for the third period. Breeana guessed he was still angry and decided to guard her from a distance. That was fine by her. How dare he criticize her marriage, something he knew nothing about?

He was a machine without feelings, hollow inside, the perfect alpha male to take on criminals and protect the innocent. He just didn't give a damn about those he protected. She was a job to him, nothing more. Except, he wanted to sleep with her, that much she could see. But sex for the sake of pleasure versus commitment to a loving relationship was a bridge she couldn't easily cross.

Glancing in her son's direction, she was dumbfounded. Sully stood behind the WARRIORS' bench, watching her. She read his lips when he told her to stay put. By this time, her father and Laura had joined the crowd, no doubt breaking speed limits from Mallard Bay to make the last period of play. It was her dad who added some clarity to the situation, explaining Sully had played hockey during his days at the university.

"He and I talked a little about the military college and its hockey program the night of the fire, after you were in bed. He called me to make sure everything was okay at the clinic. Anyhow, I was wired, couldn't sleep a wink, and somehow we got to talking hockey. He asked me not to say anything. I guess he didn't want it to appear he was bragging, especially to Cody."

Breeana's heart did a happy dance inside her chest. Maybe she didn't really understand the kind of man Sully was. He might disguise it well, but he obviously had some feelings. He hadn't wanted to usurp her husband's place as the hero in her son's eyes.

That says a lot, doesn't it?

The score was still 2-2 with only a minute left in the final period when Sully called time-out.

"What's he doing, Dad?"

"He's shortening the bench," her father replied. "He's going for the win. In tournaments like this, it's important to get as many points as possible. A win is worth more points than a tie."

"I don't understand."

Her father whispered in her ear. "With one minute left, Sully's using the best players to get the winning goal."

The whistle blew. Cody won the face-off and broke for the net, streaking down the ice without his wingers. He wound up to take the shot, drawing his stick back. An opposing player hooked him from behind. Cody slid sideways, plowing head first into the net. The goal posts jumped their moorings and slammed into the boards. Cody sprawled on his stomach and didn't move. Breeana leapt from her seat, intent on reaching her son. Her father grabbed her jacket and held her, pulling her back down beside him.

"Sully's with him, Bree. Let's wait and see if he calls you down. You don't want to embarrass your son in front of his teammates."

"Dad..." Even knowing he was right, Breeana clenched and unclenched her hands, fidgeted in her seat until Sully got Cody up on his feet and skating toward the bench. The crowd went wild as the referee called a penalty shot on the play.

Breeana released the breath she held. *Thank God, Cody is okay.*

Sully reined Cody in and they talked for a minute before her son nodded. Then tapping his helmet, Sully sent him back out to center ice.

Her father nudged her shoulder. "See? What did I tell you? Cody's fine. He's taking the penalty shot himself."

Breeana sat frozen in the stands, wishing the game would just end. Her son must have one heck of a headache after sliding into the net. She wouldn't breathe easy until she checked him herself and made sure he was all right.

The whistle blew. Rounding center ice, Cody picked up the puck on the second pass and skated for the net. The goalie came to the top of the crease, cutting down the angle, meeting him head-on. Deking left instead of right, Cody backhanded the puck. The goalie went down and missed with his glove as Cody buried it, top corner.

"Yes, he's got it!" Laura leapt from her seat ringing a cowbell. The fans cheered. There was a lot of back slapping on the ice as the WARRIORS celebrated their victory. After shaking hands with the other team, the boys headed to the locker room.

Breeana got caught up in the crowd and streamed into the lobby with the others. Standing shoulder to shoulder with Laura, she stood on her tiptoes and scanned heads, looking for her father with their coffee orders. A man approached through the throng calling her name. He wore the yellow jacket of a tournament official.

"I'm Breeana McGill. Is something the matter?"

"Your son got back to the locker room and started vomiting, ma'am. His coach says there's no cause for alarm but the kid seems to be disoriented. We've called an ambulance. It'll be here in fifteen minutes."

Fifteen minutes?

"What's the locker room number?" Breeana demanded. "I need to see my son."

He angled his chin at the stairs behind her. "They're in number ten."

"Listen, I'm going there now. Have someone watch for the ambulance and escort the EMTs the second they arrive."

"I'll do it myself, ma'am. I'll go outside and wait."

"Thank you."

She tugged on Laura's arm as the tournament official pushed his way back through the crowd. "Tell Dad what's happened. I need to check on Cody."

Without waiting for an answer, Breeana shot down the nearest stairs, taking them two at a time. The downstairs hallway was dank, cold and dark. She guessed it must circle the perimeter of the ice surface, but it didn't give any view of the arena itself. She must have missed the signs pointing to the locker rooms.

She ran full out, anxious to reach Cody and help with his injuries until the EMTs arrived. Offshoots of the tunnel spread out around her like spokes in a wheel. She wasted precious time searching each of them to find the right locker room.

Bare bulbs shone sporadically along each darkened corridor. Many of them broken or burned out beneath rusted grills, casting the tunnels in an eerie glow. Muffled voices ricocheted off cinderblock walls, but she couldn't get a fix on where the voices originated.

Where is everyone? Shouldn't there be people milling in the corridors?

She continued through the maze of tunnels until she found locker room number ten in the last corridor she searched. She was breathless by the time she reached it, her chest heaving, a growing uneasiness penetrating her spine.

Why is the team's locker room so far away from the stairwell? And why isn't someone waiting in the corridor for the EMTs to arrive?

She burst through the door and got her answer. The room was empty. The steel door slammed shut at her back with a decisive clunk. A key turned in the lock. She was alone. She was a prisoner. *This can't be happening!* That murdering-psycho-madman was down here somewhere. It was the only thing that made any sense. She had raced into his trap like a steer to the slaughterhouse. She sucked in a deep breath and processed her last calming thought.

Cody wasn't injured. It was all a sham, a clever trap based on her love for her child.

She would die because she had fallen for the oldest trick in the book.

WHERE THE HELL DID she go?

Sully leapt the stairs three at a time and made for the lobby. Damn it, he'd told her to stay put. One minute she was there and the next she was gone, swallowed up by the throng heading for the door. He battled through the crowd as fans poured back down the stairs to grab seats for the next game. Laura and Jack rushed him when he reached the lobby.

Why isn't Breeana with them?

"Where's my daughter?" Jack snapped. "And how's Cody doing?"

"I haven't seen Bree. I thought she was with you. Cody's fine. What in blazes are you talking about, Jack?"

Sully's gut tightened as Laura and Jack filled him in on the ruse that sent Breeana into the maze of tunnels, the tunnels on the *far* side of the arena which were rarely used since the new wing was added a few years ago. He knew this because he played hockey here from time to time for charity events.

"When Laura showed me the staircase Breeana went down, I got concerned," Jack said. "I know the old building from coming to other games, and I figured she had gone the wrong way."

"Shit!" Sully reached for his weapon where he'd tucked it into the waistband at his back beneath his jacket. His blood iced with a deadly calm as he wrapped a hand around the familiar grip. "Find Cody and stay with him until I get back. Call 9-1-1. I need back up. Now."

"Wait! Where are you going?" Jack shouted.

"To get Breeana back."

Sully sprinted through the double doors back down to the rink. With no time to waste, he took the shortest route to the old locker rooms by cutting across the ice. Slipping and sliding his way between players doing warm-up drills before the next game, he took a puck to the ankle.

Hobbling and cursing, he kept on running toward the steel doors on the far side of the ice. Seeing the Glock in his hand, arena security chased after him. He waved them off with his badge and barked out an order to lock down the arena.

Frantic to reach Breeana, he plunged through the old entrance to the locker rooms, his pistol sweeping in a firing stance. She was down here somewhere with a killer. He couldn't afford to make any mistakes. He kicked himself for leaving her alone upstairs. He might as well have hung a sign around her neck, saying 'Take her, she's yours.'

Chapter 7

The sounds of scampering and squeaking reached Breeana along with their stench before she saw them pour out of the shower area. Sewer rats, too many to count. She guessed they hadn't eaten in a while.

Will they attack? One made a mad dash in her direction.

Yes, they would.

Breeana had never been afraid of rats, at least not the laboratory variety. But these rats were a new and terrifying species to her. Their oversized teeth seemed anxious to sink into fresh meat...a fresh kill...to sink into her. They caught her scent and the frenzied race to reach her was on.

Was this how it would end for her? Death at the hands of a madman, to be torn apart by rodents? No, not if she had anything to say about it. She vaulted onto the nearest bench and hauled herself up the cinderblock wall to the clothes hooks screwed near the ceiling. Clinging to those hooks with shaking hands, and ankles, she screamed at the top of her lungs.

Then she saw it, a pink, beaded rosary hanging by its silver chain from the hook nearest her head. The psycho had left her another calling card.

The rats below her were frenzied, whiskers twitching, beady eyes brightening with the knowledge dinner was only a hairsbreadth away. They stampeded over each other, leaping through the air and sliding back down the wall mere inches below her spine.

Soon they clambered up a pipe on the opposite wall and scurried along the overhead conduits slanted in her direction.

"Oh, dear God! Help me! Help me!" She screamed, imagining those gnashing teeth ripping at her flesh and dropping her to the ground.

SULLY THREW HIS WEIGHT against the door, again and again, listening to her agonizing screams and imagining the worst hell had to offer. The door wouldn't budge and shooting the old locking mechanism didn't release it. There had to be another way in. Then he remembered.

The bathrooms connected these old-style locker rooms. He should know. He'd had enough fights with the opposing teams in them as a teen. He raced to the next locker room and, *thank you Jesus.* The door was unlocked.

His mind registered the cages stacked in the shower stalls as he charged through the shower area and into the next room. It took him about a nanosecond to size up the situation. His stomach heaved. Rats, lots of them. *Fuck.*

"Get ready to jump!" His shots rang out and the rats started to fall. Breeana seemed paralyzed as the surviving rats fell upon the others, tearing flesh away from the bones of their fallen comrades that lay twitching on the floor.

He reached her in two strides, wrenched her into his arms, and raced for the door. He slammed it behind them with mere seconds to spare. The rats hurled themselves against the other side of the door.

"Holy hell, that was way too close." Sully pulled her against him and held her tight. He doubted he had the strength to move anytime soon. He buried his face in her hair and inhaled the flowery scent while running his hands over her body. He did not want to think about what could have happened. "Do you need a doctor? Did they hurt you?"

"No, no. They didn't bite me, but they almost scared me to death." Her eyes were dark pools of terror when she turned them toward him. "How did he do it? How did he know the room would be filled with rats?"

Sully wrapped an arm around her shoulders and started the long trek out of the tunnels. He tried his cell phone, but there was no signal. They were in a dead zone. "He planned this, Bree. He trapped the rats and brought them with him. I saw the crates he used in the shower stalls. These old tunnels and locker rooms are hardly used anymore. He must have found a way in from the outside. It had to take him a few days to bring in so many of them."

"He did it after he missed killing me at the clinic." Breeana grabbed hold of his hand as she shuddered. "There's a rosary hanging on one of the hooks in there. You'll need to get it. And someone should talk to the tournament official, the one who said Cody was hurt and in that locker room."

"Don't worry, we'll take care of it. But, Animal Control has to gas the rats before I'd risk letting anyone back in the room. Once that's done, the forensic team will go in to gather evidence. I'll get Millette out here to detain the jerk who lied to you, as soon as I raise him on my cell phone."

"Thank you for saving my life," she said, so trusting, it tore him apart inside. The look on her face finished him off.

"I'm nobody's hero, cookie. Don't thank me when I almost got you killed."

"You're selling yourself short, Sully." She got in front of him and stood on her tiptoes, wrapped her arms around his neck. "You shot the rats and carried me out of the room."

He let out a groan and pulled her closer, capturing her face in his hands. He slanted his mouth over hers and, taking his time, tasted what he had almost lost tonight. The cold reality shot through him. She was more than just a woman under his protection. She was the woman cracking the defenses around his obstinate heart.

"Listen, if I'd been with you, where I was supposed to be, it never would have happened. I give you my word, Bree...I won't let you down again."

But, even as he said the words, a nagging doubt wouldn't let go. How had the killer known she would be at the arena today? He must have known in advance to carry out such an elaborate scheme to kill her. Hell, the psycho had trucked in the rats to take her down.

Sully's insides quaked, his brain shifting to warrior mode. This was one hell of a diabolical killer.

BREEANA CHECKED HER appearance in the visor mirror, twisted her hair into a clip on top of her head and pinched her cheeks to draw some color back into her face. She still looked like "death warmed over" as her mother used to say. But it could have been so much worse. If Sully hadn't rescued her, she would have ended up as hamburger meat, with very little of her body left for anyone to identify.

From all outward appearances, she didn't look half bad, but terror still churned on the inside, making it hard to breathe. She needed to get home and pull herself together. The off ramp to Mallard Bay flew by the window at a hundred clicks per hour. "Hey! You missed the exit. Where are we going?"

"I thought we'd eat out tonight."

"What?" She was incredulous. Had the recent events not phased Sully one iota? "How can you think of your stomach at a time like this?"

"It's easy, Bree, with a beautiful woman at my side and a romantic city like Montreal at our disposal. Besides, you need time to calm down and we need to talk before we go back to the house. Jack and Cody are fine without us for a few hours. The uniforms outside the house will keep them safe."

Breeana folded her arms across her chest and silently counted to ten. "Sully, I don't want to talk about anything right now. I just want to go home."

"Why? So you can bury your head in the sand again? Not anymore, cookie."

"Oh, for heaven's sake. You're being silly."

He glanced over at her. She tried to gauge his expression but his mirrored shades tossed back her own reflection. Truth be told, she was more ticked off at herself than she was at him. Because he was right.

Despite her reluctance, he parked in the old quarter of the city. Then he plastered her to his side with an arm banding her waist as they strode the cobblestone streets to a popular café. Once inside, Sully pointed to a table in a far corner and tipped the maître d' to seat them there. They ordered drinks to start, followed by rack of lamb for both of them. They didn't speak until the waiter returned with their drink orders.

Sully held her hands in both of his, stroking her wrists with his thumbs until the shaking subsided in her fingers. She could see the raw concern in his eyes. "Are you all right?"

"Perhaps after two or three more of these strawberry daiquiris." Her attempt at a joke came out flat. Nothing could erase the horror of being locked inside the locker room with those rats. Worse than that, her fear of the man who wanted to kill her whipped through her body. If it wasn't for Sully, she *would* be dead. "I'm glad you're the designated driver."

"Hey, anytime." She watched him nurse his beer while scanning the other occupants of the restaurant over the rim of his glass. His gaze was cold and calculating as he assessed every face and every nuance of movement in the crowd. Tenseness gripped his shoulders as his gaze touched on hers then moved away again to land on another couple waiting to be seated. "I'd like to run something by you, if you're up to it."

He frightened her with his constant surveillance of the people around her, as if the maniac might have followed them there. "If it's not good news, I don't want to hear it."

"Too bad." His strong fingers brushed a stray lock of hair behind her ear. Then he cupped her chin in his hand and forced her to meet his gaze. "The attack on you at the arena was too damn close for comfort. So, now you're going to do things my way, because until the killer is caught, your life isn't worth spit."

"I don't think—"

"Just hear me out. I know you don't want to go into protective custody and I understand. You and Cody have a life, and you want to keep it as normal as possible. But, if you won't go into hiding, you need around-the-clock protection. I won't risk the freak getting near you again, Bree."

"I know you're right, but I don't want to frighten my son by changing our routine. Or give the psycho the satisfaction of seeing me running scared. Isn't there a chance he'll back off now and leave me alone?"

"Are you willing to bet your life on it? Or Cody's? My gut says he'll keep on coming until he gets it right." Sully took a small sip from his pilsner glass and laughed. It was a chilling sound, one without humor. "Wake up before it's too late. This isn't some fairytale where you get to write your own ending. You're the one who got away, remember? *Twice*. You're also the *only* one to spoil his fantasy for him. And you're the one he is determined to destroy. It's a matter of pride for him now."

Chills slid up her back and slithered back down again. "Are you expecting him to jump out of the woodwork and finish me off, for heaven's sake?"

"Oh, he can try. It's one of the reasons I'm handling your protection personally." He leaned on the table and threaded his fingers through hers across the round expanse of linen. "But that's only the professional reason. We both know there's something heating up between us. I care about you, Bree, more than I should. I can't be with you to protect you all the time, not if I'm going to oversee the investigation. So, I'm bringing in some people to keep you safe.

"And, after I catch the psycho? I'd like the chance to get to know you a whole lot better. I don't mean I only want to sleep with you. That's just part of the reason...and I'm willing to wait on that score."

Breeana thought about the sultry feelings he stirred inside her. She wondered if she dared risk having her heart broken by any man again, especially by this man who thrived in the danger zone. A man terrified of intimacy. A man she was attracted to.

Yes, I dare. Life is for the living, after all.

Tom had died over two years ago. She knew he wouldn't want her living in the isolated vacuum she had cocooned herself in. It was time to let go and move on. Removing her wedding band, she gazed at Sully and tucked it inside her purse. The twinkle in his dark eyes at her action warmed her insides.

"I'd like the chance to get to know you better, too. Now, who are these people you want to protect me?"

"They are members of my Special Ops squad. We're a reserve unit now and I can get some men together to help out. I trust them with my life, Bree, and I trust them to take care of you and Cody. They are trained to handle these situations far better than any police force. They won't let this guy get to you."

Breeana gasped, the reality of her situation finally sinking in. She tipped her chin. "So, what do we do now?"

Sully met her gaze and held it. "*We* do nothing. *I* call in my team to keep you safe."

Chapter 8

The Shepherd stood beneath a wide canopy of maple trees, gazing at the river where it churned over the rocks.

Beside him, the tournament official pulled out his wallet, added the bills he'd given him, and slipped it back inside his jacket. Uncapping a hip flask, the man chuckled before taking a deep swallow. Excitement flared when he recounted his part in capturing Breeana. "I only paid the kid ten bucks to hook her son and plow him headfirst into the net. And you shudda seen the broad. She went squirrelly when I said her boy was puking his guts out. She raced for those stairs like a house on f—"

The Shepherd had heard enough. The man would be bragging from a barstool first chance he got, so proud of what he'd done.

Palming the knife, he flicked it open on the upswing and brought it across. With one slash, steel met flesh. A clean slice opened at the official's throat, and he gagged, choking on his own blood. The Shepherd watched, enjoying the show as the man toppled forward in the river. He twitched in the shallows a moment before the undertow dragged him into deeper water.

With a hum, The Shepherd crouched, swished the blade in the river to clean off the blood, and dried it on the grass. Folding the KA-BAR, he slipped it into his cargo pants while scanning the area around him.

The lights of the town on the far shore lit the dark horizon. Nothing moved, only a breeze skimming the river. It filled his mouth with the taste of dead fish and raw sewage. He spat and swiped a hand across his lips. He'd chosen the right spot to do the sinner. The man was human waste at its finest.

The body floated farther out and finally caught the rapids. It bucked and rolled in white water and disappeared...about time. He needed to haul ass before someone spotted him. They'd find Breeana soon and all hell would break loose.

The crowd's roar melded with the music blasting through the arena doors some fifty meters behind him. *We Will Rock You* blared between hockey plays in short, staccato bursts.

He rocked tonight. *He* was the champ. He wanted inside the building so bad he got hard just thinking about it. But once Sauvage found Breeana's bloody body and sounded the alarm? The place would be locked down tighter than a prison yard and crawling with cops.

So yeah, as much as he wanted in there to see her corpse and his handiwork, he'd have to take a pass.

The parking lot was deserted with everyone still inside watching the on-ice action. Reaching the sedan, The Shepherd cranked the key and drove toward the bridge leading to the highway and Mallard Bay. He hummed his favorite hymn which poured through the speakers and thought about his work tonight.

Hoo-rah, two fist pumps in the air for two perfectly orchestrated killings. The first—God's will, and the other—well, it was God's will, too. Taking money to lure Breeana to her death was wrong, a mortal sin. The man had deserved killing.

God as his witness, The Shepherd thought he deserved a medal for what he'd done tonight, but knew he'd have to settle for a six-pack and a movie instead. A horror flick that guaranteed thrills and chills with Breeana in the starring role. Maybe not as satisfying as being live on the set to hear her screams and see the carnage first-hand, but he would deal.

He wondered if Sauvage was attacked by the rats when he sprang the door to the locker room. If the rats got by him, they would make their way to the spectator stands and cause a bloody stampede. A lot of God fearing people could get hurt if it happened. He hoped the cop was smart enough to contain the problem before it reached the innocent.

He glanced at the clock on the dash, his heart pounding. Another thirty minutes, and he'd be sprawled in front of the wide screen. He'd watch Breeana die tonight—in HD with sound surround. And he'd relive the moment over and over again.

It is God's will, Breeana...God's will.

SULLY SNAGGED BREEANA by the elbow and nudged her into an alcove at the bar's entrance as he answered his cell phone. "Talk to me."

"The Crime Scene Unit just left." Sergeant Millette waited out the sound system booming in the background before continuing. "They found cameras transmitting live video feed from the locker room."

"Son of a bitch." Sully's excitement spiked. He fought to keep his voice even, didn't want to get Breeana's hopes up. "Did they leave the cameras in place?"

"Better than that, they acted like they never saw them. Pinheads in the walls, nothing more. The signal's still active and our geek squad's tracking it now. There's an IP anonymizer on the link, but our guys say they can crack the code if the connection stays open for another minute or two. It shouldn't be long now."

The bastard may not know it yet, but once they traced the IP address they'd have his location—and his balls to the wall. Yeah, Sully loved the geek gods. They'd work their magic and get him what he needed.

He winked at Breeana and held up a finger to ward off her questions. "Millette, I want the address and a warrant ASAP. Drag a judge out of bed if you have to. And notify Tactical Response. We'll need them for the takedown. I don't want him slipping through our fingers."

"It's already in the works, Lieutenant. SWAT's standing by and our guys are heading in now. I sent Sanchez to sit on the judge. He'll have the warrant as soon as we have an address."

"Let me know the instant you hear. We move on my command. Nice work." He closed the connection.

"You want to tell me what's happening?" Breeana pushed out of the entryway and onto the sidewalk. A death grip on his hand, she tugged, pulling him behind her, closing the distance to the Tahoe. He hit the remote and lifted her onto the passenger seat. "Do you have a lead?"

Sully slid behind the steering wheel and fired up the engine, trying not to think about how good it had felt with his hands wrapped around her slim waist. "I'll fill you in later. Right now I need to get you home."

"No...no, you don't." She drew in a steadying breath as he pulled into traffic and lightly touched his arm. "Right now you need to be with your squad, Sully. You're waiting on an address and you don't have time to drop me anywhere. I'm going with you."

Sully's eyes narrowed as he mulled over his options.

Damn, she makes sense. Time was the enemy and he had none to spare. Still, he couldn't protect her on a takedown, wouldn't take the chance on something going wrong. "I'll radio a squad car and transfer you to them on route."

She crossed her arms over her chest. "Now wait just a—"

"I don't have time to argue with you, Bree." The stubborn woman didn't know when to quit. She'd been through hell tonight and acted like she wanted more of the same. Or maybe she felt safer with him. Hard to tell, but either way, he wasn't buying.

His cell phone buzzed and he punched speaker. Millette rattled off the address, a warehouse in Mallard Bay on the waterfront near the pier. Sully disconnected, hit the bar lights and siren, and booted it for the highway. Speed dialing the MBPD, he requested a unit meet him at the off ramp to transfer Breeana to them. They could take her home where she'd be safe and out of the line of fire.

"Sorry, Lieutenant, we've got an armed robbery in progress at an ATM machine. The dickheads dragged it out of a wall with a trailer hitch. We don't have any units available until we have them in custody, unless we send the unmarked parked at Dr. McGill's house. It's your call."

Breeana stiffened, her eyes blazing in the dim interior light. "You *promised* me Cody and my father would be kept safe. Don't you dare pull their protection."

Terrific. There was nothing like being caught between a gunfight and a red-headed, fire-breathing woman. He'd take the gunfight any day of the week; it upped his chances of survival. Sully gritted his teeth and growled, knowing full well Breeana wouldn't cooperate if he pulled the cops off her family's guard detail. "That's a negative. Keep the unit at Dr. McGill's residence."

"Roger that, Lieutenant."

There isn't any other choice. He'd leave her in Tactical's on-site command center while they raided the warehouse. But, he didn't like it. "Happy now? You get to hang out where the action is."

"Right, I really want to get close to the scumbag. I just thought you'd get there faster if you didn't have to drop me off." She stared straight ahead, hands shredding a tissue in her lap, anxiety tightening her features. "You think you'll catch him?"

Breeana had a way of touching his soul at the worst possible times. He should be thinking about what lay ahead, not trying to ease her fears. Reaching across the console, he squeezed her hand. "We have a good chance. It's our best shot."

Hitting the off ramp at breakneck speed, Sully cut the siren and navigated the streets to the warehouse district. He stopped half a block down when he spotted Tactical's armor-plated truck and the string of cars pulled in behind it.

Millette and Clemente approached when he angled out of the Tahoe. Sanchez, Lemieux and Bruno stood off to the side. "You have the warrant?"

Sanchez patted his vest. "We're good to go, Loot."

Sully nodded, rounded to the passenger door, and hauled Breeana to the asphalt. If his squad was surprised, no one said a word, not that it mattered to him. He kept her close, brought her round back of SWAT's office on wheels, and rapped hard. As soon as the door opened, he pushed her inside ahead of him and shut the door.

Quite the set up. Infrared images played across video screens, the outside of the warehouse lit up from every conceivable angle. Phones rang while two men dealt with the calls while tapping their keyboards like well-oiled machines.

SWAT's commander, Luc Renault, stood off to the side. A taciturn guy, he was late forties and built like a fireplug dressed in full body armor.

Luc held out his hand. Sully took it, and they shook, "It's good to see you again, Sauvage. I hear you want the lead on this one. That's against procedure, and I can't let you do it. Sorry, man, but SWAT goes in before your team."

"Yep, I know. By the way, how are Millie and the boys doing?" Sully touched Breeana's arm. "Luc and I served together in the military. We've known each other for a long, *long* time."

Luc hesitated when Sully turned the conversation to his family. Not surprising, since he knew where Renault's skeletons were buried.

"Everyone's great. Millie and I are coming up on our tenth anniversary soon."

"Well, be sure to tell her I said hello. By the way, did she ever find out about the time in Beirut when you got lost in the hotel, and...?"

Renault clamped his shoulder, held up a finger to silence him, and glanced at his men working the computers. "You wouldn't."

Sully leaned in and whispered in his ear. "It pains me to say this, but I would."

"You must want the son of a bitch real bad to risk putting me in shits-ville with Millie. You want the lead that much?"

"You have no idea." Sully waited a couple of beats, then grinned when Renault finally nodded agreement, his gaze flickering to Breeana who stood motionless inside the doorway. It was time to do what he did best, catch a monster. "This is Dr. McGill, the woman our perp is fixated on. I need her locked down here while we nail the guy."

Renault motioned to a swivel chair with a grandiose gesture and guided Breeana to it. "If I'm reading Lieutenant Detective Sauvage right, I should handcuff you to the workstation to ensure your safety. Or, you could give me your word you'll stay put. What'll it be?"

"I won't move. I promise." She tossed Sully a you-are-so-dead glare. He ignored her, switching mental gears to focus on the warehouse.

Renault nodded and turned back to him. "What's the plan?"

"I need the blueprints."

Sully leaned over Renault's shoulder as the other man brought up the schematics on a laptop. "As far as we know, it's open warehouse space with a small office at the back...right here." He pointed with an index finger. "The warehouse hasn't been used for a couple of years. There's a small window in the office and six bay doors across the front and back with loading docks."

Sully breathed easier. No basement and an open concept building meant less places for assholes to hide. Their serial killer may not work alone, although there was no evidence to prove otherwise. Still, better to plan for a party than get their butts kicked or get dead.

"I want my team to infiltrate and SWAT outside covering the exits."

"You got it." Renault grabbed a headset and tossed it to him. Sully checked the signal; it worked fine. He'd be tied into SWAT at all times. Another few seconds and they synchronized their watches.

"Give us three minutes to get in position."

"I'll kill the infrareds before you start moving. What I don't see can't get written in my report." Renault nodded toward Breeana. "I'll coordinate from here and keep eyes on Dr. McGill."

"Make sure you watch her." Sully spared Bree a glance. She stared at the monitors, looking shell-shocked and pale. He knew her husband had died on a military op. *Can she handle this?* "Breeana, don't sweat it. We'll get the creep."

Her chin came up and she glared his way. "Suck lemons, Sauvage. Just get back here in one piece."

Yep, she can handle it.

He exited, moved to the Tahoe, and popped the hatch. Taking a deep breath to focus his emotions, he strapped on his Kevlar vest and grabbed the assault rifle someone from SWAT handed him. After checking the load and pocketing extra ammo, he was good to go.

Renault confirmed through his headset—SWAT was in position and the infrared cameras were off. Sully's homicide team took off. It was pitch dark. Security floodlights must not be in the budget for the unrented space. His men trained their flashlights on the ground while making their way to the back of the warehouse. Logic said the computer was in the office. They needed immediate access to the room.

Clemente used bolt cutters on a garage door and snapped the lock. Lemieux shoved the door up the few feet they needed to roll under. It shrieked and rumbled on its track. Sully grimaced. Whoever was in there knew the posse had arrived.

The interior looked like a junk heap of scrapped trucks and heavy machinery, making for numerous places to hide. *Open concept, my ass.* He flinched when a rat scuttled across his foot. He hated the fuckers, especially after what had happened to Breeana earlier tonight. *Focus. Get your bearings.*

Clemente and Millette broke left to do a sweep. Sanchez and Lemieux went straight up the middle while he and Bruno veered right.

An eerie glow reflected off slatted blinds on the interior window of the office. He signaled Bruno to go wide, and they approached it from opposite sides. Sully edged close enough to the window to peer through the slats. The computer still recorded video feed from the arena locker room. He scanned the shadows around it looking for their perp. Empty, no one hiding in dark corners. His gaze swung back to the monitor, touching on something almost hidden by the computer tower—a bundle of explosives with a cell phone attached.

"Everybody out! The building's rigged! Fall back! Fall back!"

Renault repeated the order through the headset while Sully and his team scrambled for the door. They rolled through and gained their feet, picked up speed, and raced for the field behind the warehouse.

Jesus. No ground cover.

Millette took the lead like a marathon runner on speed. He raised a hand in the air, shouting something about a drainage ditch. Everyone else followed, their legs pumping and minds hell-bent on survival. Sully guarded their six, did full visual sweeps for anyone with a rifle. Or, God forbid, the flash of a muzzle. His squad was easy pickings if the freak got the urge to bag a few cops.

Once his men blew into the ditch, Sully stopped searching for snipers. He cranked up his own gears and burned rubber, his thighs churning like pistons. One Mississippi, two Mississippi...still twenty meters out. Ten meters...five, just five more, *thank you God!* As he dove for the drain pipe, the world exploded.

RENAULT PINNED BREEANA'S shoulder before she could leave the chair. "Sit back down or I swear I'll cuff you."

"Are you crazy? Did you see the explosion? I have medical training. There are people out there who need help!" *Where is Sully? I need to do something. He could be hurt or dying.*

"Hold up. The only thing out there you need to worry about is the freaking maniac who is trying to kill you." Renault placed his hands on the arms of her chair and leaned in close. "He's willing to mess with cops to do it, lady. So let Sauvage do his job. Wait until we get a headcount and stick to the chair like you're glued into it. Got it?"

She nodded. Renault turned back to the other men inside the control center. They spoke through headsets to their team. Everyone was accounted for in their squad, no serious casualties. But they couldn't raise Sully with repeated tries. The minutes ticked by, Breeana's fear edging toward full blown panic. She scanned the monitors searching for his familiar face. Nothing. Smoke billowed and flames leapt skyward.

Three fire trucks arrived, followed by rescue vehicles and several patrol cars, the scene a nightmare of confusion. Firemen pumped water from the nearby shore of Lac St. Louis through hoses and trained them on the blaze. She could see Renault's men, pushing close to the flaming building with the firemen, looking for...

She couldn't sit there feeling helpless another minute. She lunged for the door. Her hands banged the release bar and her feet hit the ground before Renault could stop her.

She ran toward the blaze. *Oh God, oh God, oh God. Please, don't let Sully be dead!* People shouted to each other; no one noticed when she slipped by them. The grass burned around her feet while smoldering timbers ignited more flames. Sounds distorted, smoke tore at her lungs, the heat of the fire almost pushing her back.

She kept on, stumbling, had to find Sully. She tripped, would have fallen but someone caught her. Tears flooded her eyes, and she couldn't see a damn thing.

"Breeana? Jesus H. Christ! What are you doing out here?" *Sully. His voice.*

His strength wrapped around her like a protective shield. He lifted her in his arms and turned his back on the blaze. By the time they reached the command post, he swore a blue streak. She didn't care. He could swear at her all night and she'd take it. He was alive.

Again, he banged on the back door and again, Renault opened it for them. "Where the hell have you been? You're a sight for sore eyes, man. What's the status on your squad?"

"They're all accounted for. No casualties, although we'll all be a little deaf for a while." He plunked Breeana back in the swivel chair, checking her for injuries. She pushed his hands away. His face was black, his clothes torn. A trickle of blood ran down his sleeve from where Bruiser had bit him. The stitches must have opened. He snarled at Renault. "How did she get out there?"

"Give me some credit, Sauvage. I sure as hell didn't cut her loose. Dr. McGill's a menace to herself and everyone else. The shit hits the fan and she takes off like a damn adrenaline junky."

Sully snorted. "Why doesn't that surprise me?"

"I'm not deaf, you know. I'm sitting right here."

"Yeah, and that's a miracle in itself," Sully snapped. "If the explosion didn't get you, the freaking perp could have snatched you out from under our noses."

"He's not here." She glared up at him, swiping at the smoke still clouding her vision. "Do you think he's that stupid with all the cops and firemen fighting the blaze?"

"No, he's far from stupid, Bree." Sully crouched in front of her and stared her down. He was angry, so angry he scared her a little. "And, he's here. The explosion was detonated by cell phone. He was close enough to watch us when he triggered the blast."

Well, when he put it that way... "Look, I'm sorry, okay? I thought I could help."

He shook his head, reached for a thermos, and poured her a mug of coffee, handed it to her and moved to the door. "Please, stay inside this time. There's a bathroom down the hall if you want to clean up."

It was another three hours before they made it out of there. The sun was up, a new day already beginning when they pulled into Breeana's driveway. She unlocked the door while Sully answered his phone, talking in a low voice for a few minutes before disconnecting. The house was quiet. Her father and Cody must still be asleep.

"The case is really pissing me off." Sully pulled off his sidearm and holster, placing them on the counter. "Every time we get a lead, the trail ends."

"What's happened?"

"Our geek squad discovered the computer in the warehouse was linked to a second one at a different location. They were in the process of tracing it when the bomb went off. It wiped out the connection, making it completely untraceable."

"Crap. He's good at covering his tracks."

"Exactly."

Bad news, for sure, but it was the next call that upset Sully the most. His shoulders tensed and his jaw tightened.

"Who was on the phone? What's going on?"

He glanced her way, studied her as if debating telling her anything more. "It's been one hell of a day and night. You sure you want to know?"

"*Yes*, I want to know."

"The police in Laurelville found the tournament official who sent you into the tunnels. He's dead. They pulled him out of the river an hour ago, one block from the arena."

Breeana sighed, making coffee while she listened, her courage hitting an all-time low. "So, we're right back where we started with no witnesses and no clues."

"Maybe not." He wrapped his arms around her from behind and kissed her hair. "I also got word last night from the precinct near the shipping docks in Montreal. Witnesses reported seeing a white van with Pest Control insignias on its sides a few days ago. The driver was trapping and crating rats for removal. Exterminators kill rats, Bree. They don't haul them away."

She turned in his arms. "You think it's the killer?"

"That would be my guess. The dockworkers joked about it when they reported him. They thought the guy was a whack job. We have a warrant for the dock's surveillance videos. I sent Clemente to take a look."

Breeana reached around him, pulled mugs from a cabinet, and poured the coffee. "Well, at least it's something."

"Wait, there's more. While we were at the game yesterday, some of my team hit pay dirt interviewing the families of the cold case drowning victims I told you about. The first victim possessed an identical rosary to the five we already have in evidence. Her rosary was also wiped clean of prints. That cinches it, Bree; the killer has operated undetected in Mallard Bay for at least thirteen years."

The empty carafe slipped from Breeana's fingers and crashed to the floor. "Holy Mother of God."

Chapter 9

Breeana's breath stalled in her lungs with every glance she dared at the stockroom where she had almost lost her life earlier in the week.

No doubt about it. Going back to work is hell. She should accept her father's offer to work without her for a few more days. Concentrate on staying alive; come to terms with her grief over Miranda's and Rainey's murders before returning to their veterinary practice.

Sully would be on board with the plan. As it was, he shot her a glare that spoke volumes. She knew he worked around the clock to guard her, until he could get the members of his Spec Ops squad in place.

"Keep hyperventilating and you're going to pass out." Sully pushed away from the wall and stepped in behind her. She shivered as his hands encircled her waist and he pulled her against him. "Listen, cookie, I'm not going to dance this jig with you. You've had two close calls in a matter of days. You've lost your closest friends and a killer is fixated on you. So, what are you doing here?"

His more than capable hands kneaded the tension out of stiff shoulders. His touch was almost enough to cause Breeana to agree with him. But, she refused to be weak. If she faltered now, she'd lose what little remained of her sanity. She inhaled his masculine scent for one brief moment before pushing away from the strength of his arms. "I'm staying. I need to keep busy to get my life back on track."

"You are one obstinate woman, you know that?" He sighed, dropped his hands to his sides, and stepped into the hallway. "If you change your mind, I'll be right outside the door."

The morning passed slowly, but the familiar routine helped soothe her frayed nerves. She and Laura settled into the rhythm of tending the animals passing through the clinic doors on a typical day. Healthy puppies and kittens brought her joy when she needed it most. There was also the sorrow of helping elderly Annie and Bill Barlow. Their beloved feline companion of more than twenty-two years passed on to the next world with both dignity and love.

Breeana performed the unhappy task and made arrangements for Tux's cremation at their request. She suggested they might take a trip to the local animal shelter, if and when they were ready to adopt another four-legged friend.

Annie mopped her eyes with a tissue before speaking. "Well, it's nice of you to suggest it, but we've already decided to get a Maine Coon this time around. We've had our names on a waiting list with a breeder for the last six months, since you told us Tux wasn't going to get any better."

Bill nodded and Breeana couldn't quite hide her surprise. "Wow, that's a lot of cat, close to twenty-five pounds. And it will require special care. Are you sure it's what you want?"

"Oh, we're sure." Bill said, stroking Tux's fur even though the cat was already at peace. "We're ready for the new little one, aren't we, Annie? We've read all the literature available on Maine Coons. We'll give it a good home, Breeana, with lots of love. We even have a screened-in play area, right outside the back door, with a tree to climb."

"Yes," Annie agreed. "Our Tux loved being outside on summer mornings, perched in his tree and master of his domain. Tux wouldn't want it to go to waste. He'd want us to give another cat a good home."

Breeana tucked a velvet blanket around the 'sleeping' Tux. "Well, I'm happy for you. I hope you'll tell me when the new little one arrives. I'd love to meet him, or her."

"You'll be first on our list," Annie said. "Bill spoke to the breeder last night, after Tux didn't wake up for his evening meal. The breeder was sympathetic and moved our names to the top of the adoption list. He's invited us to see some kittens tomorrow. Twelve-weeks-old and ready for good homes."

"That's wonderful," Breeana said.

"And that's not all," Bill added. "We told him you and your father are the only holistic veterinarians in the area; and while you practice conventional veterinary medicine, you search for less invasive and natural cures rather than always relying on prescribed medications and surgeries. The breeder was impressed and said he'd recommend you to his clients."

"That is so nice of you. Thank you for your recommendation."

Annie and Bill left the clinic at lunch hour. Breeana took her sandwich into her small office, closed the door, and tuned in an easy-listening radio station.

She could hear Laura and Sully bantering back and forth in the empty waiting room. She guessed they could entertain each other for a while. She noticed her mail stacked in a pile on a corner of the desk. Several days worth had accumulated since she'd been gone, mostly advertising, with the exception of one small padded envelope that caught her eye.

Assuming it was samples from one of her suppliers, she slit open the flap and upended the envelope. A dainty silver anklet trickled into her fingers. She recognized the chain immediately. It was Miranda's. Also nestled in her palm was a pair of gold and amethyst earrings belonging to Rainey.

Breeana morphed into a full-blown panic attack. Pain cleaved her lungs and squeezed out the oxygen. Her heart rebounded in her chest like a ping-pong ball gone wild. The walls threatened to close in around her. *I have to get out of here!*

Desperate to escape, she raced down the hallway and through the waiting room. Whipping by Sully and Laura, she was out the front door before anyone could stop her.

"What the hell?"

"Leave me alone!" she cried, knowing Sully would follow her.

He closed the distance between them as she flew into oncoming traffic. He didn't try to stop her. Instead, he waved his badge in the air and cars screeched to a halt. The sound of horns blasting didn't slow her down. Breeana sprinted for the beach. Her feet hit the sand and her legs drove harder and faster. She couldn't stop herself.

A kaleidoscope of sights and sounds whirred by her. The blur of sunbathers chatting, children building sand castles and squealing with delight, victory cries from the volleyball court—all overriding the labored sounds of her breathing. Dead fish smells on the summer breeze assaulted her. Her pulse pounded in her ears. Her stomach threatened to heave.

"Bree, freaking hell, will you stop running?" After another few seconds, Sully caught her by the waist and brought her down in the sand, cushioning her fall with his body. "What the heck has gotten into you?"

She doubled over and retched between his feet. She gagged, on and on, with nothing left but dry heaves twisting her insides. When she finished, Sully maneuvered them to a clean spot in the sand, crouched on his haunches, and drew her up against him. She hung onto his knee, wept, and rocked back and forth in his arms. A keening sound escaped her lips. She clamped her fingers there, trying to hold back the dreadful noise while dragging air into her depleted lungs.

"Easy, Bree, take it real easy." Sully scanned around them, his holster unsnapped, his hand on the butt of his firearm.

Shell-shocked, Breeana sobbed and cursed, clinging to him until she ran out of steam. Sully remained silent during her meltdown, his muscles tensed for action, a vein pulsing his temple. She could only imagine what he must be thinking.

When she could breathe without the ragged wheezing sound, his assessing gaze cut to her face. He wiped tears from her cheeks with the pad of a thumb and squeezed her nape. "What happened back there?"

Emotion choked her windpipe at the softness of his voice. She tried hard to form coherent words, but nothing came out. How could she make Sully understand while she blubbered all over him like a crazy woman? In desperation, she opened her hand and the jewelry clenched in her fist caught the sunlight. "M-Miranda's...R-Rainey's...someone s-s-sent these to me."

He cupped her chin for an instant, then snagged a plastic envelope from his jacket pocket and held it beneath her fingers. "I'm sorry, baby. Slip those into the bag for me. I have to take them as evidence."

"B-but I want to keep them," she moaned. "Will you give them b-back to me, when it's a-all over?"

"You know I will, if it's what you want." He brushed a tangle of hair off her face and swept a kiss along her forehead. "I'll ask you again when it's time. But these mementoes won't give you fond memories of your friends."

Breeana expelled a shuddering breath, realizing he was right. "P-please don't let Cody find out about this. He's driving me crazy as it is. Now, he'll worry more."

"You've got it. There's no reason for him to find out. The taskforce will keep this kind of evidence away from the media."

She stared at him and nodded, the strain of the last few days causing her shoulders to sag. "About Cody...I don't want him staying with me right now. It's too dangerous. Can you arrange for him to stay somewhere else until you get the bodyguards here?"

"I can try, but it won't be easy. Cody won't want to be separated from you and he's going to put up one hell of a fight."

Breeana leaned against his chest, his heart beating strong and steady beneath her cheek. She stared out at the water, looking for answers. Should Cody stay with her? Or stay somewhere else?

"I don't care what he wants. I just want him safe."

FREAKING HELL, JOELLE had been right on the mark. The bastard collected souvenirs from his kills. He had sent those mementos to Breeana knowing full well they would send her over the edge. The son of a bitch had probably watched through binoculars while she freaked out on the beach. There were a lot of boats in the bay today. He could be on any one of them.

A fury grew inside him, a rage so deep his body thrummed with it. For the first time in all his years of police work and Spec Ops assignments, he craved vigilante justice. The animal would die if Sully was given any kind of an excuse. He would put him down as surely as he would a rabid dog. A serial killer was nothing but a preying, torturing, killing machine, one without remorse or a human soul.

In his experience, too many psychopaths pleaded the insanity defense and got away with murder. It happened more often than people realized. He only had to look as far as his sister to prove the theory. The psycho she had profiled for the RCMP had walked on bail while awaiting trial, because of a sympathetic judge. Joelle had disappeared soon afterward.

His Special Ops buddy, Hawke, had tracked them down, but it had taken three days to find Joelle. Sully and Theo, his brother, had arrived on Hawke's tail, too late to do anything but cry for their sister. The damage to her had been done. Her tormentor had slipped through their fingers. Now, Joelle carried the scars, ones people could see and the others she hid from the world. She would never be free of the night terrors. Hell, neither would he.

Sully forced himself back to the present. He had a monster to track and no time to worry about the past. His focus on Breeana, he wiped the sweat from his brow and lifted her from the sand. No way would he risk Joelle's scenario repeating itself, especially not with Bree. He would go up on murder charges first.

HIS CELL PHONE RANG and Sully checked the readout. Cody. He answered before it went to voice mail.

"It's about time you picked up, Lieutenant!"

"Cody? What's up? Is something wrong?"

"Naw, I just wanted to tell you I had a gigantic brain fart. And you'll never guess what I figured out? You've got the hots for my mom and you're doing your damnedest to split us up."

Sully understood where the boy was coming from, although he wouldn't admit it. It had to be hell for the kid to be pushed away from his mother's side, even for his own protection.

"I know it's hard, pal, but it's for the best until—"

"Come off it. Don't bother pretending. But, guess what? It ain't gonna work, you muscle head."

"Hey!" Enough was enough. "Come on, calm down. You're old enough I shouldn't have to spell it out for you. This is a police matter and you don't belong in the middle of it. It's why you've been separated from your mother for a few days, and it's the *only* reason. My interest in your mom is purely professional, contrary to the brain fart you've experienced. It's my job to keep her safe and that's all I'm doing. I have no ulterior motives here."

"The way you stare at Mom is downright disgusting."

"You're blowing this way out of proportion, Cody. I'm telling you, there is nothing going on between your mother and me."

"Save it for someone who cares. You've got a thing for her, all right. And, let's get something else straight. The only protector my mom needs is *me*. We've been a team ever since my dad died. We were doing just fine until you showed up. I'm not going to be shoved aside by some super-stud cop who's ogling my mother and licking his chops. Have you got that?"

If nothing else, Sully admired the teen's resolve and his instincts to protect his mother. He was also bang on the money where his feelings for Breeana were concerned. "Look, where is this coming from? Sure, I like your mother a whole lot and I guess it shows. But I've never thought about taking it any farther. And I won't, at least not until the case is wrapped up."

"You're so full of it. No wonder your eyes are brown. Just leave my mom alone."

"Sorry, but that's not going to happen. After we catch the killer, I'm planning to ask her out on a date, like normal people do. I would like to have the chance to get to know her better. Is it such a bad thing? Your mother is a beautiful woman, Cody, even if you don't think about her in those terms. Isn't it possible she gets lonely from missing your father? Doesn't she deserve another chance at happiness?"

Cody's bark of laughter shot over the line. "I'd say you're dreaming in 3D. As far as I'm concerned, things are fine the way they are. She doesn't need you, Lieutenant, so go out and find yourself another conquest and take my mom's name out of your little black book."

"I'm sorry you feel that way, but like it or not, I'm here until your mom tells me different. Then I'll go, but only if *she* wants me to go. In the meantime, how about we call a truce and work together?"

"Work together? What a laugh. The goon squad won't let me get anywhere near my mom."

Sully moved the phone away from his ear as it disconnected. *Shit.* Cody was furious and he didn't blame him. The kid hadn't been advised on his mother's request to keep him out of the loop. The boy had been separated from her for two days, forced to stay with his grandfather and the MBPD uniforms guarding Jack's house until Sully could get his Special Ops buddies in place protecting the whole family.

The kid wasn't stupid. He sensed his mother was still in danger and he wanted to be with her. Breeana, on the other hand, wanted him out of harm's reach. It was a no win situation and the back and forth arguments caused him a mammoth headache.

Sully's phone rang a second time. He prepared to do battle once again as he answered the call. *Patience, my man, have patience.*

"Hey, Cody, did you forget something?"

"Sorry to disappoint, but I'm not Cody."

His brother's voice came through the line with a chuckle.

"Hey, Theo, it's good to hear from you. How's the lawyering business?"

"About the same as the homicide business, I'd imagine. Booming. If it's not real estate law, it's corporate, estate planning, wills or prenups. What can I say? I don't have a life, which is why I'm returning your call."

"It's about time." Sully heard a beer can being liberated as the tab popped and a satisfied grunt on the other end of the line indicated his brother was taking a sip. "What are you up to?"

"Vacation, brother, mixed in with a little business. I'm taking a month at the lake, starting now, and I want you to join me for a few days. If you've got something going with a new lady, you can bring her along."

"I can't, man. I'm neck deep in a serial killer investigation involving her and the case has hit a major firewall, which is why I called you." Sully raked a hand through his hair and along his bearded stubble. He could shave twice a day and still have a five o'clock shadow. "It's not good, Theo. Someone wants her dead and he'll keep on trying, unless I can get to him first. I've called in the team, but you're the first one I've been able to actually speak with."

"Isn't that all the more reason to get her the hell out of Dodge, until everything is in place? No one will search for her here and if they do, I'm already with you, bro. I've stocked the fridge with enough food to feed an army, not to mention copious amounts of beer on ice."

When Sully still hesitated, Theo dangled the carrot. "Bro, you bring her here, or I'll come to you. But, we can just as easily make contact with the rest of the unit from my place and it might be safer for your woman. What do you say?"

What Theo said made sense. He was also a firearms and martial arts expert. It would be a relief to have an extra pair of eyes watching Breeana's back. Between them, they could keep her safe. Added to that, the lake was isolated. The perp would have trouble following them there. Sully glanced at his watch. It was just after eight-thirty. He calculated how long it would take them to get on the road. "Let me clear it with my captain, see if I can shake loose for a few days. I'll get back to you."

When Sully placed his next call, Captain Jean Hébert needed some convincing. He'd go to the wall for his men, but he was nobody's fool. "I'd like to take Dr. McGill out of the city for the weekend, Captain, to keep her out of danger."

There was a distinct pause on the other end of the line before Hébert spoke. "How many from the homicide team are going with you?"

"None, sir."

"What? How do you expect to see danger coming without your squad riding shotgun?" Hébert asked. "Have you suddenly developed ESP? Look, Sully, you know as well as I do it's impossible to predict what the nutcase is going to do next. How do you know he won't follow you?"

"He might, but I'll be ready if he does. I'm hooking up with my brother, Captain."

"Ah, I guess that changes the odds in our favor. How is Theo, by the way? Being a lawyer must seem pretty tame compared to his...other interests."

"I'll give him your regards, Captain."

"What about your squad? Can they handle things without you for a few days?"

"They won't need to, sir. I'll be in constant contact by cell phone, and I'll request a police chopper in an emergency."

"Fine, you may proceed. And Lieutenant?"

"Sir?"

"Keep Dr. McGill close, but not *too* close."

In other words, keep my dick in my pants.

"Right. It's under control." *Liar.*

Breeana entered the sunroom as he disconnected. "My brother called a few minutes ago. How would you like to head to the mountains for a few days? We can swing by your father's to pick up Cody and be on the road within the hour."

She sank to a bar stool and shot him a guilty look. "I forgot to tell you. Cody's not here. He and Dad left this morning with the hockey team. School finished yesterday for the summer, and there's a tournament in Toronto all weekend. I'm sorry, I should have said something. It's just I thought it was safe, since they'll be out of the city."

"It's not the end of the world, and it's not your fault. The Mallard Bay cops should have kept me in the loop. I guess the idiots are over there guarding an empty house. Still, let's not take any chances. A buddy of mine on the Toronto force owes me a favor. I'll give him a call and set things up. He'll arrange around-the-clock protection for Cody and your father while they're in his jurisdiction."

THEY EASED ONTO THE highway an hour later. Sully's glance cut between the rearview mirror and the lanes stretching ahead of them. Breeana said nothing as he drove the Tahoe deep into the mountains. He pulled off on secondary roads from time to time to search for anyone following. No lights crept up on them out of the dark, and he seemed satisfied.

Bruiser and Bear panted in the back seat.

"Will your brother mind the dogs coming along?"

"Not even a little. Theo owns the island and his house is the only one on it. Believe me, once he gets a load of these guys he's not going to mind, unless they drink his beer."

Breeana almost choked on his last comment. "Um, they have been known to take a slurp or two. Dad's a bad influence, I guess."

He chuckled. "Maybe I should pick them up their own six-pack, just to be on the safe side."

"You're really funny. I think they can survive for a few days without it."

Pulling into the docks at Silver Lake, Sully grabbed their bags while she freed the dogs from the confines of the back seat. Noses to the ground, Bear and Bruiser sniffed their way from one end of the boat landing to the other. Then they waded into dark water, their silhouettes outlined by a crescent moon in an almost cloudless sky. The parking area was grass. A family of deer stood off to one side near the edge of forest. The scent of pine wafted the air. Breeana filled her lungs with it, glad to leave the smell of the city behind. A few moments later and pinpoints of light rounded a distant bend of shoreline. The boat altered course and roared toward them.

"There's Theo," Sully said from behind her.

His breath ruffled the curls at the back of her neck. It took all of her willpower not to lean into him. She was better off if she didn't get too close. *Fess up, girl, you drool every time he gets within breathing distance.*

"How can he drive so fast in the dark? Isn't he worried about crashing into something?"

"There's no way it would happen," Sully chuckled. "My brother's got eyes like a cat."

The Bayliner docked and Breeana and Theo introduced themselves. The dogs leapt into the bow and the boat reversed thrust. Sully drew her beneath the convertible top as they travelled down the winding twists of lake. She relaxed for the first time in a long time, settled into a bucket seat, and watched the brothers with interest.

In the dim dashboard lighting, she could see Sully and Theo were strikingly alike. Yet, she would recognize Sully anywhere. She was attuned to him now—his broad step across a floor, the clean male scent of him, how his mouth quirked with a grin, or his brows furrowed in a scowl, and the low cadence of his baritone. His traits were indelibly stamped on her brain, and maybe in her heart.

Sully had promised to wait for sex until after the case was solved. She knew he meant every word. Breeana regretted the agreement but, then again, she blamed herself with her prim and prissy attitude. Well, except for the night of the fire when she hadn't been thinking clearly. Her hormones had raged that night. She would have slept with him for sure, if he'd asked. Now she worried she would exceed her use-by date and he wouldn't be interested in her at all.

Another half hour and they sat on a screened deck extending from the living room along three sides of Theo's wood and glass home. The house smelled delicious, a mixture of wood smoke and piney breezes. A magnificent view of Silver Lake shimmered below her in the moonlight. Breeana sighed with appreciation while nursing a Brazilian coffee.

She barely noticed as Sully filled Theo in on the murders in Mallard Bay and the attempts on her life. His brother listened, only stopping him with the occasional question. An hour went by before Sully pushed from his seat on the couch to refill their drinks in the kitchen. Theo used the time to question her about Cody, her veterinary practice, and her life in general. She guessed it was his way of steering the conversation away from himself. He seemed to have something unpleasant on his mind.

Placing another Brazilian coffee in front of her, Sully sank to the couch beside her again, his hand claiming her knee, his calloused fingertips working their magic. A spark of heat ignited her core and radiated like a flash fire throughout her body. Breeana clenched her thighs and brushed his hand aside. He winked at her, shot her a bad-boy grin, and slid his arm across the back of the couch to caress her nape. *Oh my, does anyone have a fire extinguisher?*

Apparently unaware of her discomfort, Sully turned his attention back to his brother. "What's got you acting like your balls are in a vise?"

"You remember Sarah Davidson?"

"She's the old gal who owns the next island, right?"

"That's her."

"I remember now. What's going on?" Sully clamped his teeth together as if bracing himself for what was to come. "Has something happened to her?"

"I'd say so. She died two nights ago." Theo paused to take a sip of beer. His hand shook as he placed the beer stein on an end table. "Her death looks suspicious, bro."

"Shit. Is there anything I can do?"

Theo grimaced. "Not yet, but thanks for asking. The provincial cops are conducting an investigation. Let's see what they find out first."

Chapter 10

Sully awoke the next morning to the sound of a woodpecker *rat-a-tat-tatting* against the oil drum outside his bedroom window. Still half asleep but instantly wanting her, he shifted and stretched across the bed to snag his woman for some good loving. Except, she wasn't his woman and she wasn't there. *Of course not. You'd have to be having a physical relationship for her to be in bed with you, you moron.*

Breeana had slept in one of the other guest rooms last night. But he knew he had gotten to her when he'd caressed her knee. Hell, he had given himself a major jones with that little maneuver. He had also set himself up for a late night dip in the lake before he could get his body settled down enough to sleep. So much for his promise to his captain. He'd tossed it overboard without so much as breaking a sweat.

Sully pulled on shorts and went in search of Breeana. Sounds of laughter floated up from the dock. He poured himself a coffee and sauntered barefoot outside to the deck. Sunshine reflected off clear water as he zeroed in on her, a flash of yellow bikini and tantalizing flesh skimming the waves. At the sight of her, instant arousal arced through him. *Hell, I've got it bad.* He glanced away in order to get his body under better control, again wishing she had been in his bed when he'd opened his eyes this morning. But, life wasn't always fair.

She swam with Bear and Bruiser, diving down when they got too close and bobbing to the surface in a different location. The killer dogs were into the game, yipping and tongue-lolling while they attacked the waves and charged after her through the water.

"Hey! Mermaid or not, you'd better not let those beasts catch you, or they're going to drown you out there."

"There's slim chance of that happening, Sully. If I need help, I'll holler." Her laughter rippled across the bay as she dove deep to steer clear of the mutts.

Theo, clad in cut-offs and sunglasses, lounged on an Adirondack chair on the wharf with his Glock by his side as he scanned the horizon. "Sully, it's about time you rolled your old carcass out of bed."

"Old carcass? Right," Sully snorted as he sank into a matching chair, rubbed a hand along his rock solid six-pack, and checked the time on his watch. "The fourteen month age difference between us doesn't make me an old man. Besides, it's only eight o'clock and I'm not a morning person, not when I don't have to be anywhere."

He sipped his coffee and rolled it back over his tongue. "Thanks for watching Breeana."

"Well, she's a damn pleasure to watch. If I'd known there would be days like today, I would have become a lifeguard."

"Better get your own woman to fulfill those fantasies, little brother," Sully growled. "The only guy doing any mouth-to-mouth resuscitation on Breeana is me."

"Relax. She's only got eyes for you, man. And, I respect the private property signals you're sending me. Just remember, I want to be best man if you two tie the knot."

"Sorry, but if it happens, I'm reserving the spot for my future son. Would you settle for being an usher?"

"Hey, are you kidding me? I'd settle for being the flower girl, just to see you walk down the aisle. So, when's the big day?"

"Who knows? We're still in the cop and assault victim stage. We don't even have anything going on."

"But, you're interested?"

"Hell, yes, I'm interested. But I'm still a long way from doing anything about it. You know I'm not good at long-term relationships," he admitted. "Now, can we talk about something else?"

Theo threw back his head and roared with laughter, then stopped at the low growl emanating from Sully's throat.

"I mean it, Theo. Change the subject."

Theo tossed his hands in the air, as if in defeat. "Relax. Listen, have you heard from Hawke yet? I tried calling him last night, before you arrived, but I couldn't reach him."

Sully had first met Jake Hawkins at the Royal Military College in Kingston where they had roomed together and become fast friends. After graduating from RMC, they were both deployed with the Royal Canadian Regiment, prior to joining Special Operating Forces, Joint Task Force 2. The fates must have been smiling, because after finishing law school and joining the Régiment Canadien Français, Theo had also joined JTF2. Together, they had seen action in several war-torn hellholes Sully would just as soon forget. It had been baptism by fire for all of them.

"Not yet. He's the last person I'm waiting on. Got word from Micah, Reece, Law, and Hunt; they're on their way. Hawke's working a case right now. He'll show up when he can."

"No doubt," Theo agreed.

Hawke was now a chief investigator with the RCMP. "He'll be here."

"Sure, unless the stalker scenario in Houston heats up for our little sister," Theo surmised. "You know the RCMP takes care of their own, and Joelle was one of them when she was a profiler. She's also a Canadian citizen, and the Prime Minister is a huge fan of her thrillers. Hell on wheels, Hawke will be working with the FBI to handle her protection if anyone so much as sneezes in her direction."

"You're right. The PM will see to it. Jeez, it never rains but it pours. We'll have to sit tight and see what develops." Sully's gaze drifted back to Breeana in the water. His priorities came into sharp focus. Her safety and catching the madman who stalked her were his prime objectives. His *only* objectives. Anything else would have to wait.

THEY ARRIVED BACK IN Mallard Bay early on Monday morning. Breeana didn't bother to wait for Sully and Theo before she hopped out of the Tahoe and headed for the house. Sully had called Cody while they were still on the road, telling him to watch for them. With Theo here to help out, her son was coming home. She turned the key in her door lock, anxious to turn off the alarm and clear a space for the gym bags the men hoisted from the car trunks. Just as her hand touched the handle, a bear of a man threw open the door, yanked her inside, and slammed it behind her, leaving the dogs and her bodyguards on the other side. She screamed at the top of her lungs, her heart inching up her throat.

Sully and Theo tore into the house, their guns drawn.

Glaring at the man who had hold of her, Sully holstered his weapon. "Jesus Christ, Hawke!"

"Yeah, great to see you guys, too." Hawke's gaze narrowed when he and Sully exchanged glances over her head. "I came as soon as I heard, once I got some good people in place to keep an eye on Joelle."

Breeana could only gape as she stared past the man with thighs the size of tree trunks and all around good looks to see four more ruggedly handsome men in her living room. They were big men, really big men, like Sully and Theo. They all carried guns, really big guns, also like Sully and Theo. They were also arrogant jerks for breaking into her house.

She drilled a finger at Hawke, chest level, and gave him her best glare. "Just who do you think you are…scaring me half to death?"

"Chill, Bree," Sully chuckled behind her. "You're going to hurt the poor devil if you don't ease up. He's a delicate little creature."

"Put a sock in it, Lieutenant," Breeana growled.

Hawke bent to her level, a grin splitting his face from ear to ear. "She's a snarly little hellcat, I'll give her that. I'll bet she eats nails for breakfast."

Sully laughed. "Good guess. She washes them down with battery acid for good measure. Dr. McGill is a regular force of nature."

"Well, her skinny little body needs some work at the gym if she expects anyone to take her big mouth seriously."

Breeana almost punched him, just to prove how strong she really was. "You're not funny, *bird-man*. You and these other cavemen probably damaged my alarm system breaking into the house."

"Alarm system? Is that what it is?" Hawke roared with laughter. "Someone should tell your alarm company not to leave the wires exposed on the outside wall of your home for everyone to see. My ninety-year-old kindergarten teacher could take her arts and crafts scissors and snip 'em, before rolling herself through the door in her wheelchair, easy as pie. Hell, she could use a credit card to open the flimsy lock of yours."

"Well," Breeana sniffed. "I may be a little lax on home security, but I do have guard dogs. It's still no excuse for what you did."

"Take a look at these killer guard dogs, boys. If they get any scarier, they'll be licking our boots."

It was true. Bear and Bruiser were dashing from man to man with their butts waggling, anxious not to miss out on the patting and stroking taking place with every nudge of their furry faces. After the laughter died down, Sully made the official introductions.

Breeana already knew who Jake Hawkins was because she had overheard Sully and Theo talking about him in connection to their sister. He was both RCMP and the pilot for their Special Ops squad. They claimed he had an uncanny ability to get inside people's heads and read their minds. She wondered if the brothers were to be believed on that score.

Next was Reece 'Rocket' Morgan, the demolitions expert and civil engineer of their unit, a man who still carried his heart on his sleeve for a woman from his past, according to Sully. Law Logan was their logistics guru, followed by Hunter Ryan, a linguistics expert. And last, but not least, Micah Rivera was an electronics wizard, mechanic, and all around flirt. Sully said Theo was the team's number one sniper, and all of them could pinch-hit for one another at any given time.

She learned from the others it was Sully who commanded their missions and took responsibility for the sometimes outrageous antics of the wild bunch. Breeana wasn't surprised. She might as well face it. He lived for action and adventure.

Micah took Breeana's hand and pressed her palm to his lips. "I'm proud to be of service, ma'am. If you feel the need for some quiet conversation, or a few hours away from these idiots, call on me. I'll help you forget all your troubles."

"Whoa, Mom, I think I heard the same line on a television movie last week." Her son was home from the tournament, dropping his hockey gear with a thud, arriving in time to hear Micah's remarks. "King Kong was trying to convince the damsel in distress at the top of the Empire State Building he was really a great guy, and not some big hairy ape."

"Ah, the kid has a mouth on him just like his mother's," Micah drawled.

"Right, Mic," Sully said, looking like he wanted to rip Micah's head off. "Get used to it, because he's your responsibility. You're going to spend every hour of every day with Cody. Wherever he goes, you go. Don't let him out of your sight. Are we clear?"

"We're real clear, Sully."

"Good. Law, you're on this detail, too. Cody, I want you to take some time filling these guys in on your schedule. Don't try to pull any funny stuff with them, because they will mop the floor with you if you do. Understand?"

"Sweet. Micah can deal the dirt on how to impress the girls with his expertise. Not!"

Ah, yes, Micah and Cody would get along like cats and dogs, Breeana smiled as she pictured it. Law had his work cut out for him running interference between those two.

"Hunt, your assignment lives next door, Breeana's father, Jack Forest. You can settle in over there in a few minutes. The rest of you will guard Breeana. Now, let's meet for ten minutes before everyone splits up."

Breeana asked, "Cody, would you make a pot of coffee and bring it out to the sundeck for us?"

"Bree, you don't need to bother with the details. Why don't you help Cody, or unpack, while I go over a couple of things with the guys?"

If Sully thought he would delegate her to the kitchen, he had another 'think' coming. "Ah, no, I'm as much a part of this as anyone. I have a right to participate in the planning."

"Planning? What planning?" he said over his shoulder as he showed the others to seats on the sundeck. "It's just a simple review to make sure everyone has their orders straight."

"Sully?" Hawke interrupted, clearing his throat. "If you're going to yell, try to keep it down to a dull roar. Okay? Breeana has something to tell you and I don't think you're going to like it. There's no reason to let the entire neighborhood in on our conversation."

Oh, oh, Hawke had a strange look on his face which caused Breeana to wonder if he actually *could* read her mind. Maybe Sully was right about that.

Sully's gaze locked on hers while he appeared to brace himself for some unpleasant news. His jaw tightened until she thought his teeth would shatter. "Okay, cookie, spit it out. What's on your mind?"

"Well, aren't we cozy?" Breeana picked at her fingernails and took in a deep breath, smiling sweetly. "Now that everyone is here, and I'm so very well protected, I wondered how you can use me to catch the psycho. Because it seems to me, I'm the best chance you've got."

Sully glared daggers at her. Time ticked by, and Breeana figured she might have time to knit a pair of socks while she waited for him to answer.

His face a mask of cold fury, he choked out, "The meeting is over."

"Hold on a second, bro," Theo said. "If Breeana is willing to bait the trap, we can control all the angles and minimize the risks. Why not let her take a shot at it?"

"Have you lost your freaking mind?" Sully barked. "Can you guarantee we can eliminate the danger to her and her family? You know the odds, Theo, and they aren't in our favor. The killer is a maniac. He is not going to stick to our schedule, he's not going to fall into a trap and give up without a goddamn fight. I will not—repeat, *not*—allow her to be one of his victims. I've already seen what the madman can do, first hand."

Reece added his say to the mix. "I think she's right, boss. We've done this before and we've been successful. Can't we at least think about it?"

"Hell, no, not this time. I'm not willing to risk her life."

"But, Sully—"

"You have my answer, Bree. It isn't open for discussion."

Breeana shook her head, anger flaming her cheeks. "And, if you don't catch him? Then what? Are you going to keep me surrounded by your people for the rest of my life?"

"Damn straight I am, if that's what it takes to keep you safe. I'll do whatever needs to be done, cookie. So get any thoughts of playing the heroine out of your obstinate brain."

"SO...THAT WENT WELL." Breeana sat on the deck with Hawke watching the sun set over Lac St-Louis, while Reece and Theo fired up the barbeque. Cody was at the arena with Micah and Law, but would be back soon. Sully had stormed out after their impromptu meeting earlier. He had called an emergency meeting at the office with his task force. She had no idea when he would return.

"Breeana, you have to move inside while I put a call in to the alarm company and a locksmith. We need to have your security system upgraded."

"No, Hawke. You are not going to touch my alarm system. I want it left exactly as is, the locks on the doors, too."

He shot her an incredulous look. *Ah-ha. Maybe the mind-meld thing doesn't work as well as he thought.*

"Why would you want to do that?"

"I want this to be over. If we don't beef up security, my stalker will have an easier time breaking in. Then you guys can catch him in the act."

"Come on, I thought you agreed to let us do our jobs?" Hawke ran a hand over his raspy jaw and frowned. "Sully expects us to protect you and that's what we're going to do. It isn't open for discussion."

"Can't you bend the rules a little?"

"No. Not in this instance. Not anytime, as a matter of fact. What Sully says, goes. Don't think you can divide and conquer because it won't work. Not with any of us. Now get off the chair and come inside where I can keep an eye on you. Please."

Breeana swung her legs over the side of the chaise longue and marched into the house under Hawke's watchful gaze. He'd made his point; her idea of swaying the troops to her way of thinking wouldn't work.

Crap!

She was terrified of being attacked by the psycho again and that was the real issue. She knew living a life of fear would destroy her and obliterate any hope she had for a future with Sully. She didn't want him thinking of her as a victim, someone to be protected and handled with kid gloves. This was the reason she refused to hide under the bed until the killer was caught. And the sooner Sully understood how she felt, the better.

"QUIET DOWN, PEOPLE. Take your seats. We have a lot of ground to cover."

Sully's detectives, Marie Matisse, and eight uniforms grabbed their coffees and notepads, before gathering around the conference table. "It's been over a week since the last attack on Dr. McGill at the arena. What do we have on the van used to transport the rats?"

"Not much that's worth anything," Millette muttered. "We were able to get the plate number off the dock security video but the plate was stolen. However, we did manage to locate the van. It was abandoned in a quarry near Ormstown, a late model white Econoline. It was stolen the same night as the fire at the veterinary clinic, from a rental agency near Magog."

"That's only an hour from here. What about the logos on the van, Millette? He must have had the van painted somewhere."

"It's a no go, Lieutenant. The Pest Control insignias were magnetic strips. They were also pilfered, came from a legitimate extermination company's van. Our guy went to their lot and ripped the signs off the same night he took the van from the rental agency.

He couldn't steal the extermination company's vehicle because the security gates were locked. He scaled the fence to grab the signs, and then made do by stealing the rental."

Vince Marshall, a seasoned cop with more than ten years on the force, added, "The van was sanitized, Lieutenant, except for rodent droppings. No prints, candy bar wrappers, used tissues, crumpled bits of paper, pens, drinking cups...nothing. Our perp was careful not to leave any evidence behind."

"You're missing something there. Did you check the outside? Maybe the guy pumped gas and got his fingerprints on the gas cap? He must have filled up somewhere, hauling the rats to the arena and then driving to Ormstown to dump the van. He also might have checked under the hood for oil or other fluid levels. His prints could be on a dipstick, for Pete's sake. Do I need to tell you how to do your job?"

"No way," Vince said, visibly shaken by the reprimand. "I'll notify the lab to go over it again."

"Good thinking, Marshall, and make sure you're there when they do it. Do we have a picture of the guy on the surveillance videos?"

"No, at least nothing we can use." Clemente offered. "He kept his head down and his face hidden under a ball cap. With those bulky coveralls the guy wore, it's impossible to even get an accurate take on his body type."

"Why am I not surprised?" Sully bit back a frustrated groan. "He knew the cameras were rolling, and he knows police procedure. Small wonder he's gotten away with murder for so many years."

"You're right." Clemente agreed. "There are so many forensics shows on television these days, almost anyone can figure out how to cover their tracks."

"Wrong answer, Sal. I want you to go back to the docks and pull every security tape they've got. Our guy knew the cameras were there because he had already scoped out the location. I want every license plate number off every vehicle down at the docks between the date of the clinic fire and the rat attack. Check with the guards at the gates for their records and get started on screening those videos. Our killer showed his face sometime, unless he's invisible."

"I'm on it, Loot."

"Good. I also want some of you tracking down the crates he used to haul the rats. Where did he get them? What about the coveralls and ball cap he wore? Did he buy them at a uniform store? Come on, people. We need answers."

"Lieutenant, we're doing our best," Millette challenged.

"Sergeant, if you want sympathy—you'll find it between shit and syphilis in the dictionary. That's the only sympathy you'll get from me. A woman's life hangs in the balance here. The creep has already gotten to her twice. If I were an insurance salesman, I sure as hell wouldn't be selling Dr. McGill life insurance policies for the foreseeable future. Let's get our act together."

Sully called a ten-minute break and got himself back under control. The whole thing made him crazy, more so since Breeana insisted on setting herself up as bait. *No bloody way is that going to happen.* He noticed the detectives shooting wary glances his way as they filed back into the room after the break. He couldn't blame them.

"Okay, let's move on. What about the rosaries? Have we got a hit on those yet?"

"Yes, we caught a break there. A shipment of rosaries was stolen from St. Patrick's Cathedral fifteen years ago," Millette said. "You won't believe it, but the church secretary is still the same woman who placed the order, an old doll named Hannah Grimes. She remembers the twenty-five rosaries being delivered by parcel post. They disappeared from the rectory on the same night. The break-in was blamed on some local thugs working the area. They were known to police for home invasions and stealing electronic equipment."

"That doesn't make sense, Jacques. There's a huge difference between stealing stereos and televisions, that are easy to unload, and a shipment of rosaries with no street value. I want you to get over to St. Pat's and have another talk with the secretary."

"Sure thing, Lieutenant. The church office is closed for the night, but I'll be there when it opens tomorrow. Is there something specific you want me to ask her?"

"Get a list of parishioners for the time when those rosaries were taken. My gut says the theft was an inside job."

"You're thinking our perp had a score to settle with the church and that's why he stole the rosaries and started killing women?" Sal asked.

"Nope, not our guy. I believe he's a predator who can only achieve sexual gratification by killing his victims. I think he's impotent."

Marie smacked her palm on the table. "Of course. That would explain why no semen was present on Rainey Dubé or Miranda Greene, or any of the other women in the cold case files, according to their autopsies."

"Exactly. His religious beliefs are only the excuse he uses for committing the crimes. If he thinks of these women as whores, they become fair game." Sully drummed his fingers on the tabletop and leaned back in his chair to ruminate. "But I'm betting he attended services at the parish he stole those rosaries from. And he may have stood out in the congregation. Millette, take Sanchez and some uniforms with you and see what you can find out. Canvas the neighborhood. Talk with the church secretary, the priests, and anyone else from the parish who was a member fifteen years ago."

"It's too late to go door-to-door now." Millette said, after glancing at his watch. "We'll start first thing in the morning."

"You and Sal can spend some time tonight with Lemieux and Bruno. Fill them in on your other cases, since they'll pick up the slack until we catch the guy." Sully turned his attention to the coroner. "Marie, what about the autopsy report on the tournament official? Please tell me you've found something to point us in the right direction."

"I wish I could. Serge Lacroix's throat was slashed before he hit the river, and that's about all I can tell you."

"Let me guess, there's no trace evidence on his body."

"If there was anything to be found, it washed away in the water. His pockets were empty, other than a booze flask and a wallet containing five hundred dollars. Only the vic's fingerprints were on the flask. Forensics is trying to retrieve prints from the money, but the bills were stuck together. I'll let you know if they find anything."

Sully nodded, shut his laptop, and stood up. "There's a buffet set out for everyone in the cafeteria—pizza and salads. Grab some dinner and then get started on your assignments. Millette, make sure everyone knows what they're working on. I'm out of here. You can reach me on my cell phone anytime, day or night. Be sure to keep me updated on your progress."

As if on cue, his cell phone chimed the opening anthem of *Hockey Night in Canada.* Caller ID registered the call as coming from the hospital in Mallard Bay.

What now?

Chapter 11

Sully paced the corridor outside of the emergency room while he waited to see his brother. According to the EMTs who'd brought Theo in, he had plowed his Corvette into a telephone pole. The EMTs recognized Sully from other crime scenes and provided a quick rundown on his condition.

Their diagnosis included possible cracked ribs, bruised sternum, and a nasty cut over an eye. There was also damage to his larynx from impacting the steering wheel. Nothing life threatening as far as they could tell, but an ER doctor would have to make that evaluation.

Shit. This could keep Theo on the injured list for a while.

Stopping at a vending machine, Sully inserted enough coins for a cup of coffee then moved to a bank of windows. It was pitch dark outside, his reflection staring back at him from the glass. He stood motionless, his jaw clenched tight while the wheels spun in his head. Flipping his cell open, he hit Hawke's number on speed dial. It was answered on the first ring.

"Where are you?"

"At the hospital. Theo smashed up his car."

"That doesn't sound like him. How is he?"

"From what the EMTs tell me, lots of bruises, contusions, and possible cracked ribs." Sully exited the hospital and walked a few paces from the electronic doors. "Listen, it might not be an accident, Hawke. Alert the other guys and keep them on their toes tonight. But don't say anything to Bree and Cody. They have enough to worry about."

"I'll take care of it. I'll see you when you get back." Hawke disconnected the call.

Sully pocketed his phone and returned to the ER. He wanted to evaluate his brother's condition for himself before sounding unnecessary alarm bells for his own family. San Antonio and Houston were a long way off for his folks and sister to travel if Theo would be back on his feet in a day or two.

Hell, he had survived JTF2 with some harrowing experiences under his belt. He had the scars to prove it. He was more than tough, and Sully predicted a fight with a telephone pole wouldn't slow his brother down for very long. Of course, when he saw him, it was difficult not to flinch and show any signs of sympathy. The man looked like shit with his forehead bandaged and his eyes blackened. He lay on a gurney in the ER, a curtain separating him from a pregnant woman in the next bed.

"Hey, bro, it's about time you got here." Theo's voice was little more than a croak. He struggled to get his legs over the side of the gurney. A blue hospital gown slid from his shoulders and landed in a puddle on the floor. The only thing saving his modesty was a pair of black silk underwear.

"Great boxers, man."

"Yeah, the ladies like them. I'll have to give you the name of my tailor. Breeana's a classy woman and she might appreciate a man wearing something finer than those packaged tighty-whities the guys in the unit like."

"I'll keep it in mind. How are you doing?"

"I'm good to go. I'd have checked myself out of here, but my witch of a nurse hid my wallet and clothes, plus my car will be in surgery for a while. I had her towed to the usual garage servicing her. My mechanic says he made the sign of the cross when he saw her. Sarcastic bastard."

Theo reached under the gurney with a sharp intake of breath, grabbed the lock box containing his Glock and tossed it to Sully. "Here, carry it for me. Let's make tracks."

"Hold up," Sully said, as he pushed his brother back down on the gurney. "If your nurse hid your clothes, it's because you were being a stubborn jackass about staying in bed, and you aren't ready to be released yet. Let me talk to a doctor first."

"Sure, talk all you want. While you're talking, I'll grab myself a cab in my manly underwear to Breeana's house. I'm pretty sure she'll pay the cab fare when I tell her you wouldn't help me break out of here." Theo glared as he sat up again. There was no mistaking the Sauvage determination. "I'm going, whether you like it or not. No way am I letting you have all the fun."

"Theo, sit your ass back down, or I swear I'm going to handcuff you to the bed rail."

"Back off, Sully. It wasn't an accident. I was run off the road because someone doesn't want me on the team protecting your lady. We'll all have to watch our backs now. What do you have to say about that?"

"Okay, okay. Let's roll, but I'll sign you out first. And, you'd better be telling me the truth. If this is just an excuse to get you released from the hospital, I'm going to drag your ass back here. You can tell me what happened in the car."

"Yeah, yeah. Is there anything else, Mom?"

There really wasn't much more for his brother to tell him, just enough to convince Sully Theo's instincts were correct. The driver had hit hard and made his escape fast. He had never slowed down and never reported the accident. Their unsub had tried to take Theo out of the equation and the reason was obvious. He didn't want the brothers teaming up.

Sully had every confidence in his homicide squad. But, he and Theo together—with Hawke and the other guys—now that was a force to be reckoned with. For the first time in a long time, he felt he held the upper hand. The killer had panicked, maybe because he was about to make another move against Breeana.

Come on, just try to get close to her again, you prick. We'll be ready.

Cody shot a look at Theo as they came through the door and engaged his big mouth. "The next time you leave the house, I'd better be riding shotgun. What happened?"

"He was out joyriding and smashed up his 'Vette. It's nothing for you to worry about." Sully knew the boy was scared. It was understandable. If the freak could get to Theo, he could get to his mother. Reece and Hawke lowered Theo into a chair and propped his legs on an ottoman. Breeana covered him with a quilt and handed him a couple of painkillers with a glass of water.

"Have a heart, Doc. Don't you have anything stronger than this for my giant headache? These are over-the-counter meds," Theo grunted.

"Sorry, champ. You could have a concussion. If you had half a brain, you would have stayed in the hospital where you could be monitored by all those pretty nurses."

"You've never met Nurse Ratched," Theo snapped. "The woman is three hundred pounds of muscle, mean, and bad breath. And while my other nurse was very cute, had minty breath and wanted to give me a full body massage, his name was Simon and he really wasn't my type."

"You're stuck with me then." Breeana brought an ice pack to his forehead and laid it in place. "I'll be waking you every two hours and asking you a bunch of silly questions, just to make sure you still know who, and where, you are."

"I guess if you must, you must." His brother had a wicked, puffy grin on his battered face. "Will you hold my hand, in case I have pain or bad dreams during the night?"

Sully hadn't missed the fact Breeana was already dressed for bed. Her little pajama T-shirt and shorts in thin, jade-green material were enough to give a man a heart attack. Her auburn hair was a riot of curls cascading down her back. Her shapely legs and pink toenail polish added to the fantasy. She had rushed straight from the shower when Cody sounded the alarm Theo was hurt.

Sully inhaled. She smelled like sin, pure and simple, a mixture of sensuous lotions, shampoo, and desirable woman. His vision turned red when he noticed the tent forming in Micah's pants across the room.

No, oh no, over my dead body, cookie! Get your little Florence Nightingale tush into the bedroom and cover yourself up. I'll stand guard in the hallway in front of your door for the night—unless you want to invite me in...

"Bree, it's nice of you to offer, but my guys are capable of taking care of Theo. They all have medical training. Why don't you go tuck yourself in bed with a book?"

"Sully, why don't you shove that notion where the sun doesn't shine?" Breeana whirled on him in a flash and went nose-to-chest with him, standing on her tip-toes for those added few inches of aggression. "You have got to be kidding me, you big idiot! My life is a mess and you really expect me, the little woman, to go to my room and read some lovey-dovey romance novel while you testosterone junkies handle what's important?"

"Hey, I'm not saying that." *She wants a war? Hell, I am just the man to give her one.* "But I don't want you standing around here half-naked in front of my men. Is it too damn much to ask?"

Breeana blinked once, then twice, her hands on her hips and anger sparking her eyes. "Well, why didn't you just say so? I'll run upstairs and change into one of my frump outfits. Will army fatigues and combat boots do?"

Sully pulled her to his chest and murmured in her ear. "Face it, cookie, a suit of armor couldn't hide that beautiful body of yours."

Breeana tossed him a look that caused his guy parts to shrivel. "And how would you know, big man? Unless you're looking in places you shouldn't."

Oops. "Forget I said anything."

"Hey, Lieutenant!" Cody hollered from across the room. He was setting up the DVD player and widescreen, a bowl of popcorn nestled against his chest. "If you don't quit manhandling my mother, I'm going to go over there and pop you one."

Sully sighed and released his hold on Bree. His forehead touched hers for a brief instant and he chuckled. It was going to be one hell of a long night.

BREEANA CAME INTO THE kitchen and elbowed Theo and Sully out of the way. She wanted to see what they were cooking. Whatever it was, it smelled awful.

She lifted the lid off the soup pot. "Blechh! What is this slop? And why are there eyes staring up at me?"

"Mmm, I've really outdone myself this time, cookie." Sully licked his lips and gave the concoction another stir, before laying the wooden spoon on a saucer to catch the drips. "You're going to love it. The guys in the unit call it slumgullion. It's a mishmash of whatever food's available at any given time, especially when we're on foreign soil or on an op."

"Oh my gosh, it's all I can do not to gag at the smell. You mean it's what you eat when you're living off the land?" she asked.

"Well, yeah. It's a variation, because the recipe is never the same," Sully explained.

He seemed so proud of his concoction she almost hated to burst his bubble.

"This particular slumgullion is the result of what's available in your fridge, Bree, which included fresh trout."

"Sully," Theo offered, "Maybe Breeana would prefer the head and tail cut off the trout."

"I don't see why, bro. What with the leftover pasta, cheese, twice-fried beans, curried rice with a couple of eggs on top, I think the trout gives the dish a touch of class."

"Kind of like a finishing garnish," Theo agreed. "I'll get the plates and call everyone to the table for lunch."

"Hold it right there." Breeana couldn't take it anymore. If she didn't get the putrid smorgasbord out of her kitchen, she wouldn't be responsible for what her stomach did next. She grabbed the pot from the stove and pushed past Sully and Theo as she headed for the garbage cans at the back of the house.

"What's the matter, Bree?" Sully asked as he reached around her to open the door. "You want to eat at the picnic table? Theo, bring the plates outside."

Without a word, Breeana hopped down the outside stairs, bumped the lid from the closest garbage pail, and dumped the vile-smelling slumgullion into the inner bag. Then she took the pot to the outdoor tap and hosed it down.

"Cookie!" Sully croaked. "What have you done with our food?"

"Consider yourselves relieved of kitchen duty, guys. From now on, there will be no slumgullion cooked in my house. The next thing you know, Cody and his grandfather will be copying down your recipes. My stomach couldn't take it. Any questions?"

Sully and Theo stared at each other before they shrugged their shoulders and Sully said, "Just one. What do you want to have for lunch?"

"We can order chicken from the local barbeque."

"Well, it won't taste nearly as good, but I guess we can make the call." Sully muttered as Theo reached for the take-out menus.

"Honest to God, the woman is scary. Can you believe she threw out our slumgullion?"

"You're right, bro," Theo said. "Breeana obviously has no taste. Why don't you tell the other guys what she did to our food while I order up the chicken?"

SULLY NOTICED MICAH trailing Cody to the door when the bell rang forty-five minutes later. He worked from home today and had Sergeant Millette on the line. The whole working from home gig had seemed like a great plan—stay close to Bree, spend some quality time with her son—but he was in quicksand, sinking fast where she was concerned. Not the best if he wanted to maintain the professional distance he needed to do his job, but he didn't want to leave her, which told him plainly he was in big, big trouble.

With his gaze glued to Breeana, he barely noticed the pizza boxes Cody carried when he blew by him headed for the kitchen. Still, the sight tripped something at the back of his brain.

"There's still no sign of Hannah Grimes, Lieutenant. We've got an APB out on her, but so far, no luck. The woman's disappeared without a trace."

"Hell. Where would she go? There's no way she vanished into thin air unless she's dead, maybe another loose end tied off by our psycho. I want the crime lab to go over her house from top to bottom. Find me something, Jacques, and then get back to me."

Sully hit disconnect and suddenly, it hit him. Theo had ordered *chicken* for lunch. He leapt over the couch and stampeded to the kitchen. Cody was already downing his second slice of pizza by the time he managed to get hold of him. He knocked the pie out of the boy's hands. Then he grabbed him around the waist and propelled him into the nearest bathroom, already shoving his finger halfway down the kid's throat. Cody fought him tooth and nail, twisted around, and bit down hard on his finger.

"Cool it, pal! I don't want to hurt you, but you have to get rid of the pizza. And I'd like to keep my fingers while you're doing it."

Breeana heard the commotion and came running. She caught on to the emergency and took control of the situation, managing to calm down her son.

"It's okay, kiddo. Sully thinks the pizza is bad. You need to get rid of it, honey. Now. We're right here with you."

Cody stared at his mother and Sully. "Let me get it straight. You want me to hurl the best meal I've had all day?"

"You got it, tough guy; we want you to puke your guts out," Sully insisted, fighting the urge to panic.

Cody sank to the floor in front of the toilet bowl. "Okay, back off, man. You could have just said so, instead of jumping all over me."

Hawke stuck his head in the doorway while the boy retched up his lunch. "Micah's got the car started and Reece is checking out the perimeter. We're ready to roll whenever you are. Is there anything else we can do?"

"Yes," Sully barked as he held Cody's head. "Gather up the pizza before the dogs eat it and get it to the lab. Be sure to wear gloves, in case there are prints on the boxes."

Theo was out in the hallway and he leaned forward over Hawke's shoulder. "I'll take the pizzas to the lab, bro. The other guys can ride with you to the hospital. I'll meet you there."

"Good idea. Thanks." Sully reached in his pocket and threw Theo the keys to his Tahoe. "Hit the siren and burn rubber all the way."

The boy was already pale and sweating. His legs were rubbery when Sully helped him to his feet. Whatever was in those pizzas seemed to race through his system at an alarming rate. Law waited with a cold compress to wipe Cody's face. Breeana grabbed for it and dashed for the front door. Sully and Hawke held Cody between them and brought up the rear.

The kid stumbled and started to sway. "Uh, I don't feel sooo good."

Sully struggled to get a better grip on him before he slid out of his grasp. "Law, keep an eye on Breeana and call the hospital from your cell. Tell them what's happened. We won't know what we're dealing with until we get the lab results, but they need to be prepared. We should be at emergency in ten minutes tops."

He set the alarm and hit the lock on his way out the door. After settling Cody in the back seat between him and his mother, he gathered the boy to his chest, pulled out his cell phone, and called the lab. The hospital needed the results as fast as possible. Law dove for the front seat beside Micah, while Hawke and Reece brought up the rear in a second SUV. Sirens blasting, they were on their way.

IT WAS SIX ANXIOUS hours before Breeana could let out a sigh of relief. Cody was resting in a hospital room after responding to treatment. She pulled the covers up over his lanky frame and sank down in the chair beside his bed. She clutched his hand through the guard rail and listened to the beeps of a medical device monitoring his vital signs. His stomach had been pumped and neutralized with charcoal to offset the effects of the drug. An IV dripped hydrating fluids into his arm. It had been touch and go for a while, but the doctor said he would fully recover.

"Relax. He's going to be fine." Sully squeezed her shoulders encouragingly.

"And what if it happens again?" Her voice constricted with fear and something else, something much stronger, the ferocity of a mother protecting her young. "The maniac almost killed my child just to get to me."

"You're right. It was a close call and we can't take any more chances. But I don't think killing Cody, or anyone else, was the bastard's real intention. He miscalculated the dosage and used too much of the tranquilizer." Sully moved his big hands from her shoulders to knead the knots along the back of her neck. "It is you he's after, and *only* you. He planned to waltz into the house and grab you after we all passed out from the doctored food."

"I don't care what he was thinking, when the end result would have still been the same. You heard what the ER doctor said. Cody's tox screen showed enough tranquilizers in his system to bring down a small elephant. My God, Sully, my son could have died!"

Her father barreled into the room with Hunt and Theo close on his heels, in time to catch the tail-end of their conversation. "Damn straight. You have to get him out of here, pumpkin. It's the only way to keep him safe."

"He won't want to go, Dad."

"I don't give a horse's patootie. I've already talked to a buddy of mine who runs a summer hockey camp in New Brunswick. I filled him in on the details and everything is arranged. Cody is going to camp as soon as he's well enough, even if I have to drag him there kicking and screaming."

Breeana agonized over making the right decision to ensure her son's safety. Should Cody go, or should he stay? As if reading her thoughts, Sully took a stand and agreed with her father. He made no bones about it.

"It's too dangerous for him to stay with you any longer. The faster we move him away from here, the safer he'll be. Micah and Law are Cody's guard detail, and they will handle his transport. They will also protect him with their lives, Bree. What do you say?"

"Hey, what's all the yelling about?" Cody moaned from the bed. He tried to open his puffy eyes. "Can't a guy get any sleep around here? I heard what you said and you're wasting your time. I'm not going anywhere, Mom..."

Breeana swept the hair off his forehead and planted a kiss on his sweat-dampened brow. She watched as sleep reclaimed him, whispering against his ear. "You don't have to go, kiddo. No one can force me to send you away."

"What did you say? Can you hear yourself talk?" The tension in Sully's grip jolted her as he wrapped his fingers around her biceps and tugged her to her feet. "You need to clear your head and get your priorities straight. A good meal will help, and I don't mean hospital food. There's a place right across the street. Your son will be fine with Law and Micah for an hour."

"I am not leaving the room." He edged her closer to the door before she could dig her heels into the slippery linoleum.

"Bree, I know you don't want to leave him, but you'll be able to see Cody's room from the restaurant window. We won't be far away. And Mic or Law will call us if there's any change in his condition. I promise.

Breeana twisted in his grasp and caught his glance. The raw concern in his eyes was enough to stall the flow of curse words threatening to spill out of her mouth. Sully cared...he really cared about them. With the realization, she released a pent-up sigh, wrapped her arms around his waist, and surrendered to an insanity that was one-hundred-percent Sullivan Sauvage.

His strong heart thumped a reassuring cadence against her ear. His big hands warmed her back and eased the panic along her spine. Such simple actions, yet her fear dissipated like mist before a rising sun.

"You aren't alone in this." Sully tipped her chin with a knuckle and brushed a kiss along her temple. "We'll keep Cody safe. You have to believe we are going to nail the bastard."

Breeana savored the temporary respite and relaxed for a few seconds against him before pushing away from his chest with her open palms. "Give me a minute to grab my purse and freshen up. Then we'll go."

The freak summer storm began just as Breeana watched her father and Hunt jog across the street. They would all catch a quick bite and bring back take out for Micah and Law.

"Come on, Sully. I'll race you before we both get soaked to the skin."

"You're on, cookie, but be prepared to lose."

They both took off; laughing and jostling for position, although Breeana knew Sully measured his pace to let her keep up with him. He would not let her out of range, not even for a second.

Thunder boomed above their heads. A deluge of rain mixed with hailstones pummeled the steaming pavement around them. Lightning flashed in the distance, enough for Breeana to see Reece, Hawke and Theo close the gap on the diner. She increased her own speed, determined to beat Sully across the parking lot.

For the first time in weeks, she felt lighthearted. The icy terror gripping her for days lessened with every splashing footfall against the asphalt. Faster and faster she ran, swerving around Sully and sprinting ahead of him. Just as she closed the distance to the restaurant, an uneasy feeling gathered in the pit of her stomach. Something was wrong. Terror gripped her and wouldn't let go.

Go back to the hospital now! Cody needs you!

Sully overshot her and skidded to a halt, swiping the rain from his eyes. "Hey, why'd you stop when we're almost there? Don't tell me you're afraid to lose?"

Cody's in danger!

With no logical explanation for the thought, Breeana knew she was right. She didn't hesitate. She pivoted and tore back in the opposite direction. A moment later, she flew through the hospital doors before Sully could stop her. There was no time to try and convince him.

Her blouse and jeans were rain-soaked. Rivulets whipped off her clothing as she sprinted through the corridors. Sully shouted behind her, but she didn't slow down. He made it to the service elevator in time to shove his arm through the slot before the doors closed on his face. Once inside, he seized her roughly by the shoulders and shook her.

"What in bloody hell do you think you're doing?"

"Cody's in trouble!" The horrifying words spilled from her lips like dialogue from a horror flick. "I know I'm right!"

His eyes grew cold. His jaw tightened. She couldn't blame him for thinking she was insane.

"Listen, my own gut instincts have been right more times than I can count. If you sense Cody's at risk, I'm willing to bet the farm you're right."

He drew his firearm and pushed her behind him. "When these doors open, I want you to stay on the elevator and wait for the others to get here. Is that clear?"

"Yes," she agreed. Adrenaline surged her bloodstream as they slowed to a halt on the sixth floor. She tasted bile, swallowing hard to push it back. Body vibrating with fear, her white-as-a-sheet reflection bounced off the metal interior and mocked her. By the time the doors slid open, she could barely stand.

A tall, hospital-garbed man wearing pop-bottle glasses and a surgical mask leaned against the elevator wall. He stood beside a blanketed body on a gurney. A foot protruded from the blanket with a toe tag attached. Breeana recognized the blackened big toe of the foot—Cody's foot. And Cody's ankle—a strawberry colored birthmark etched on the bony nub.

"Cody! Dear God, we're too late!"

"Police! Get your hands behind your head!" Arms holding a firing stance, Sully's gaze locked on the man standing in front of them. "Put your hands behind your head and step away from the gurney. Do it now!"

"You murdered my son! You son of a bitch!" Breeana lunged without thinking. She threw herself out of the elevator, clawing and kicking, punching with her fists. Sully grabbed her from behind and tossed her against the elevator wall. Too late. He lost his shot.

The bastard plowed the gurney into them and knocked them both to the floor. Then he disappeared into the nearest stairwell.

Cody toppled from the gurney, a moan escaping his lips.

"Jesus, he's alive. Bree, stay with him." Sully leapt to his feet and shoved the gurney aside. Leading with his gun in a two-handed grip, he left her cradling her son on the floor.

Chapter 12

Another elevator pinged. Theo stuck his head out the door.
"Hold up!" Sully shouted. "Hawke, the perp's in the stairwell. Get after him. Reece, watch Breeana and Cody."

Sully boarded the second elevator while medical personnel lifted Cody back on the gurney then charged down the hall with him. Theo hit the button for the garage. Where the hell were Micah and Law? No answer on either of their cell phones. He assumed the worst—they were either down, or dead.

"I'm going to kill that sack of..." Sully watched the numbers above the door as the elevator descended, got on his phone to brief Millette. "Lock the hospital down."

"I'll call it in. We're on our way."

Hospital security and local law enforcement would have to do the job until his homicide team arrived. *Fuck.* He flipped his cell phone shut and clipped it back on his belt. "I hope we're not too late."

"We'll catch the bastard if we beat him to the garage," Theo said. "He has to have some kind of transport. How else would he get Cody's so-called corpse out of here?"

"If you get a bead on him, take him down."

"No problem."

The elevator doors slid open at the garage entry level. Oversized laundry trolleys lined the walls in front of the first bay door. Theo leveled his Glock while Sully took his boots to them, knocked them flying. No one hiding inside.

A second loading area contained pallets of supplies being unloaded from an 18-wheeler. Theo boarded the box and herded two men off. A few others stood around having coffee, including the driver. Sully scanned their faces and body types, lowered his gun, and flashed his badge. "Everyone take off. Now."

The third stall was empty. Lightning reflected off wet pavement beneath the partially raised door as the other men ducked under it and fled.

A hearse from a local funeral home loomed large in the fourth bay. *Bingo!* Sully held his weapon in a two-handed grip, approaching along the far wall, while Theo took the driver's side.

They moved in sync, staying low as they inched forward. Heart pounding, adrenaline rushing, Sully's finger steadied on the trigger guard. The slightest movement, or sound from inside the hearse, and he'd fire, straight down into it. He knew Theo would do the same.

Brothers in arms and not just by blood, they had fought side-by-side for years—often in worse situations and always watching each other's back. He'd give his left nut for his brother's safety, but hopefully, not today. The hearse was empty.

Theo whispered in the gloom. "You figure it's stolen?"

"Hell, yes." Sully eyed the hearse and faked a yawn. "I'm tired, bro."

"Uh-huh. I suppose you want to take a nap?"

"That's the plan."

"Pleasant dreams. And keep your head down. I might miss when I take the shot."

Theo edged toward the semi again and crawled under it. Sully almost laughed as he slipped inside the hearse. Hiding in back was only a precaution. Theo wouldn't miss. He never did.

THE HEARSE WAS A BUST, an hour wasted before Sully headed back up to the sixth floor. He reached the double doors of the Intensive Care Unit and peered through the glass. A beehive of activity surrounded Cody, Micah and Law. Hawke had called him to relay the news. His guys were still alive and kicking.

He couldn't see Breeana, but he knew she was with Reece and Hawke in the adjoining waiting room. She wouldn't stay away, not while medical staff worked to revive her son. Sully could only imagine how devastated she must be. He and his team had let her down. A powerful rage shook him, but he shoved it aside. He couldn't indulge now. He had work to do.

Five minutes later, he stood grim-faced with Jacques Millette and Sal Clemente in Cody's hospital room. The psycho had left his calling card. A rosary hung from the IV stand clamped to the kid's bedrail. But, it was the letter taped to a wall and addressed to Breeana that floored all of them.

"What did you just put in an evidence bag?"

Sully turned and saw her standing at the foot of the bed, pale-faced and shaken. Something inside him unraveled.

I don't want to scare her more than she already is, but someone has to open her eyes to what the beast is capable of. She has to send Cody away for his own protection, and forget the insane scheme of hers to set herself up as bait.

Watching her tear across the hospital parking lot—away from him and into danger—had been enough to make his knees grow weak and his heart stall in his chest. The evil bastard had slipped through his fingers again, almost succeeded in taking Cody with him this time.

Theo still watched the hearse in the garage, but Sully figured their perp had escaped before the hospital was locked down. He shrugged, sealed the evidence bag, and handed it to Breeana.

"Here, see for yourself."

"What are you doing, Lieutenant?" Millette shot him a disapproving glare. "She doesn't need to see it."

"Oh, I think she does, Sergeant. Dr. McGill needs a reality check." Sully watched Breeana's knuckles whiten and her fingers tremble as she clutched the evidence bag and read the computerized words, printed on standard stock paper.

DEAR BREEANA,

Are you missing your son? If you come to me, I might let your boy go. Otherwise, I'll send him back to you one piece at a time. I wonder...can he still play hockey without his fingers and toes? His fate is in your hands.

I'll be in touch.

The Shepherd

Sully pried the evidence bag from her gripping fingers and handed it off to Clemente, who monitored the crime scene techs working her son's hospital room.

"Cody's leaving here tonight, Bree, as soon as the doctor says he's fit enough to travel. Any more objections?"

Breeana could barely nod her head in agreement. She was speechless with horror after reading what The Shepherd had in store for her child. He would have killed her son in front of her; she had no doubt, once she showed up for her own slaughter. She started to list to one side but Sully moved to support her, encircling her waist with a strong arm and guiding her out of the stuffy room. He waved off Hawke and Reece who stood in the hallway by the door.

"Easy, cookie. Take shallow breaths."

Breeana clung to him, paralyzed, no longer capable of holding herself up, or placing one foot in front of the other.

"I'm sorry I let you read the letter."

At the sound of his voice, Breeana's temper flared and got her sea legs under her as nothing else could. "That's the biggest load of bullshit I have ever heard you shovel, Sauvage. You're not sorry. You *wanted* me to read that abomination. You're punishing me, because I haven't been the good little soldier you expected me to be."

"You couldn't be more wrong. I just want you to face goddamn reality. Let your son go. He needs to get off the lunatic's radar before it's too late. He needs to get the hell away from you."

"Are you taking the boy to a safe house?" Millette's voice cut in from close behind them.

"That's need-to-know information and you *don't* need to know," Sully snarled.

Breeana winced. It wasn't Millette's fault the hunt for the man, who called himself The Shepherd, decomposed faster than road kill in the noonday sun.

Sully turned to the sergeant and clasped his shoulder. "Just do what you do best, Millette. Focus on the evidence and follow-up on any leads. And make sure Clemente has the crime scene techs go down to the garage after they finish up here. I want the outside of the hearse gone over before it's towed to the lab."

"Right, Lieutenant."

Sully let out a long breath and turned back to Breeana. She knew her gaze was hateful. She couldn't help it.

How dare he act like I don't give a damn about my son's safety?

"Do you think I can't figure out my son is in danger?"

"Can you? Then try acting like it. Do you understand what a psychopath is? Can you even say the word?" Sully struggled to lower his voice with visible effort. "Cody was lucky this time, if you want to call it that. I'm begging here...let my team move him somewhere safe. I couldn't stand it if anything else happened to him. And I know you couldn't live with yourself if this maniac makes good on his threats.

"He will use every means at his disposal to get you where he wants you, Bree. Please, if you don't care about your own life, at least eliminate the risk to your son, before it's too late."

"I care about Cody's life, *and* my own life!" She choked back a sob and her voice hardened with conviction. "All right, you can take Cody out of here, but only on one condition. My father goes with him or the deal is off."

Sully sent her a tight smile. "Consider it done."

The letter was Breeana's wake-up call. She understood her father's life wouldn't be worth the price of a gumball if the killer moved on to him next. Sully pulled her to his side, his arm wrapping around her like a steel band. She didn't resist, since his next words almost choked the life out of her.

"By removing Jack and Cody from the mix, The Shepherd will come straight for you now. Which means, no more charging off in dark parking lots, or anywhere else. From here on in, Bree, you'll toe the line and do as I say."

The Shepherd...what sort of moniker was that for someone without a conscience or a soul? Did he really believe himself to be compassionate and kind?

I'll see you in hell! You won't get my son in your clutches again!

Stiffening her spine, Breeana pushed herself from Sully's embrace and swallowed her panic. "Put your plan in motion for Cody's and my father's safety. I'll be in ICU if you need me."

A few minutes later, she stared through the ICU window. Cody, Micah, and Law were still unconscious, their beds lined up against the far wall. With Micah and Law hooked up to oxygen until the effects of succinylcholine—a muscle paralyzing agent sometimes used on animals—wore off.

The drug was probably stolen from her clinic on the night of the fire. She had missed inventory but assumed it was destroyed by the blaze. The medication was dangerous if given at high doses.

"I can't believe the bastard got the jump on Mic and Law." Hawke scowled. Pressing a cup of coffee into Breeana's fingers and a comforting hand on her shoulder, he steered her to a chair in the waiting room. "Even if he was disguised in hospital scrubs, they should have known something was up when he came into the room."

"Why would they?" Breeana argued. "When I saw him, he looked like he belonged here, right down to an ID badge. They had no reason to suspect him, and probably assumed he was Cody's doctor making his rounds."

"In our line of work, we don't *assume* anything. More to the point, how the hell did he manage to nail both of them with syringes?" Anger fueled Reece's words. "All I can say is he must be one hell of an actor. If I didn't know any better, I'd swear he's invisible."

The chief resident pushed through the ICU doors and joined them, wiping sweat from his brow with a hairy forearm. He was built like a linebacker. Breeana thought he'd look more at home on a football field than in a hospital ward. "The worst is over and the men have stabilized."

"Can you be more specific, Doc?" Reece demanded from his position by the door.

"It means they're breathing fine on their own and their hearts are beating at a normal rhythm, although we'll keep them sedated until the drug completely eradicates from their systems." He turned his attention to Breeana, a smile creasing his lips. "Your son is doing fine, by the way. It seems he slept through all the excitement. Don't worry, he should be up and around in a day or two."

"Thank you." Breeana turned out of the waiting area and made a beeline for the nearest bathroom, tears of relief streaming her face. She rounded the corner, with Hawke close behind her, and thought she saw Cody's hockey coach up ahead. In a flash, Ben Prewitt disappeared into the stairwell at the far end of the corridor.

Impossible. She must be seeing things. Ben couldn't have known about the attack on Cody. There was no other reasonable explanation for him to be here. Exhaustion must be playing tricks on her, making her see things that weren't really there. *God, will this nightmare ever end?*

A MILITARY TRANSPORT helicopter lifted off from the hospital parking lot at five the next morning. Breeana watched from the ground along with Sully, Hawke and Theo. A lot of strings were pulled between the police force and the military to set the plan in motion. A flight crew, doctor, and full contingent of passengers were onboard. Sully said no flight plan was filed. And no one knew the final destination of the passengers, not even the flight crew assigned to their transport for this leg of the journey. Once the chopper landed at a predetermined location, the passengers would be met by other members of Sully's military unit and would be relocated to an undisclosed location.

Reece and Hunt were on the helicopter. They would guard Jack and Cody until Micah and Law were once again up to the task. It could take another few days, according to the flight doctor who was now responsible for their recovery.

Breeana watched the take-off with a smile on her lips. *Find Cody and my father now, you sick freak!*

A few minutes later, she and Sully were seated in the restaurant across the street from the hospital. Sully pointed out the obvious with a raised eyebrow. "You have to eat something. Starving yourself isn't going to help matters."

The waitress topped off their coffees as Breeana continued to push congealed eggs around on her plate. It was only five-thirty but the café buzzed with early risers. She knew she looked a mess and didn't need a mirror to tell her. Her clothes were still damp from the storm, her skin clammy and cold from the air blasting out of ceiling vents. Her make-up and hairstyle were yesterday's memory. She felt like a dishrag after mopping up kennel spills. All things considered, she thought herself lucky to be still vertical and not sliding under the table to catch a few winks.

She glanced Sully's way and her abdomen scrunched into a ball of heat. He looked sinful in jeans and a tee with a gun clipped to his waist beneath a loose, black linen jacket. How could the man be so unflappable and yummy after he had whisked Cody to emergency, then challenged The Shepherd to save her son's life? Not to mention overseeing evidence collection and the investigation into Cody's poisoning and attempted kidnapping.

"I'm hungry. I just can't seem to get the food past the lump in my throat. I miss Cody and Dad already. I'm worried sick about them."

Sully tugged her hand across the table and squeezed her fingers. "You don't have to worry about your family anymore. They are beyond The Shepherd's reach now, and Cody has nothing but time on his hands to recover. You heard what the doctor said. He'll be bouncing out of bed and nagging the rest of them in no time flat."

"I suppose." She managed a wan smile. "Kids always recover faster than the rest of us. He'll go postal when he finds out he's been whisked away from the action though. At least I won't have to deal with the fall-out."

"See? There's always a silver lining if you search hard enough." Sully winked, reached for his wallet, and threw some bills on the table. "If you've finished playing choo-choo with your food, let's go."

She grabbed her purse and slid from the booth. "I have time for a run with the dogs before clinic hours. The fresh air will wake me up."

"Do you have to open the clinic today?" He grasped her elbow as his gaze scanned the crowd in the diner. "Don't you have an emergency number listed when the clinic is closed?"

"Don't go there," she said, tossing the curls in motion around her head. "We agreed it would be business as usual until The Shepherd is caught. I expect you to honor our agreement."

"I'm willing to do it. I'd just like you to catch some sleep before you croak from exhaustion. Does reasoning with you always have to feel like steering a course blindfolded through a minefield?"

She ignored his sarcasm as they hustled to the Tahoe, and he unlocked the doors. "Why do I need to rest? You didn't get any more sleep than I did last night. I don't see you wanting to go to bed."

"Ouch. I always want to go to bed with you. I'm hard just thinking about it. As far as sleep goes, I'm used to taking catnaps from my military training."

He paused to shoot her a sexy grin. "Theo and Hawke can run the dogs. How about snoozing when we get back to the house? I'll wake you in plenty of time to get to the clinic. Or, we could have wild chimpanzee sex. I'm ready to do my part."

That gave her something to think about. Would she be able to sleep? No, definitely not. She needed something, someone, to help her forget. She wanted Sully—his strength and the comfort of his body—to get her through this nightmare. Confusion ran neck and neck with desperation and the knowledge she wanted the man on so many levels. He was her sanity. She was already halfway in love with him. And yes, soon he would be her lover. He just didn't know it yet.

"Hey, I'm only teasing you about the sex, trying to lighten the moment a little." He hugged her waist and smoothed a kiss against her temple. "Come on. Let's get you home."

Chapter 13

The walls of the beach house closed in around him. He couldn't breathe. Tears of anger and disgust blurred his vision. The Shepherd sank to the floor, hugged his knees to his chest, and rocked back and forth. He focused on steadying his breathing.

How can everything be so messed up?

Breeana, a whore who didn't respect God's word, was alive. The Lord had called her home, trusted The Shepherd to send her on her way. And yet, she still breathed.

Why can't I get the job done?

He gulped in air, hung his head in despair, swiped a sleeve across his runny nose, and crawled to the side of the bed. Clasping his hands together, he heaved his elbows to the mattress, planted his knees on the hardwood floor, and prayed for guidance.

Eventually, it came to him—the reason for his failure. *It's the Devil's work. He wants to keep her for himself.* The Shepherd prayed fervently for Breeana's eternal soul. He also implored God to give him the tools he needed to snatch her away from Satan.

After all, he couldn't use her family anymore. The cop had moved her son and father out of reach this morning. Heaven help him, he'd seen the helicopter take off from the hospital and had almost blasted it out of the sky. But, he couldn't follow through, not with so many innocents on board. They didn't deserve killing. Maiming? Sure, if it taught Breeana a lesson. But he wouldn't kill an innocent...not unless she forced his hand.

It was far better to keep his anger focused on his quarry. *Yes, Breeana must die soon.* The list of women who didn't know their place kept on growing. God needed his help; he didn't know what to do. He couldn't go to the next name on the list, not until Breeana was sacrificed.

Above all else, he had to be careful. No more hidden cameras tracking back to him. And last night at the hospital was lousy planning. He'd almost had a coronary when Sauvage popped out of the elevator with the bitch riding shotgun. He barely had time to escape, and he'd ditched his disguise—another dumbass move. What if the cops found it? They could lift his prints off the eyeglasses and hospital ID. Or maybe they'd find hair follicles, or skin cells on the hospital scrubs.

No more mistakes.

The end game for Breeana will come soon. The Lord has ordained it, and the Lord is never wrong.

"BREE?" THE HOUSE WAS so quiet Sully could hear a pin drop, and Breeana was easing down on his bed. He must have dozed off the second he hit the pillows. He thought he was dreaming at first, before he hauled himself into a sitting position and caught her naked silhouette against the backdrop of closed louvers covering the windows. *What the hell is she doing?* When she threw back the covers and slid the protection over his erect member, he knew.

"Did anyone see you come in here?" he croaked, sweat breaking out on his body as he moved to Red-Alert mode. *God, she is beautiful.* Everything he wanted. Everything he shouldn't have. It wasn't right. He wanted to take her hard and fast. He knew she deserved better.

She shook her head and whispered in his ear. "No, Hawke and Theo are still out with the dogs."

Shit. Sully was so wide awake now his body parts argued for control with the sane part of his brain that knew he should push her away. Breeana climbed on top of him, her teeth scraping his neck as her hands roamed further south to circle his equipment. He stilled her furtive movements, his palms gliding down her slender arms.

Her sweet musk engulfed him. The honeyed scent clung to him like a homing device. It tempted. It teased. Not good. Breeana needed the comfort of his embrace right now, not him ramming himself into her.

She also deserved church bells and bouquets, while he was the poster boy for love 'em and leave 'em. Nothing would change because they exchanged body fluids. He craved her, but was he man enough to keep her? It had to stop before he did something stupid. Like take what she offered, and say to hell with tomorrow.

He tried to move her off him. She clung like Velcro around his neck. *God, I am only human.* He wanted to shove his tongue into her amazing mouth until he stroked her tonsils. But, he had no business seeking redemption with a woman like her. "Go back to your own bed. Get the hell out!"

She steadied herself on his lap and met his eyes. "I'm not going anywhere."

"If this is your way of thanking me for keeping you alive and saving your son, you can forget it."

"Sully, I..."

"Shh...hear me out." He cupped her face with his hands and almost lost himself in the emerald hurt of her eyes. *Have mercy.* "I'm a lone wolf, cookie. I always will be. While I want to know you better, I'm not sure I can give you what you need. If you want rough and meaningless sex, then I'm your man. If it's a long-term relationship you're after, you are in the wrong bed."

"I'm not afraid of you." She looked him straight in the eye and feathered kisses across his jaw. "What I *need* is for you to get down off the soapbox and make love to me. I'm so hot, Sully, so very, very hot. I'm burning up. You're the only one who can help me."

Point taken.

He could feel her pulsing heat as she positioned him beneath her and slid herself down his rock-hard shaft, inch by agonizingly slow inch. Her body arched, her small hands dancing across his chest.

Hell, he wasn't a saint. He was locked and loaded with a round already in the chamber. He latched onto her creamy breast, nipping and suckling every delicious inch. One hand cupped her sweet ass and squeezed, his fingers parting the indent there. His other hand circled the bull's-eye shielded beneath her auburn curls. He penetrated those curls and stroked her delicate nub, already slick with moisture. Joining the rhythm of his busy fingers, his penis thrust itself home.

"Come for me," he groaned. Breeana trembled and mewled. He tongued her breasts again, licked his way from one pointed peak to the other while he caressed the swollen silk of her sex. The scent of her fiery heat drove him to a frenzy. He gentled the kiss and eased off on the tension. He had to slow down, back way the hell off. She was delicate and small to his hard and mean. He didn't want to hurt her. "Tell me what you want, Bree."

"Damn you for stopping." She hitched in a ragged breath, her head falling forward as a sob parted her lips. Her hands stilled on his shoulders. "I want you. Now."

No woman had ever made him want like this. He was torn between her fragility and his need to take himself home inside her. The need to protect her from his big, bad self battled the need to lose himself in her softness. It tore at his heart. But, pleasure won out. He gave up the fight and rocked his hips against her. Breeana moaned, her muscles clenching around him. Together, they rocketed into another dimension.

Sully grabbed a shower while Breeana slept, stepped back into his boxers and flopped on the bed. She opened her eyes, stretched like a kitten and snuggled against him. Sully prodded her about the change of heart. "I thought you wanted us to get to know each other better before we made love."

"True, I did."

"I am grateful, cookie, but how did you end up in my bed?"

Breeana smiled and poked him in the ribs with her elbow. "It was when you told me you didn't want me parading around half-naked in front of your friends the other evening. I got hot and bothered because *you* were hot and bothered. Then I thought, if we could get sex out of the way, we could just go about our business. Micah would quit flirting with me, and you could focus more on finding the killer and less on what I was, or wasn't, wearing."

"Ha," he snorted, "like that's going to happen. Mic is a natural born flirt. He'll keep after you like a tick on a deer. And, I'll want to rip your clothes off every time I'm in the same room with you."

She sighed against his neck, her lips planting a kiss there. "It could be arranged."

Sully laughed. No other woman had ever affected him the way she did. She stunned him. She made him feel alive. She smelled like a rain forest, sultry and hot. He reached for her again, moving down her length to the juncture of her thighs.

"Your calves belong draped over my shoulders. Then there are your thighs...and..." His tongue slid home, gliding across the molten heat of her sex.

"Sully?" She moved her hands as if to stop him, stunned confusion clouding her gaze. He was beyond the point of doing the gentlemanly thing. Breeana whimpered as she rode to climax. He kept pace with her, laving and stroking, increasing and slowing until she shattered against him. He brought her down easy, hyped by her body's responses and humbled by her trust. He ignored the ache in his groin as he pulled her against him and smiled. "You can tuck the purple vibrator in the back of your closet from now on. You won't be needing it."

As the words left his mouth, he wanted to take them back. He knew he shouldn't encourage her, or a relationship. *What the hell was I thinking?* Releasing a long breath, he realized he was in a world of shit where she was concerned.

SULLY NEEDED A SOLID lead on The Shepherd. The investigation had stalled, and day after day, he watched the tension build in Breeana. Hell, she barely spoke to him anymore. He passed by her bedroom door, thought about knocking, and changed direction for the kitchen. *What's the use? She won't answer anyway.*

Theo grabbed two beers from the fridge and tossed him one. "Where's Bree?"

"In her room, resting." Sully sank into a chair across from his brother.

Theo twisted the cap off his beer and took a swallow. "Look, bro, you have to drag her out of there. We've barely seen her in days."

"*You've* barely seen her?" Sully grabbed his brother's arm. "You mean to tell me she's holed up in there all day long, too?"

"Yeah, that's what I'm telling you, man, except for when she's working at the clinic. When she's home, it's tough pulling her out of there for meals."

"I didn't realize, Theo. I'll talk to her in the morning."

"All right, bro. Let me know if there's anything the rest of us can do."

It was no big surprise, because Breeana hadn't made another appearance in Sully's bedroom either. And while his body protested, he understood. Being separated from her family and living in fear had to be hell. No small wonder she didn't want to talk to anyone.

She also needed sleep. Romping with him between the sheets wouldn't give her that. Still, he wondered if she kept her distance for another reason. Was she still determined to set herself up as bait for The Shepherd? The thought stayed with him when he crashed for the night. He had the mother lode of all nightmares.

Killers and victims haunted his sleep on a regular basis, but this nightmare was different. Breeana had the starring role. She reached out to him, begged him to help her, blood spattering the white silk of her gown. *Dear Christ!*

Sully snapped awake and raced to her bedroom, almost colliding with Hawke in the hallway. He just about puked with relief when he opened her door. The hallway light bathed her. Curled in on herself, she was a tight ball of nerves gripping the edge of the mattress. He sank down beside her and hauled her against him, tucking her head under his chin. He needed to hold her.

Breeana jerked awake at his touch and cracked an accusing eye in his direction. "Why hasn't he come for me yet?"

Her voice was soft and husky from sleep. Just the sound of her tightened his groin muscles. He wanted her. He ached to touch her, to pour himself into her, to make her forget the only way he could.

Right, dirt bag. Go ahead, take advantage of her while she's still reeling from the separation of her family and facing the prospect of being caught by The Shepherd. How about keeping your damn hands to yourself and cutting her some slack?

He clenched his jaw against the throb in his groin. "Are you so bored with life you need The Shepherd to attack you to break the monotony?"

"Don't be obtuse. It's the waiting that gets to me. I don't know how much longer I can stand it."

"You'll stand it as long as you have to." He tunneled a hand through her hair. He wanted to bury his face in its fragrant softness, flip her over, and kiss her brainless.

"Patience was never my strong suit. I want it to be over, Sully. I want my family back!" She shoved his arms aside and tumbled out of bed, grabbed some clothes from the dresser, and padded to the bathroom.

The hallway light shone through the thin fabric of her nightshirt and Sully stifled a groan. As much as he wanted to, he didn't go after her and try to calm her down. He knew if he didn't stand strong for her now and expect her to do the same, she would break. Then they would both be lost.

He watched her disappear before grabbing the phone and dialing Millette's cellular. It was the middle of the night, but who cared? "I got your message. What's up?"

"They found a floater out by the Ste-Catherine locks a few hours ago. Marie Matisse will perform the autopsy later today. Her preliminary findings are the body matches Hannah Grimes' general physical description. It looks like another murder, Lieutenant."

Sully cursed. "Did you find anything at her house to indicate she knew her attacker?"

"Nada. Whatever Ms. Grimes knew, she took to the grave with her. The old priest, Father Mike, is trying to put together a list of parishioners for the time the rosaries were stolen. It will take some time. St. Pat's records aren't computerized and the priest says only God knows where Hannah Grimes archived anything."

"Does he remember anyone who might fit the bill for our unsub?"

Sully knew it was a long shot. His sister had already explained psychopaths rarely exposed the dark side of their personalities to ordinary folk. Still, Hannah Grimes knew something and whatever it was had gotten her killed. Maybe she had shared her suspicions with someone else at the parish.

"While the priest is big on longevity, he's real short on memory. I don't think he can remember what he had for breakfast this morning, let alone dig through the past. The old guy's a touch senile. I'm afraid Hannah Grimes was the only one who could have told us anything useful."

"Whatever she knew, she can't tell us anymore. Keep after the diocese for the list of parishioners. Our killer's name could be on the list."

"Right, I'm on it."

"How's Sal doing with the surveillance tapes from the docks?" Sully asked.

"He's still running license plate numbers. Nothing's jumped out at him so far. There's a lot of ground to cover."

"Make sure he stays on top of it, Jacques. And call me if the lab finds anything useful on the pizza boxes or hospital evidence, including the hearse. Sooner or later, The Shepherd will screw up and leave proof of his identity behind."

"There is one other thing," Millette offered. "The pizza delivery guy hasn't turned up at his apartment. No one has seen him since he delivered at Dr. McGill's house. His friends think he's camping at Long Sault."

"Find him."

"Sanchez and Lemieux are already on it. I have another lead to chase down."

Millette hung up and Sully tossed the phone across the bed. He still had nothing but a shitload of questions and no answers. He also wondered what other lead Millette was working on. He wouldn't put it past him to hoard information, didn't think of him as a team player.

He rasped a hand along the stubble lining his chin. Four in the morning and Breeana was already up for the day. He might as well shower, shave, and get started himself.

Chapter 14

The Shepherd snapped out of a dead sleep with a gun in his hand. Someone had tripped the silent alarm. Swinging his legs over the side of the bed, he headed for the back window. With a bird's-eye view, he saw the cop right away. And recognized him. *The idiot.* He was zigging when he should be zagging to get to the front door.

Silent and steady, he slid the window wide. Easing over the sill, he dropped onto the porch roof and then to the ground. Moving with stealth, he shadowed his visitor, inching through the undergrowth running from the curb to the front of the beach house.

He watched the cop pound on his front door. *Dumb-dumb.* Did the guy really expect to be invited in for a cappuccino? When he rapped again, The Shepherd shook his head. The cop's gaze moved to the car parked in the drive beside the house, recognition kicking in. He squinted at it a moment then swung back to stare at the door; so focused, he never heard death approach from behind.

The Shepherd's fingers tightened on the Sig Sauer P226 equipped with a sound suppressor. The cop swiveled too late, the muzzle pressed tightly against his temple before he could make a move.

"Raise your hands and drop your weapon."

The cop did as he was told.

"Nice try, Sergeant, but I can't oblige you today." Leaning in, he hissed in his visitor's ear. "No, the Lord still has plenty of work for me to do."

The Shepherd fired two quick rounds into the cop's skull, and then cursed himself. He should've made him walk to his car first. The SOB weighed a ton. As he dragged him through the underbrush, he checked his sight lines. Everything looked good. No nosey neighbors to contend with at this late hour.

Reaching the cop's beat-up ride, he popped the trunk and heaved the body inside. A clear plastic bag lay tucked in a corner. His hospital scrubs, glasses and ID.

Yes! All wrapped up nice and neat. No evidence lying around for Sauvage to find.

He started the engine and put the pedal down, roaring away from his hideout, eventually parking on a side road near the edge of town. He left the keys in the ignition and jogged five kilometers along the water's edge, back to his wreck of a beach house. He couldn't be late for work today.

Breeana had to die.

"YOU LOOK LIKE YOU'VE been ridden hard and put away wet," Breeana teased as she wandered back into the bedroom. Fresh out of the shower and feeling better than she had in days, she couldn't help but stare.

Sully still sprawled in the middle of her bed. His rock-hard body drew her gaze. Even his bed-head endeared him to her. God, she had it bad for the man, but she couldn't satisfy her cravings for him again until her son was safely home. *It wouldn't be right; would it?*

Sully wanted her. It didn't take a genius to figure it out. His manhood bulged in the front of his boxers. She knew from experience he had the equipment of a stallion. He also knew how to use it. She longed to touch him. Taste him. She fought the sexual pull, swallowed, and almost choked on her saliva. Then she blurted the first words popping into her head. "Do you want to go for a run?"

He rolled out of bed and drew her into his arms. "Jogging isn't the first thing that comes to mind, but I suppose it will have to do. But, let's wait until the sun comes up...we'll trip over ourselves in the dark."

"What?" She peeked through the slats on the bedroom window, surprised to see it was still dark outside. Her resolve to abstain from sex vanished the instant his arms banded her. "Maybe we do have time for a quick nap."

"Did you say quick?" Sully ran his hands under her T-shirt. He sighed, his fingers blazing a trail along the sides of her breasts. "There is absolutely nothing quick about what I'm going to do to you."

"Mmm, I like the sound of that."

Breeana stood on her toes and wrapped her arms around his neck. His lips slanted over hers and she surrendered. Easing her onto the bed, he followed her down. Covering her with his hard-muscled leanness, he balanced his weight on his elbows and pulled her T-shirt and bra above her head. Her arms twisted within the folds, imprisoning her in cotton handcuffs as he kissed his way down her neck to suckle her breasts.

"You are so incredibly beautiful." His eyes raised and held hers for an instant, burning desire evident in his gaze. "Live in the moment for both of us. I need you, Bree."

Breeana moaned as she allowed his claim on her body. His gifted hands finished undressing her, his mouth laving every inch of her. She writhed with want as he slowly, expertly tasted and explored, stimulating every nerve ending she possessed. Just as her body arched toward release—on the precipice of climax—he stopped.

He stripped out of his boxers, suited up in a condom he took from her nightstand, and smoothed a roughened palm over her rib cage. "Let's not rush things. I have all the time in the world to take you to heaven."

Breeana felt her cheeks flame with embarrassment. "I can't move my arms because they're caught in the T-shirt. And you can't get gratification if I don't...give back." She tried unsuccessfully to squirm from his embrace.

Sully lifted his head on a groan, his gaze boring into hers. "Watching you is what I want right now. It's a powerful turn-on for a man to pleasure his woman."

His woman. A slip of the tongue, or did he really mean it?

Licking her belly, he planted a kiss there. "You know, you take my breath away."

With those words, he rolled off her and released the T-shirt and bra from her wrists, scooped her up in his arms, and wrapped her trembling legs around his waist. Breeana felt weak with pleasure and yet impatient for more. His lovemaking was explosive. She couldn't get enough.

The scent of their sexually charged bodies rose and fueled their passion. His lips slid up her neck to capture an earlobe between his teeth. She dragged his mouth back to her own. Their breath caught and mingled. She kissed him senseless, feeling the heat, knowing she was on fire for him.

Breeana throbbed with the need to be one with him. Sully smiled, gripped her bottom, and carried her through to the bathroom while whispering in her ear, telling her exactly what he wanted to do to her with words she could never repeat. The coarse hair on his chest rubbed sensuously against her breasts.

One flick of his wrist and the shower jets pulsed warmly against her back. He slipped inside her and held her in position, her legs riding his hips. The words he breathed into her mouth were potent with promise. "Hold tight, cookie. I'm going to take you places you've never been before."

G-spot city. Sully was a man of his word.

Breeana couldn't say for certain what surprised her more. The best sexual experience of her life—or the realization she was incredibly head-over-heels in love with this man. As they clung in the afterglow of lovemaking, his heart played a powerful crescendo against her ear, an answering rhythm echoing in her own chest. The barriers surrounding Sully's heart seemed to crack a little bit more as he gave her another glimpse of the gentleness beneath his gruff exterior.

It was in his touch as he smoothed the hair off her face and kissed the tender spot beneath her ear. In his gaze as it flicked over her in a possessive sweep that said *mine...all mine.*

He didn't have to say anything. Some men couldn't express how they felt, and Breeana sensed Sully fell into that category. Yet, when he made love to her, it was more than the joining of their bodies in a dance as old as time. It was a melding of kindred spirits who had somehow managed to find each other in spite of gruesome circumstances. When he held her, as he did now, there was no need for awkward conversation.

He *loved* her.

"WHAT DO YOU MEAN YOU forgot to tell me you saw Ben Prewitt at the hospital the other night?" Sully ran an exasperated hand through his hair and arched an eyebrow at her. "Seeing someone flee a crime scene isn't something you neglect to mention to the officer-in-charge."

"Oh, come on, Sully. Everything happened so fast, I just forgot about it. Okay? Do you have to make a federal case out of it?"

"Would it make a difference if I did?" He picked up the tray containing croissants, fruit, and cheese, and then strode out the door to the sundeck.

Pouring coffee into mugs, Breeana added spoons, the creamer and a bowl of sugar to a second tray and carried it out behind him. Hawke and Theo leaned against the deck railing watching the sunrise, a brilliant orange ball hovering just beyond the beach. Breeana thought she might enjoy the view if she wasn't so frustrated by Sully's attitude and all his pacing.

Damn. How can he make love to me so thoroughly one minute, as if I'm the most precious person in his universe, and yell at me in the next?

She placed the tray on the picnic table, snagged a cup for herself along with a plate of fruit and cheese, and moved to the far end of the deck. "Anyway, Ben couldn't have hurt Cody. Trust me, he isn't The Shepherd."

"Whoa," Theo mumbled under his breath, sending a grimace Hawke's way. "Breeana, I think you'd better quit while you're ahead."

"And why isn't Prewitt The Shepherd?" Sully scowled into his coffee mug, taking a swig of the hot brew while he continued to pace. "Is it because you feel it in your bones? Or did you consult the *Ouija* board? Tell me, Bree...what proof do you have?"

"I don't need proof to know what I feel. Okay, fine," she shot back. "Waste your time checking out a guy who could no more hurt my son than have a sex change and dance around in a hot pink tutu!"

Hawke pointed in her direction with his mug. "Sully, there's no reason to get bent out of shape with Breeana about it. There was a lot going on that night for all of us."

"You said it." Theo heaped a plate with buttered croissants and jam then eased his big frame into a chair. "It's understandable Breeana forgot about seeing the coach, considering what happened to Cody."

"I get the message, guys—loud and clear. You can both quit defending her." Sully plunked his mug on the deck rail, its contents splashing over the sides. He extended an arm and pulled her against him, an almost smile quirking his lips. "Call me crazy, Bree, but I'm still going to interrogate Prewitt and check out his alibi for the times in question, just in case your hotline to the ether world is way off beam."

Breeana started to respond when Sully's cell phone rang and he grabbed for it, effectively ending their conversation. It wasn't long before he broke the call and snagged his jacket from the back of a lawn chair. "*Unfreaking believable*. Clemente just told me Sergeant Millette was found stuffed in the trunk of his car. He's been shot. It's a miracle he's still alive."

"How the hell did it happen? Did he bust in on a drug deal, maybe get caught in a turf war?"

"Not in this town, Theo," Sully shrugged into his jacket. "I'm guessing he went toe-to-toe with The Shepherd. It's the only case he's working on. The fool must have held back information. *Shit!* I'm heading over to Millette's crib now. It's possible he has evidence stashed somewhere."

He nailed Breeana with a concerned glance. "You stay close to Theo and Hawke today. I mean it, cookie."

She was so unnerved after hearing about the assault on Sergeant Millette it took her a few seconds to respond. She placed her mug on the picnic table with shaking hands. "Don't worry. I'll stick to these guys like glue."

"Make sure you do." Sully took the stairs and crossed the grass. He climbed into his Tahoe and started the engine, rolling down the window. "Theo, Hawke, don't let her out of your sight for one second. I don't care if she's in the shower; one of you had better be standing on the other side of the shower curtain with your eyes facing the door."

"I'll toss you for it." Theo and Hawke called to each other as they flipped a coin and waved Sully off. He laid rubber out of the driveway.

"DR. MCGILL?"

Breeana listened on speaker phone as she shuffled through the charts Laura handed her with the morning's schedule. "Speaking. Can I help you?"

"It's Jenny from the alarm company. There's been a break-in at your residence. The police are waiting for you before they go inside. Apparently, you have dogs in the house?"

"Good Lord!"

Breeana was safe from The Shepherd as long as she stayed at the clinic. She knew Theo and Hawke guarded her every move. The waiting room was filled to capacity with patients. Everything was normal, or as normal as could be expected under the circumstances. No one could hurt her. Logically, she knew these things, yet common sense deserted her during the phone call.

She couldn't think. *What should I do? Do I go home and risk facing The Shepherd? Would Sully want me to do that?* She hadn't heard from him since he left her place this morning.

Theo stood right beside her and quickly took control of the situation. "I'm Theo Sauvage, Lieutenant Sullivan Sauvage's brother. Contact the lieutenant immediately at homicide and advise him of the situation. I'll be at Dr. McGill's address within five minutes. And, advise the responding officers to send for back-up and *not* to enter the house until the lieutenant arrives to take command. The serial killer the police are searching for could be inside the house."

"Theo, they can't shoot their way inside my house," Breeana pleaded as he disconnected the call. "The dogs could get caught in the crossfire."

"Relax," he said, squeezing her shoulders. "My brother knows what he's doing."

As jumpy as a cat, Breeana paced circles in her office after Theo left to join the police at her house. If the psychopath showed, Sully would take him down. But, what if something went wrong? As much as she wanted The Shepherd caught, she couldn't live with herself if anything happened to Sully. She was head over heels in love with him.

Shoot. When did that happen? She headed to the coffee pot, only to realize she didn't need any more caffeine because she was jittery enough already.

Confused and scared out of her wits, she dropped into her desk chair and again poured over patient charts for the walk-in clinic, unable to grasp one word on any page.

Calm down. Sully will call me when it's over. He'll be fine.

Chapter 15

Sully pulled up behind Sal in Millette's driveway. After locking the Tahoe, he eyeballed the house, a no-frills bungalow with gray aluminum siding, white trim, and a fallen down front porch. "I guess Millette isn't into carpentry."

"He's not much for gardening either, unless crabgrass is the new thing." Clemente stepped lightly up the sagging steps, flipped the doormat aside to find a key beneath. "See, what'd I tell you, Loot? Every cop I know hides a key under the mat for emergencies."

"Then you must know a lot of dumbass cops." Sully pulled on rubber gloves, used the key, and turned the door handle. No beeps. No alarm system. He entered the living room. Dust balls clung to orange shag carpeting. Brown beanbag furniture and a vinyl recliner, circa 1960s, completed the nightmarish decor. Pizza boxes and empty beer cans littered the coffee table. "Looks like Jacques kept to himself. Didn't do much entertaining."

"Yeah, welcome to the man cave." Sal toed an overflowing ashtray aside as they moved forward to a central hallway. "What are we looking for?"

"Evidence on The Shepherd. It could be anywhere."

"Man, I'm really not cool about Millette. I mean, I know he's a cop...and he's been shot in the line of duty, but the truth is, I'm pissed about a lot of things. I never really liked the guy, Loot. I don't trust him."

"Don't worry about it, Sal. I have mixed feelings about Jacques myself. The important thing is to do our jobs and find something leading us to the shooter."

"All right. You got it."

Clemente got started in the living room and Sully headed for the kitchen, opening the freezer. Nothing but TV dinners and a half-finished bottle of vodka. Condiments and a six-pack of beer occupied the fridge.

Is this what living for the job can do to a man? Should I worry about my own state of mind? Shaking his head to clear the thought, he replaced it with a new one. *Not since Breeana came into my life. She makes all the difference—makes me whole. And thank Jesus.*

While he searched, Sully mulled over Sal's words regarding Sergeant Millette and thought about his own feelings. If anything, he felt too much compassion for the man, because of the crapper Millette called home and the fact he'd been shot. Yeah, he regretted the violence against the sergeant—even if his gut said Jacques brought it on himself by holding back crucial evidence. It was the only thing that made any damn sense. Hell, if he'd known who The Shepherd was and kept the information to himself, it was obstruction of justice.

Why feel sorry for someone when he may have cost other women their lives...could still cost Breeana her life. *Shit, don't go there!*

He snapped the lid on his anger and continued to search, checking the oven, dragging cereal boxes, coffee cans, and pasta containers out of cupboards. He ripped everything apart. *Nada.*

Sal tackled the bedroom and study while Sully moved on to the bathroom. Next up was the basement. A mountain of sealed cardboard boxes took up half the space, as if Millette had moved in years ago and never bothered to unpack. He was also a collector—balls of twine, empty liquor bottles, old newspapers, tin cans. You name it, the sergeant salted it away. Sully checked out the washer and dryer, and even opened the furnace door, just to be sure. Nothing inside.

When dispatch rang on his cell phone, he welcomed the distraction. "This is Sauvage."

"Lieutenant, Dr. McGill's security company called. Someone's tripped the alarm at the doc's house. Your brother and some MBPD uniforms are there now, waiting for you to take charge."

He thought for a minute. "Call Tactical and get a SWAT team there; STAT. MBPD can handle the perimeter. Have them set up road blocks and patrols on the water as well. Dr. McGill's house borders the lake."

"I'm on it, Lieutenant."

He disconnected. "Sal!"

Clemente met him at the top of the stairs. "Yeah, boss?"

"I'm taking off. There's been a break-in at Dr. McGill's residence."

"No shit? Let's boogie."

"Thanks, but I've got back-up on this one. You stay here and search the attic."

Sully hit the bar lights and siren and burned rubber. Dodging in and out of traffic, a sick feeling nailed him in the gut. Was The Shepherd somehow making a move on Bree by staging an invasion at her house? It made no sense, since she wasn't even there.

And was he stupid enough to set off the alarm system? *Hell, no.* The guy was smart, way too smart. The tripped alarm seemed like a diversionary tactic.

But what does the bastard hope to gain? Sully knew it was only a matter of time before the shit hit the fan, yet he still had no clue to The Shepherd's identity. One thing he did know...he had to be ready.

DETECTIVE CLEMENTE rolled to the curb outside the veterinary clinic and hopped out of his unmarked. Hawke called to him and came out the back door to meet him. Sully's Spec Ops buddy must remember him from the night at the hospital. Yeah, their paths had crossed during the foiled kidnapping on Dr. McGill's son.

"What's up, Detective? Is there any news on Millette's condition?"

Clemente strolled up to him, scanning the parking lot before moving his gaze to Hawke. "He's still holding his own, for what it's worth. He's in a coma. Even if he survives, the doctors think there could be brain damage and paralysis."

Hawke shook his head. "A hell of a price to pay for not following police procedure."

"Tell me about it. I never figured the sergeant for a loose cannon, but it looks like he screwed up. Even if he fully recovers, he's finished on the force. No one would take a chance on him again. They'll pension him off."

"Really sucks, man. So, what brings you here?"

"The lieutenant got the message about the break-in from the alarm company. He's on his way to Dr. McGill's residence to check it out. But, he's not convinced the break-in is legit."

Clemente watched the back door to the clinic for signs of movement; no one watching from inside. The parking lot was still deserted. His gaze swung back to Hawke. "He thought you'd need a hand protecting the doctor until he and his brother get back here. You never know what The Shepherd is going to do."

"Right."

Clemente could see gears turning inside Hawke's head. *The prick knows I'm lying. Yeah, I should have realized.* The lieutenant never left anything to chance. He would have called Hawke to tell him, if he'd really sent him there on protection duty.

He slid the Taser from the back of his waistband, wrapping his fingers around the grip. It felt cool to the touch and gave him the power. A big guy like Hawke would crash and burn after only one hit. *Aw shucks, you're protecting a whore. And now you're gonna pay up.*

Clemente struck with the speed of a viper, hitting Hawke square in the chest with the weapon. Hawke fell to his knees, pitched sideways, and rolled onto his back. Sweat broke out on the guy's brow, and Clemente watched it roll over his temple before he grabbed his ankles.

Using a tugging motion, he dragged him behind a dumpster. Even so, Hawke swore while he drooled, as if he thought he could still overpower him. Guess he hadn't counted on the two-by-four he pulled from the dumpster.

"Shit." Hawke flailed, trying to roll out of the way. He didn't get far.

"What did you expect, defending a bitch like her?" Blood spurted when wood connected with flesh and bone. Clemente saw the blood spatter and almost cringed. Sure, he was The Shepherd, but it didn't mean he enjoyed the task. Hawke was one of the good guys. Still, he'd stood between him and Breeana. That would never do.

LAURA WAS IN THE EXAMINING room, soothing a Great Dane, when a police detective slipped into Breeana's office and closed the door. He flashed his badge and introduced himself. Breeana frowned, staring at him, pen poised over the file she updated.

Why did he close the door? "What's going on, Detective? Is Sully all right?"

"The lieutenant sent me to get you," Clemente said. "Good news, Doctor. The team nailed The Shepherd inside your house."

"What?"

He sidled over to her desk and leaned in close. "The lieutenant wants me to bring you down to the station for a line-up, to see if you recognize the creep."

Breeana couldn't say how she knew, but she *knew* the detective was lying. Maybe it was the way he eyed her...detached...like a cat stalking a mouse and waiting to chomp its head off. She sucked in a breath, scanning her desk for anything she could use as a weapon. There was nothing, except for the pen clutched in her fingers.

Stall for time. Don't let him know you're nervous. "The lieutenant knows I can't leave the clinic when I have patients to see. Tell him I'll have Hawke drive me downtown after clinic hours."

Trying to look anywhere but at his face, her gaze landed on the cuff of his shirt sleeve.

Blood. Oh, God. Where is Hawke? She opened her mouth to scream. He was on her in a flash. His fingers squeezed a pressure point in her neck. Before she could fight back, her vision went dark, and she pitched forward. The last thing she saw was paperwork as she slumped over her desk.

Chapter 16

Sully passed Theo a Kevlar vest and shrugged into his own. They drew their weapons, checked their load, and grabbed headsets. Six of SWAT's best officers were suited up and waiting for them. "I want two of you around back. The rest of you are with me."

"Here, use this," he said, handing the door key to the mountain of a man with the battering ram. Approaching the house, Sully could hear the dogs barking and growling—not a happy sound. "I'm first inside. No one shoots the dogs."

They breached the door in seconds. Sully snagged Bear and Bruiser's collars and motioned to the stairs; signaling two officers up and the other two down to sweep the basement. He and Theo took the ground floor. The living room was clear. After scoping out the bathroom, Sully motioned the dogs inside and closed the door. The kitchen, study and sunroom appeared undisturbed. He could hear footfalls overhead and then the 'all clear' on his headset; ditto from the men in the basement a minute later. Everything seemed untouched, except for a broken window in the living room and the rock someone had heaved through it. SWAT moved outside.

"The Shepherd was never inside the house, bro," Theo said, opening the bathroom door to let the dogs out.

"Otherwise Bruiser would have ripped him apart," Sully agreed, bagging the rock. "The dog's got a score to settle with him for killing his mistress. So, why trip the alarm in the first place?"

His cell phone rang, and he grabbed for it. As he flipped it open, a hysterical voice came through the line.

"Lieutenant Sauvage...thank God!"

"Laura?" he asked, his heart cranking into overdrive.

"I think something terrible has happened!"

"Talk to me." Motioning to his brother, he held the phone to his ear and raced for the Tahoe. Right on his heels, Theo slid into the passenger seat. He started the engine; hit the bar lights, and stepped on the gas, squealing out of the driveway on two wheels. "What's going on?"

"Breeana and Hawke have disappeared. I don't know where they are. Breeana would never leave the clinic with patients waiting!"

"I'm on my way."

Sully roared into the clinic parking lot just minutes after receiving the call, his heart pounding like a battering ram. He and Theo were out of the SUV, racing for the back door when they spied blood on the ground, trickling from behind the dumpster edged up against the brownstone.

Don't let it be her. Please.

Theo nudged his shoulder, calmed him down. "Give me a hand."

They rolled the dumpster aside. Sully's knees went loose for a second. *Sweet Jesus, Hawke.* Bloody and unconscious, a gash ran from his temple to the top of his head. His eyes rolled. His pupils were dilated. Still, he had a faint pulse. Thank God for that blessing.

Theo used his jacket to staunch the blood flow. Sully called for EMTs from his cell phone as he charged through the back door of the clinic. A quick search of the consulting rooms and the stricken look on Laura's face said it all. Breeana was gone.

Taking Laura by the arm, he drew her into the office. "Before Breeana and Hawke disappeared, who else was at the clinic?"

Looking pale-faced, Laura's hands trembled as she said, "I-I don't know. There was no one else here. O-only the clients still out in the waiting room."

"Come on, Laura, think. Something must have happened." Sully poured a cup of coffee laced with sugar and placed it in her hands. "Where was Bree the last time you saw her?"

"Wait. I remember now. I was in an examination room with a dog for a few minutes. Breeana had stitched him up and gone to her office to write up the chart. I only noticed she was gone when I brought the dog back out to the waiting room. I-I asked if anyone had seen her or Hawke leave. But, no one saw anything."

No leads to follow. For a few minutes Sully couldn't think straight, couldn't breathe. He could only react through his years of training and do what needed to be done. He had never before felt so powerless.

Lord Jesus God. The Shepherd had his woman and he didn't know how to get her back. Hell, he didn't even know who the bastard was. He cursed Millette's stupidity for the hundredth time. He wasn't unsympathetic—the man's life hung by a thread and he had paid heavily for withholding evidence—but now Breeana was snared by the freak.

He ignored the little voice in his head, the one insisting she could already be dead. He refused to believe it. No. The bastard was angrier with her than he had been with any of his other victims. He would keep her alive and make her suffer before he killed her. *Gawd damn.*

The EMTs loaded Hawke into the back of the ambulance while Sully dialed Clemente's number. "Sal? Send crime scene techs to the veterinary clinic. STAT. Dr. McGill's been snatched by The Shepherd."

CLEMENTE ALMOST LAUGHED at the naked fear in the lieutenant's voice. He glanced over at Breeana, slumped unconscious on the seat beside him. The tinted windows on his unmarked proved to be a blessing. They shielded her from the passing gazes of motorists as he waited for the light to change at an intersection.

"The whole case has gone straight to hell, Loot. I'll notify the criminalists right away. What else do you need?"

"Get over to Ben Prewitt's and bring him in for questioning. Be careful, Sal. He could be The Shepherd. Take Sanchez and Lemieux with you to pick him up. You can reach me on my cell if you need me."

"Hey, I'm on it. I'm still at Millette's completing the search, but I'll leave right away. Where will you be?"

"I'll let you know. Call me back when you have Prewitt in custody."

Clemente disconnected and reached over to clasp Breeana's hand. She was so beautiful, curled up on the seat beside him like a kitten. She belonged to him for as long as he wanted, until he sent her to the Lord.

Only one more loose end to take care of—the kid from juvie he'd paid to break the window at Breeana's to trip the alarm. He'd find time to kill him later.

BREEANA AWOKE SLOWLY, as if from a fog. She had the mother of all hangovers. Disoriented and confused, she rubbed her forehead. What had happened?

The room was cold and dank. The mattress she lay on was lumpy and reeked of urine and mildew. *Where am I?*

Sitting up was a dizzying experience. She raised a hand to her aching neck and a chain rattled, pulling taut from a ring bolted to the wall. She was handcuffed to the wall by her wrist.

With that realization, everything else came rushing back at her. *The Shepherd.* Detective Sal Clemente was the killer. He had kidnapped her.

Terror struck in a rush. It twisted up her spine and threatened to paralyze her limbs. Breeana steeled herself to keep from passing out. She would *not* hyperventilate. She was *not* going to die.

"Hey, Breeana?"

His singsong voice reached out from the shadows. Excited. Like a kid waiting to open the best birthday present of his life. Her gaze widened as she searched the darkness for a glimmer of movement. Nothing. Her heart tumbled in her rib cage. The man was a deranged lunatic. Her life was in his hands. She froze and clenched her teeth to keep them from chattering.

Where is he? She could smell him—the sweet-sour odor of donuts on his breath and nervous sweat radiating from his pores. She almost retched, swallowing hard to push back the bile.

"If you have a brain in your head, you'll let me go, Clemente!" The strength of her voice steadied her. She'd always been good at bluffing in poker.

"I can't do it, my darling." The detective separated himself from the gloom and moved toward her. His sick smile ghosted in light coming from a solitary window high up on a wall. Bending low, he crouched on his haunches, running a finger along her cheek, capturing her face in cold fingers. "Poor baby. I hated to hurt you, you know."

Liar. Fear welled inside her like a living thing. She jerked from his touch. Wrestling with panic, she refused to allow him to see it. He would feed on her terror and use it to destroy her. "Stay away from me, you sick pervert!"

"Tsk, tsk. Such talk, Breeana. And such bravado."

Coward. Unshackle my wrist and I'll show you bravado. One well placed kick and you'll be singing soprano while I boot it for the door.

As if reading her thoughts, his hands trailed from her face to the column of her neck. His fingers coiled like snakes, wrapping themselves from her collarbone to her ears. She stiffened, bit back a scream. His reach was longer than hers. If he tightened the pressure, she would die. She stared into the face of death. Such bland features, it was hard to believe they hid the soul of a monster.

The Shepherd shook his head and chuckled. His fingers loosened their grip. "I think we understand each other. However, I'm afraid we'll have to postpone our little chat. Duty calls, you know. The lieutenant wants *me* to help him catch The Shepherd. Can you imagine? He's relying on me, Breeana. I can't disappoint him. But, I'll be back soon. Then we'll have more time together. Meanwhile, make yourself comfortable."

"Drop dead, you freak." She raised her head, jutted out her chin, and glared at him. "You won't get away with it. Sully is going to kill you when he catches you."

"Darling girl, I've been getting away with murder for years. Doing the Lord's bidding as He sees fit." Clemente threw back his head and roared with laughter. "The lieutenant doesn't have a clue who I am. So, who's going to stop me? Hmm? Do you really believe Sauvage can protect you from the Lord and what He has ordained?"

"Maybe not," she said, her voice shrill. "But I know he can protect me from a maniac like you."

Breeana worked saliva into her mouth and spat full in his face. Clemente swiped at the spittle hanging from his chin with the back of a hand. "You will do penance, you disgusting witch. When I get back, we'll see how brave you really are."

"Wait! You can't keep me chained up. I need to use the bathroom." Any excuse would do, just as long as he released her from the chain on the wall.

"Why, of course. Let me show you to the toilet."

The filthy bucket Clemente kicked toward her clattered to a stop at her feet. "It's the maid's day off, so I don't have any little guest soaps or fluffy towels, but I'm sure you'll manage."

She could hear his sick laughter as he made his way to the top of the stairs. There was the thud of a door closing and then absolute silence. She was alone with her terror.

Push it back. Don't think about anything but getting out of here. You're on your own. Sully can't help you now.

Her eyes adjusted to the dark space around her. The walls seemed to be a mixture of crumbling cement and earth. She must be underground, which would explain the dampness permeating the air. She could make out dusty jars filled with jams and pickles on planked shelves lining a far wall. An antique apple-peeler was shoved into another corner.

There were boxes of empty jars, lids and sealing wax. Bins of rotten vegetables were scattered about the room. She must be in a root cellar. The house had to be old because newer homes didn't have underground storage. She guessed she was down by the lake. The newer developments were out by the highway.

She heard a squeaking sound before she saw a mouse scuttle across the floor and head for a vegetable bin. *Ugh!* She'd seen enough rodents at the arena to last a lifetime. *Enough.* She was breaking out of there.

Her hands grabbed for the chain shackling her wrist. She tugged as hard as she could, and cement dust crumbled from around the ring anchored to the wall. The cement was old. She might be able to pull the ring out if she worked it back and forth. Steely determination seized her. She visualized the ring coming loose and releasing her from this hellhole. She would escape.

Cody needed her. He was only thirteen. He needed his mom, would be devastated if she didn't make it home. And Sully? He would blame himself for letting The Shepherd hurt her...kill her. She wouldn't give them up without a fight. She hadn't told Sully she loved him, and she wanted the chance.

Chapter 17

"Where are you?" Sully barked into his cell phone.

"I'm at the hospital," Theo said. "After you dropped me at Breeana's, I grabbed our bags and used her Pathfinder to get over here. It's not looking good for Millette, by the way. He's still in a coma."

"What about Hawke? What's his prognosis?" Sully didn't want to think about his best friend and the shape he was in.

"The doctors anticipate a full recovery, but he has a concussion. He's still out for the count, and I don't know when he'll be able to tell us anything."

"He may not know anything." Sully tensed his fingers on the steering wheel. "He might have been hit from behind. Stay with him, Theo, in case he wakes up."

"Roger. Where are you?"

"I was at Millette's house again. I tore the place apart, but didn't find anything useful on The Shepherd. We may never know what evidence he had on him. And get this, the body of the pizza delivery guy who brought the pies to Breeana's was found in a ravine out by the Long Sault campground. He's another dead end, unless Marie Matisse can find trace evidence on his corpse."

"Jeez, Sully. I'm sorry, bro. But you'll find Breeana. I have a gut feeling about it."

"I hope you're right. I can't lose her." He wanted to cry, something he hadn't done since he was six-years-old and his grandfather had died of complications after a stroke.

But nothing could describe the gut-wrenching sense of loss he felt now. If he didn't find Bree in time, his life would be a black, gaping hole. He cared about her beyond reason, and prayed for a damn miracle. He needed her back by his side, safe and sound, where she belonged.

"Theo, I'm heading over to talk to the old priest at St. Pat's. Father Mike is the only lead I've got left."

"Just call when you need me. Reece and Hunt are on their way back from Cody's location. They should arrive any time now. We can meet you anywhere you say."

"Thanks, bro. Listen, it's important. If anyone asks where I am, keep silent."

"Does this include your homicide squad? What the hell's going on, Sully?"

"*Especially* my taskforce. The Shepherd knows every move we make as soon as we make it. He also knows how to hide his tracks. There's a mole in my department; there is no other explanation. Unless The Shepherd is a cop."

"Son of a bitch."

"No shit. I'll be in touch. Just be ready to move and fill in Reece and Hunt. We'll be taking down the bastard on our own. I can't trust anyone else."

ONE FINAL TUG AND BREEANA pulled the ring free from the wall. *Yes!* Then she was off the mattress and sprinting for the stairs. She reached the top landing and pounded her shoulder against the door, again and again. The hinges were old and creaked with each thrust of her body. Freedom was on the other side of that door, and she was damn well going to break through it.

Finally, the door sagged and she crawled through the opening. She landed face-first on a graveled drive. She needed to rest but there wasn't time.

Get going. Run for your life!

She pulled herself up and saw shoes in front of her. The Shepherd's wingtips. She leapt to her feet and veered around him. Clemente anticipated her move, wrenched her back by the hair, and threw her on the ground. Her elbows connected with gravel. She sat up and rubbed at the wounds, blood seeping through her fingers. Grimacing with pain, she closed her eyes.

The Shepherd moved behind her. She didn't need to see his face to know he was insane with anger. He heaved her to her feet by the armpits, spun her back through the open doorway, and shoved her down the stairs. Shielding her head with her hands, Breeana bounced down every step. Landing hard at the bottom, she couldn't move, could barely breathe. A sharp pain jabbed her side. Lord, she thought her ribs were cracked.

The lunatic was on her again in an instant, dragging her by the arm past the vegetable bins and canning equipment to a curtained recess in the wall. The skin rasped from her back with each tug on her arm as he hauled her across the cement floor. Her chance for escape from the madman was gone. But, she would stay alive, she vowed to herself, for Sully and Cody. She would see and love them again.

The Shepherd tossed a curtain aside and steered her into an alcove. He flicked a wall switch. A crude altar stood directly in front of her, the brass cross on its surface catching the light as a low-watt bulb flickered overhead. Clemente pushed her into a chair. Then he reached for a rope.

"Let me go. Please, I won't tell anyone." She clawed at him, leapt to her feet. Balling her fist, she pulled back her arm and swung at his face with every ounce of strength she possessed.

The Shepherd dodged her punch at the last second. Her hand hit the wall behind him with the force of a heat-seeking missile. Pain shot up her arm. Bones buckled in her hand, her wrist, and crunched together. She glanced down, noticed her thumb and fingers were at an odd angle. She glanced back up. The Shepherd was still standing.

Mercifully, she blacked out from the pain.

"AH, BETTER," THE SHEPHERD said to the unconscious Breeana. He slid her back onto the chair, securing her arms and legs to the spindles. Satisfied she couldn't move, he grabbed his tool kit and hurried to repair the root cellar door. He did a rush patch job, but it would hold. After all, he never knew when someone would come snooping around.

It was doubtful the cops would be interested in the house anymore. They had already searched it from top to bottom, but missed the door to the root cellar in their haste to find clues to the church secretary's disappearance. *Yeah, someone screwed up, big time. I think it was Millette.* He chuckled.

Too bad, he couldn't take his time with Breeana now. It would have to wait until he clocked in with Homicide. Before the lieutenant realized he wasn't where he was supposed to be. Still, he had time for a last peek at the woman before he charged off to save the world.

He laid his tools aside and entered the makeshift chapel. She was still unconscious where he'd left her tied to the chair. He cupped his hands to the fullness of her breasts, bent low to inhale the lemon scent of her skin. Tipping her chin up, he feathered a kiss against her parted lips. She moaned, the sweetness of her breath tightening the muscles in his groin. He felt the surge. Anger took hold. He slapped her hard.

The Lord's right about you, Breeana. You're a whore. You need to learn some respect.

Chapter 18

"**P**rewitt has a solid alibi," Clemente said. "He's living with an ICU nurse from the hospital. She confirms his story."

Sully careened into the parking lot of St. Patrick's Cathedral, shoved the car in park, and switched off the ignition. "What story are you talking about?"

"Apparently, he stopped by to see her at work on the night Cody was attacked. They were eating in the cafeteria at exactly the same time The Shepherd tried to nab the kid. Prewitt has plenty of witnesses. A lot of them are hospital staff, Loot. There's no way he pulled off the attempted kidnapping."

Frustration and nausea rolled over Sully in waves. Every lead in the case hit a brick wall. He was almost out of options and nothing brought him closer to finding Breeana. He desperately needed a break on the case, some tiny shred of evidence to point him in the right direction. He pounded his fist on the steering wheel.

"All right, Sal. Cut him loose, but I want him followed around the clock. I'm still not convinced."

"I'll get some men on it before I release him." Clemente said. "Where will you be?"

"I'm heading to the hospital to check up on Millette and Jake Hawkins," Sully lied.

"Have either of them regained consciousness yet?" Clemente asked.

"No and I don't think they're going to. Neither of them is expected to make it through the night," Sully lied again. "I'll let you know if anything changes."

He hung up and dialed his brother. Theo answered on the first ring. "Listen, I want Reece and Hunt to guard Sergeant Millette and Hawke. The Shepherd hates loose ends. Those two are sitting ducks if he goes after them at the hospital. I can't trust anyone on the force to protect them."

"Consider it done," Theo said. "We don't need to remind our guys how dangerous he is. They still remember what he did to Micah and Law, and how he almost took Cody out of the hospital under everyone's noses. And now, there's Hawke. The doctor's keeping him sedated because of brain swelling, so we still can't get anything out of him."

Sully growled. "Just tell the guys to stay alert. No one gets in those hospital rooms without Reece or Hunt watching their every move. You make sure our guys are armed."

"Got it, bro. I'll be waiting for your call. We'll find her."

"Just pray it's in time, Theo. I'll be in touch." Sully pocketed his phone and car keys, sprinted up the stairs, and rang the doorbell to the rectory. The building was a gray stone affair. Chipped mortar between the bricks and moss trailing up walls created a gloomy atmosphere. Cold and damp, it caused him to shudder.

A plump woman peeked out from behind a curtained window before opening the door. "You're the one who called from the police department?"

"That's right." Sully flashed his badge. "Are you the housekeeper?"

"I am." She chuckled. "And just about everything else around here, including the handyman. What is it you want, Lieutenant?"

"It's vitally important I speak with Father Mike. It's a police emergency, a matter of life and death."

"Follow me then. He's resting in his room." She closed the door behind him and shuffled her way along a dim hallway leading to a staircase at the back of the house. Her arthritic knees popped with every step as they climbed to the second floor. "Don't expect too much from him, mind. I know Father Mike still has his lucid moments, but most of the time he's in *La-La-Land*. Try not to upset the poor dear."

Great, just what I need, a senile priest who doesn't know reality from fantasy. Still, he had to see him. It was the only lead he had left. Breeana...he couldn't afford to dwell on what was happening to her. He needed to keep what little sanity he had left to question the priest. "I'll be discreet."

The housekeeper motioned to the first door on the right at the top of the stairs before she turned back to the stairwell. "Call out if you need me. I'll be down in the basement doing the laundry. The old dear keeps soiling his bed linens."

Sully poked his head through the doorway. He was shocked to see the emaciated form huddled beneath a mountain of blankets. The bedroom contained a narrow bed, a nightstand with a reading lamp, and a pine dresser against the far wall. The only illumination came from the lamp, a brass cross on the wall reflecting its pale glow. The windows were closed, heavy curtains drawn across to block the outside world. The room reminded Sully of a crypt in an old cemetery. Stifling hot, it reeked of decaying flesh and urine. The stench was overpowering, even to a seasoned cop like him.

A gaunt face turned toward the sound of his shoes clacking the floorboards as he moved closer to the bed. There was something about the priest that gave him the creeps. It had nothing to do with his advanced age or illness; but the cold, dead eyes staring up at him. A person's eyes were the windows to their soul, weren't they? Either the windows were shut tight in the priest's case, or he didn't have a soul.

"Where's Hannah? Why hasn't she come to see me?" Spidery fingers clutched the edge of the blankets as the priest struggled to sit up in bed.

"Hannah's busy doing other things." Father Mike obviously hadn't been informed about the church secretary's death, or else he'd already forgotten. Sully wasn't about to break the news to him. "She sent me instead."

"Come into the light where I can see you." The old fellow studied him for a time, his gaze narrowing as if trying to distinguish Sully's features more clearly in the lamplight. "What is your name?"

"The name's Sullivan. I'm a friend of Hannah's."

"Liar! Do you think you can fool me, boy? I know exactly who you are."

"I'm not lying, Father." Sully figured he had just entered *The Twilight Zone*. The old guy was nuttier than a peanut sundae, double-dipped. "I'm telling you the truth."

"The truth? Boy, you don't know the meaning of the word."

The priest's rheumy eyes narrowed. Then he inhaled on an apoplectic wheeze and shook a gnarled finger in Sully's direction. "You can't fool me. Don't you dare lie to your own father. Did saying the rosary teach you nothing?"

His own father? Was the old coot referring to his title as a priest? Or had he done the unthinkable? Was it possible the man of God had fathered a son? The sins of the fathers...Sully was going to play this to the hilt. "Hey, I never believed in the rosary, old man. But you already know that, don't you?"

"Blasphemer! The devil is still inside you!"

Father Mike clutched his pajama top and tried to rise up on an elbow. Spittle flew from his mouth. Hatred burned deep in his eyes. "Hannah should have punished you more often, lad. Did you not learn anything in the root cellar? I told her she was too easy on you."

The picture forming inside Sully's brain was so grisly it defied description. What kind of man allowed his child to be abused and then complained it wasn't enough?

"Hey! What did you just say to me? Don't make me laugh."

"Get down on your knees and pray to the Almighty. He's the only one who can save you now." The priest was turning blue, gasping for breath, and Sully didn't much care. He was not going to call for help unless he got the answers he needed to save Breeana.

"Dear Lord, the fruit of my loins is the devil's own! Satan...get...thee...out!"

The housekeeper rushed in just as the old priest collapsed, his eyes staring heavenward, as if he expected help from on high. A death rattle escaped his throat and his lips froze in a permanent grimace.

Sully was sure the Lord was turning the priest away from the pearly gates at that very moment. He wasn't a man of God, nor a Catholic. This was a vile freak, someone who had used the sanctity of the Church for his own devious purposes.

Even so, he couldn't be The Shepherd. He didn't fit the age profile. He was too old and frail to have killed those women, even thirteen years ago. Sully pressed his fingers to the side of the priest's neck to be sure he was actually dead. He was. *Good riddance.*

"Oh, the poor dear," the housekeeper clucked. "I think he's finally passed over into the Lord's hands."

"It would seem so. I'm sorry if I upset him, ma'am." Sully realized she had heard the priest's ranting all the way down to the basement. "He seemed to become very agitated for no apparent reason."

"Yes, I heard him, young man. He often pontificated about the devil and his unholy works. It was nothing unusual."

She gazed up at Sully with something akin to embarrassment in her expression. "He wasn't allowed to provide solace for his parishioners, you know. Not for the last few months."

"Was it because of his failing health, ma'am?"

"No, it wasn't because of his health. His sermons had become rather upsetting. The congregation complained about him to the Archdiocese. It was shortly afterward Father Mike's health began to fail. It devastated him, you know, not being able to tend his flock. Now the poor soul is gone. May he rest in peace."

The housekeeper busied herself, pulling a blanket up over the priest's head while Sully prayed the prick would burn in hell for all eternity. He was certain the priest's son was The Shepherd. *Who was he?*

"Ma'am? Can you give me Father Mike's full name for my report?"

"His name is Father Michelangelo Clemente. It has a lovely ring to it, don't you think?"

Clemente?

Fuck!

Sal Clemente was The Shepherd. He must have legally changed his name to his father's.

ALONG WITH CONSCIOUSNESS came excruciating pain, a body-slam of agony unlike anything Breeana had ever experienced before. It was terrifying, debilitating, and ripe with the promise of certain death. She couldn't let The Shepherd win. Her heart cried out for Sully, needing his strength to survive. To do what had to be done.

She gritted her teeth against the pain, swallowed hard to keep the bile from rising in her throat and choking off her windpipe. She forced her hand open, inch by agonizingly slow inch. Her shattered bones ground together. She came close to fainting several times. She would not give in.

Control the pain. You can do it.

It was a waste of time. Her right hand was useless. She fumbled with her left instead to untie the knots binding her wrists to the chair back. After several tries, the ropes loosened and dropped to the floor. Lucky for her, Clemente had never been a Boy Scout, or he would have tied secure knots. Easing her broken hand gently onto her lap, Breeana worked with a dexterity born of terror to untie the bonds at her ankles. Finally, she was free. She had won.

She wanted to weep with joy. *Baby steps*, she reminded herself. She would get away from the animal by taking baby steps. Not by sitting there and blubbering like a child. It took another full minute, one she could ill afford, to remove her blouse and fashion it into a sling to support her broken hand. Another minute and she was off the chair and wobbling for freedom.

The Shepherd laughed from somewhere to her right. "Congratulations, my darling. I didn't think you'd be able to get free. I could almost admire your persistence if I wasn't so angry with you."

"You sick bastard." Breeana bunched her muscles in a fight-or-flight response. It was long past time to get moving. She staggered, cutting away from his shrill voice as fast as her trembling legs could carry her. She didn't get far.

"Enough fooling around." He wrenched her by the shoulders and pitched her back on the chair. "I'm running out of patience with you. It's time to say the rosary and beg forgiveness for your sins."

"I don't know the rosary," Breeana cried out. "I'm not Catholic."

"What?" He gripped her neck. "You are nothing but a filthy liar. I saw you at mass with your friends. I watched the three of you giggling like schoolgirls as you tromped out of St. Pat's. You *dared* to laugh at Father Mike's sermon."

Breeana focused the nausea and terror away, and then pushed her mind back to the day in the cathedral, the day she had gone to mass with Miranda and Rainey who were members of the parish. She remembered the service and the despicable priest. He had sounded like a raving lunatic, tainting the scriptures to send his sexist message to everyone in the congregation. He had preached about whores and their day of atonement.

The pieces of the puzzle came together with gemstone clarity. It was why Miranda and Rainey were dead, because they had walked out of church before the priest had finished spewing his venom. And, this was why she would be the next to die. One member of the congregation had taken the priest's ramblings to heart.

"You will learn the rosary, Breeana. Or die trying."

Chapter 19

Tracking the police-issue SUV to Hannah Grime's property was a piece of cake, thanks to GPS technology. Clemente had no idea he was being followed. There were some things a military man could do better than the guys on the force. Tracking was one of them. Blending into his surroundings was another.

Sully didn't just search the terrain around Hannah Grime's house. He *became* the terrain, and was impossible to spot. It wasn't long before he picked up footprints matting the grass along the border of lawn and then followed them to the entrance of an old root cellar hidden by twisted foliage. No wonder the investigators hadn't found it. He knelt to touch traces of blood dotting the graveled entrance. Breeana was injured, how badly he couldn't tell. And The Shepherd was with her now.

Theo's voice whispered into his earpiece. "Clemente's SUV is parked in the garage. No one's inside."

"They're in a root cellar edging the property. I'm going down."

"Roger. I'll call it in and catch up."

Sully's tread was light on the stairs. He moved silently, trying hard not to think about Breeana and what he would find in the cellar.

Don't go there. You can hear her. She's still alive.

"No, you stupid, stupid girl!" The Shepherd's voice shrilled with frustration. "You made another mistake. Start again from the beginning. It's in the book. One more mistake and I'll have to punish you again."

The son of a bitch is as good as dead.

Sully crept across the floor from the main part of the root cellar and plastered himself against the outer wall of the makeshift chapel. He inched forward. In his haste to reach Breeana, he failed to notice the metal bucket lying on the cement. It connected with his foot and rattled across the doorway. *Fuck!*

"Breeana? I believe we have company." The sound of The Shepherd's voice chilled Sully's blood to ice.

"Come out where I can see you, Lieutenant. Otherwise, I'll finish her off."

Sully pushed through the doorway and into the room. He inched as close to them as he could get without spooking Clemente. Breeana moaned. Sully's chest constricted as his gaze locked on her. She was pressed against The Shepherd's body, pinned there by an arm strapped across her chest. The blade of a KA-BAR at her throat, blood from a knife prick trickled down her neck. He couldn't get a shot off without hitting her.

You rat shit bastard! That woman is my life! You will not hack her to goddamn pieces! "You don't want to do it, Sal."

"Salvatore Clemente is gone forever. I'm The Shepherd and you will deal with me, Lieutenant. Drop your weapon!"

Sully barely recognized the madman standing in front of him. There was no resemblance to the mild-mannered detective he worked with on the force. This psychopath was The Shepherd, plain and simple. He derived pleasure from murdering women and inflicting pain. He was absolutely insane.

"Do it now, or I swear I'll cut her again!"

My God, Bree, what has he done to you? Sully could see abrasions on her skin, the odd angle of her hand and wrist. He locked on her gaze and sent her a silent message. *Don't worry; we'll get out of this.*

He was sure she understood when she gave him an imperceptible nod. Then he dropped his police-issue firearm and put his hands in the air. *Where is Theo?*

"Now, take out your backup piece. Ease it out of your ankle holster and slide it over."

Sully bent low at the waist and whispered under his breath into his mic. "It's up to you, bro. Take the shot. Take the goddamn shot!"

Theo appeared at the entrance to the room like a specter, his Glock extended from locked forearms as he took precise aim. The Shepherd moved in an instant. He twisted himself and Breeana in Theo's direction. His knife moved a fraction of an inch away from her exposed throat. Finally, the break Sully needed. He raised his snub-nosed .38 caliber, leveled it at Clemente's head, and squeezed the trigger.

The Shepherd dropped like a rock as the bullet shattered his temple. Sully closed the distance, scooping up Breeana before she fell to the floor. He gathered her against him, shielding her from the worst of the carnage.

His brother holstered his firearm and heaved a sigh of relief. "Your homicide squad and the EMTs are on the way. They should be here soon."

"Theo...thanks." Sully's hand trembled as he squeezed his brother's shoulder. It had been too close—way too close.

"Don't mention it. I'll stick around, explain things, and meet up with you later."

Breeana clung to Sully and buried her face in the crook of his neck. "Please...I want to go home."

"Soon, after a trip to the hospital." He lifted her in his arms and carried her up the stairs, away from the hellhole and the stench of death. He could hear sirens wailing in the distance. They couldn't get there fast enough. Breeana trembled like a leaf, and he knew she was already in shock. Whipping off his shirt, he wrapped her in it. She wouldn't be going home tonight, that was for sure.

"It's over, cookie. It's finally over."

"SO, THAT'S WHY BRUISER attacked you at Rainey's?" Breeana managed to pull herself up higher in the hospital bed with Sully's help. He fluffed the pillows behind her head. The doctor had insisted on keeping her for a few days, and Sully wholeheartedly agreed. She'd been outvoted. While she wasn't happy about it, at least the intravenous pain meds dulled the worst of the throbbing in her hand.

"Right. The dog was really after Clemente. Bruiser knew Sal had killed his mistress and it was payback time." Sully passed her a glass of juice from the tray and helped her take a sip through the straw. "It's one of those times when I wish animals could talk.

"I think Bruiser may have also saved your life. After leaving the rosary in your bedroom, Clemente couldn't go back inside your house once you brought the dog home. He was scared to death of the Rottweiler. I remember him making the sign of the cross and drawing his weapon when I first opened the door to Rainey's laundry room. He knew Bruiser wanted to kill him."

"What I don't understand is how The Shepherd planned to get me out of the house, after the pizza was delivered with the tranquilizers. Wouldn't Bruiser have attacked him then?"

Sully bent to brush a kiss at her temple. Then he scooted her over in the bed and slid in beside her. Wrapping an arm around her shoulders, he hugged her close. Laying her head against his chest, she was comforted by the steady beat of his heart.

"Bruiser wouldn't have had the chance. He would have shot the dog while we were all out cold. But, he couldn't take the chance on coming by the house beforehand. He knew what would happen if

Bruiser went after him in front of me. He would have headed my suspect's list, for sure."

She sighed. "I'm so glad it's over. I want to put this behind us and go on with our lives."

He skimmed his fingers along her cheek and brought her mouth up to meet his, melting her with a heart-stopping kiss. Gathering her in his arms as if she was porcelain and would break, he smoothed a hand down her back. "I know, cookie, and if you behave yourself, the doctor will release you tomorrow. In the meantime, we'll just have to pretend we're already home."

"Hey, 'hot lips'! What are you doing in bed with my mom? She's injured...or haven't ya noticed?"

Cody and her father had entered the room. Sully's team filed in close behind them, except for Hawke, who occupied a room down the hall. Sully had mentioned Cody and her dad would fly back today. Her brain must be fuzzy from the meds because she'd lost track of time. Breeana could feel a flush rising from her toes to the top of her head. Sully eased away from her as Cody came forward into her arms.

"It's great to see you, Mom. Looks like I got here just in time. Boy, the lieutenant has more moves than Micah, and that's saying a lot."

"Relax, pal," Sully laughed. "It was only a harmless kiss."

"I don't know. Gramps, what do you think?"

Jack eyed Sully thoughtfully, a devilish glint in his eyes. "We'll have a private chat with the lieutenant later. I'm sure he was just about to heave his carcass out of my daughter's bed, anyway. Right, Lieutenant?"

"Not if I had my way," Sully muttered under his breath, then shot Breeana a wolfish grin, and planted another wet kiss on her mouth before swinging his feet to the floor. "We were just discussing Sal Clemente and how he managed to keep himself off the suspect's list."

"It must have given him one hell of a shock when Sergeant Millette called Rainey Dubé's death in to your homicide squad," Theo said.

"I imagine it did. All his other murders had gone undetected and the last thing he wanted was to have Homicide involved. I remember how sick he looked when I first arrived at the murder scene. He blamed it on eating cold pizza." Sully rubbed a hand along the back of his neck. "On the other hand, once we took over the investigation, he was able to manipulate the facts."

"How did he manage to tamper with evidence without getting caught?" Micah asked.

"It's not difficult, considering he worked the case. Clemente monitored the surveillance feed from the docks of The Shepherd trapping rats. He claimed a clear picture of The Shepherd never appeared on those tapes. Forensics called me an hour ago. The tapes were doctored. I'm guessing Clemente removed any video footage of himself."

"But, why did he kill the church secretary?" Reece wanted to know.

"Because Hannah Grimes was his mother. Although, oddly enough, I don't think he really wanted to kill her. But, he didn't have a choice, not when he knew we would question her. He must have been afraid she would tell us about him."

"You planned to ask her about those rosaries stolen from St. Pat's all those years ago?"

"Right, Bree. I'm guessing she knew he took the rosaries. Clemente had no idea if she'd rat him out. He knew his mother despised him. Yet, even with that, he may have wanted to keep her alive so he'd still have an excuse to murder other women. Joelle believes he envisioned murdering his mother with every innocent life he took. She also believes he had some unhealthy fantasies about her."

"Oh-oh, information overload." Cody clutched his throat and forced a gag.

"Do you know how he chose his victims?" Law interrupted, laughing at her son's antics. "I've never understood how psychopaths decide who's going to live and who's going to die."

"I know how he chose Miranda, Rainey and me," Breeana offered, trying to get more comfortable in the bed. "He followed us home from St. Patrick's Cathedral after mass. He was furious with us, because Father Mike was giving the sermon and we walked out in the middle of it, when the priest started saying incredibly vile, horrible things about women. We couldn't sit there any longer and listen to his poison."

"I'm not surprised," Sully said. "Father Mike was Clemente's biological father and the fruit didn't fall far from the tree. The priest and Hannah had been having an affair for years. And I believe they abused Sal as a child."

Breeana shuddered, and Sully slipped his arm around her shoulders again. "I can't believe a mother would hurt her son for any reason."

"I know, cookie, but remember...both of his parents were total whack jobs."

Hunt shuffled on his feet. "I guess it doesn't make much sense, but I almost feel sorry for the guy."

"Even after what he did to Breeana?" Sully carefully took her injured hand, which was wrapped in a cast, and raised it off the pillow a few inches. "I can't feel sorry for him. He killed innocent women, and my guess? He used his badge to get close to them. So, there were never any signs of a struggle. We found a tackle box in his beach shack where he hid souvenirs from his kills. Plus, he almost murdered Cody. I would kill him again if I had to.

"While I might grieve for Sal Clemente the child, I have no sympathy, whatsoever, for the man he became. The Shepherd was nothing but a cold-blooded killer who preyed on women to satisfy his sick cravings," Sully added.

"Oh, oh, Gramps," Cody snickered. "It's time to roll up my ears and tuck them in my head. It sounds like Sully's going to talk about kinky sex. Micah hasn't explained those things to me yet."

"Mic!" Sully growled. "What have you been teaching the kid while you guys were recuperating?"

"Will you relax, Sully?" Breeana saw Micah roll his eyes and wink at both her son and her father. "We only had normal conversations about the birds and bees. I would never tell Cody anything his own grandfather wouldn't want to teach him."

"I'm not so sure, Mic," Sully said, curling his lip.

"Hey." Cody's grandfather interrupted. "Why don't we let Breeana get some rest and play a little poker over at my place? I'll supply the beer and cigars."

"Sweet, Gramps. Let's go see if Hawke wants to get in on the action. We could always break him out of here for a couple of hours. Let's go, guys!"

Breeana lay against the pillows and laughed until tears ran down her cheeks and her stomach hurt. The expression on Sully's face was priceless. He clearly had no idea what life with Cody and her father was all about. After they all filed out and he had a moment to regroup, he cupped her chin in his warm hands, tenderly lifting her face.

"Bree? I love you beyond belief." He gazed into her eyes with something close to terror in his own. "It took almost losing you to realize I don't want to live my life without you. I never thought it could happen to me. I'm lousy at relationships and I don't know how this will end."

"Well, maybe it doesn't have to end," she whispered. "Why don't we take it one step at a time and see where it takes us? Because, Sully, I love you too, and I don't want to lose you."

"Aw, cookie," he groaned, carefully moving over her on the bed, still holding her face between his hands and kissing her lips. "I'm a lousy prospect for marriage. I live life in the dangerous lane and there's always the risk I won't make it home to you one night. It wouldn't be fair to you, or Cody."

Breeana's heart plunged as if it would shatter in a million pieces. She loved Sully so completely. She knew he would never hang up his shield, or stop fighting for the innocent. It was who he was. The man she loved. She was more than willing to take the risk of being a part of his life, for as long as he wanted her. "Sometimes you think too much. Go lock the door and show me how much you love me."

"Now that's something I can handle."

Chapter 20

Sully brought Breeana home the next morning and carried her upstairs to her bedroom. "How about taking a nice hot shower?"

"It depends. Are you offering to scrub my back?" She wrapped her arms around his neck and winked at him. "If you are, we'll have to hurry. Cody and my father will be back from the arena soon."

"There's an offer I can't refuse, if you're sure you're up to it. Just let me put the dogs out in the yard. I'll get the water started in a minute."

He set her down on the bed, ran downstairs, and pulled up short as two pairs of eyes drilled into him. Cody and Jack were already home. If looks could kill, Sully figured he'd be choking on his last breath right about now.

"Good morning, Lieutenant."

"Morning, Jack," he mumbled.

"Hockey practice was cancelled and we're home early. We were just about to have breakfast." Jack led them into the kitchen and reached in the cupboard for three bowls. He slammed them down on the counter next to an apple-cinnamon pie. Then he tossed the pie into the microwave and scowled in Sully's direction. "So, before you take a shower with my daughter, you'll be joining us."

"Right. Don't mind if I do, Jack." The scent of fear mixed with sweat oozed from Sully's pores. He'd sooner be facing the Son of Sam than going up against the tag team of Cody and Jack. There wouldn't be a trial. They'd go straight for the lynching, and he sure couldn't blame them.

He was guilty, caught red-handed last night in a hospital bed sampling the spoils of victory, rolling on the sheets with Cody's mother and Jack's daughter, however innocently. And, now they'd heard him talking about taking a shower with her. Maybe he should just shoot himself and get it over with. Hell, he probably deserved it.

Cody slammed the freezer door and the vanilla ice cream he carried landed with a thud on the counter beside his grandfather. Forest deftly cut the warmed pie into three slabs and smashed it into bowls. Cody followed along behind with an ice cream scoop and heaped the slices à la mode.

"Would you mind telling me what you were doing in bed, lip-sucking my mom last night?" Cody said. "Was it supposed to be your idea of mouth-to-mouth resuscitation, or what? I'd hate to think I have to slug you for hitting on my injured mom. But I'll do it, and I'll take the consequences for assaulting a police officer while I'm at it."

"There's no need to get physical, Cody. I can explain." Needing to do something with his hands, Sully grabbed chocolate sauce from the nearest shelf and squirted it over the ice cream.

"We're listening, Lieutenant," Jack said, smiling darkly as he flicked maraschino cherries over the chocolate sauce in the bowls, managing to spray Sully's shirt in the process. "We'd like to hear your explanation...wouldn't we, Cody?"

The kid was busy shaking a whipped cream canister, landing a glob in Sully's hair before maneuvering the nozzle over the heaping concoctions. "Yeah, Gramps. I leave home for a few days and come back to find this dude sniffing around my mom, even after I warned him off. It had better be good."

Sully routed around with his head in the pantry, until his hand landed on a jar of chopped nuts. Mindlessly, he opened the cap and heaped them into the bowls. "The truth is I screwed up... You know, like sometimes happens with teenagers?"

Damn! Why should he have to explain his actions to Cody and his grandfather? It was embarrassing as hell. He was a man, full grown. He shouldn't have to give the details of his love life to anybody, least of all Breeana's family.

"Well, you're no teenager," Cody scoffed. "And even *I* know you have to keep a handle on your actions after your brain leaves the building. Gramps and I have discussed it, about taking responsibility; haven't we, Gramps?"

Sully almost slid to the floor at Cody's revelation. Thirteen, and he was already discussing sex with his grandfather. He was still a kid. Wasn't he too young to be having those conversations?

"The way Gramps tells it, a man's got to keep his *screw ups* under control, unless he's planning to marry the lady in question—which would be *my* mother. Do you have anything to add, Gramps?"

"Nah, I couldn't have said it better myself. I think I'll just sit back with my breakfast and let you handle the manly stuff in the family."

Jack added bananas as the final topping to their breakfast, slid spoons into the bowls, and set them onto the table in the sunroom, nodding for the others to take their seats. "So what's the deal here, Sully?"

Marriage seems to be the deal, he thought. And if Cody and Jack had their way it was going to be a shotgun affair.

Marriage? The word stuck in his craw as he attacked the mountain of syrupy gloop dripping from his spoon and brought it to his mouth. Yet, wasn't it his need for permanency with Breeana that had confused him from the beginning?

Since he'd first laid eyes on her, in fact? Hellfire, he was hopelessly in love with her. He'd rather die than live without her. The thought struck him like an epiphany, claps of thunder and bolts of lightning zinging around in his brain. *Marriage? Why not?*

"Cody, I swear to you, I love your mother. And I do want to marry her." He caught the glance passing from grandson to grandfather but couldn't get a read on it. "What do you say? Do I have your permission to ask her to marry me?"

Jack nodded to his grandson. "The decision's yours, son. I'll go along with whatever you decide."

Cody eyed Sully as he swirled his spoon between his fingers. "Hmm, if you marry my mom, does it mean you'll want me around? 'Cuz it's a package deal, you know? I'm not ready to leave yet and someone's got to stick around to keep an eye on things when you're out doing your police and military stuff."

"Absolutely, I wouldn't have it any other way. We'd be a family, Cody." He heaved a sigh of relief and reached out to clasp the teen's shoulder.

"Hold up a minute. Not so fast." The kid winked slyly at his grandfather. "And will you promise to practice with the team and take us to hockey games at the Bell Center sometimes?"

"You bet I'll practice with the team." Sully fought to keep the grin off his face. "I'll even spring for tickets to the NHL games when I can."

Cody was on a roll. "And will you keep your hormones under control, at least until the wedding day? I don't want to have to walk around the house blindfolded, so I don't see your sick moves on my mom."

"Ah, *that* I won't promise you. It's normal for people in love to kiss and hug each other, pal."

"Well, just don't get any ideas about kissing *me*, Sully, but you can hug me if you want to, as long as it's not in front of the guys."

"The same applies to me," Jack said. "You can hug me if you want, but no kisses. Now come on, group hug before we ditch the evidence of our breakfast. God knows, Breeana will kill us all if she sees what we just put into our stomachs. What's all the mess on your shirt and in your hair, Sully? Did your spoon have a hole in it?"

Cody's eyes cut to Sully again. "So, how are you going to propose to Mom? I know! You should do it at the arena at center ice. Yeah, what a great idea. The WARRIORS can watch from the stands. Come on, what do you say?"

"In your dreams." Sully collected their bowls and headed for the dogs' dishes in the kitchen with the leftovers. "I am *not* proposing to your mother in a grungy arena with you and your socially inept, scuz-bucket friends watching. You can just forget about it. A marriage proposal is a private moment between two people who love each other. We'll fill you in on the details after it's done."

"You better not be feeding any crap to the dogs!" Jack bellowed from the sunroom, his nose buried in the sports page of the newspaper. Sully knew better than to cross Jack and promptly did an about-face in the direction of the garbage can.

Epilogue

"What a great idea you had, Dad, having a cook-out." Breeana passed him the barbeque sauce. "The whole town has shown up."

"I know. It's terrific, isn't it?" He toasted her with his beer stein as he continued to flip burgers on the grill. "It's been a few days since the god awful night when I almost lost you to The Shepherd. We have so much to celebrate."

"Yes, we do."

"You know, pumpkin, I'm not known for making long-winded speeches, but I need to get something off my chest. Sullivan killed the scum-sucking bastard and rescued you, as well as saving my grandson."

"He was amazing. But what are you getting at?"

"My question is...will the lieutenant be smart enough to hold onto you? You'd think the man would've made his move by now. I'd be real proud to have him as my son-in-law."

Only time will tell, she thought. "Listen, how about letting me manage my love life, and you focus on those burgers you're cooking."

"You're right, honey. Besides, after what everyone's been through around here, I think I'm the only one left standing who's healthy enough to cook the food."

"I know what you mean. Sully's Spec Ops team all seem a little worse for wear."

"You've got to be kidding." Jack grinned when he glanced in their general direction down by the lake. The group was swarmed with gorgeous, available females, all vying for the team's attention. "You could have fooled me. Still, Hawke is going to have one hell of a headache for another few days, according to the doctor. But, it doesn't seem to be stopping him from flirting with the Taylor twins."

Breeana tipped back her head and laughed. "I don't think the women of Mallard Bay have seen this much hunkiness since the *Chippendales* came to Montreal."

"You're probably right about that. You'd better inform the ladies the guys are leaving town in the morning."

"Will do." She ambled away from the barbeque and admired the view down to the lake. The back lawn was festively decked out with Chinese lanterns strung through the trees. Lawn chairs were gathered in cozy groupings across the wide expanse of grass. The sounds of "golden oldies" drifted on the warm summer breeze.

The scent of citronella candles floated through the air to keep mosquitoes at bay. Two long picnic tables were set up on the deck with navy and white checkered tablecloths, napkins, plastic utensils, and condiments. Tubs of ice water chilled the sodas, wine coolers, and beer.

Her father and Cody had been busy since yesterday setting it up. Now all *she* had to do was wait for Sully to pop the big question. Heck, it was time the man worked up his nerve to do it. He could take on terrorists and serial killers without batting an eyelash, and yet, he was scared of her. *Go figure?*

Sully found her alone on the dock as she watched the sky fill with a blazing sunset. He came up behind her, pulled her against his chest, planted a kiss behind her ear, and wrapped his arms around her waist. "Hey, cookie. How's the hand?"

"The pain's almost gone, but Dad will perform surgeries at the clinic for another month, until the bones mend and I can get the mobility back in my fingers."

"I don't think Jack will complain, considering he has you and Cody back."

"That's what he said." Breeana turned in his arms to stare up at him. "He has you to thank."

"Shh." He pressed his lips to her neck and held her tighter, rubbing her back in familiar circles. "It's over now. I didn't come down here to talk to you about the past. Right now I need to talk to you about something else, something I can't wait on any longer."

"What—?"

"Don't talk, just listen. Okay?" He blew out a breath in her hair. "The truth is...I mean, without you...I can't imagine..."

"Come on, 'hot lips'. Even *you* can do better than that!" Cody's head popped up alongside the dock, his body submerged underwater, his hands grasping the wooden planks to hold him in place. Three of his friends treaded water not far from him. "See? What did I tell you, guys? The man's never going to be able to pop the big question if we don't help him out."

The other boys snickered in response.

Cody grinned at Sully and winked at her. "Can we hurry it up a little, Lieutenant? Gramps is just about to serve dessert and it's an old family recipe. Smashed hot apple pie with all the fixings like whipped cream, ice cream, chocolate sauce, nuts, bananas, and cherries. Man-oh-man, I can taste it now."

Her son didn't slow down as he continued. "Now, just tell Mom you want to marry her, plant one on her, and we can all move up to the house and tuck ourselves into the pie. I have to make up for all the food I missed while I was making like Rip Van Winkle."

Sully stared dumbstruck at Cody before swiveling his head back to her.

"Well, what do you say, Bree? Will you marry me and put me out of my misery?" He kissed her on the lips and held onto her, waiting for her response as he whispered. "I love you, with all my heart."

He held his breath, as if daring to hope. It gave her a glimmer of their future together. He loved her, all right, hopefully half as much as she loved him.

"Oh, yes, I'll marry you. I think I've been in love with you ever since I met you," she whispered back. Chuckling, she raised her voice just a little. "What took you so long to ask me, big guy?"

"I'm a little slow on the upswing. But, since I've popped the big question and you've given me the right answer—for better or for worse—you're stuck with me on a real long-term basis."

He took the ring, from a box he carried in his pocket, and slipped it on her finger. "I'm just plain crazy about you, Bree."

"An emerald!" Breeana held out her hand to catch the fire of the setting sun in the shimmering stone. "Oh, Sully. It's perfect! How did you know I've always wanted an emerald?"

"I didn't know. I bought it because it matches your eyes."

"Hoo-rah!" The boys in the water high-fived each other, leaped onto the dock, and hugged her and Sully in soggy embraces. Then they were off and running, up to the house and the waiting family recipe.

"See? What did I tell you?" Cody exclaimed. "I knew Sully could ask Mom to marry him if we gave him a helping hand. It's a good thing we stuck around to give him the benefit of Micah's expertise. Did you see the rock he planted on her? Way to go, 'hot lips'!"

Breeana was helping Sully outside with clean-up duty when Theo jogged across the lawn.

"Hey, have you got a minute?"

"Sure. Let's walk." Sully wrapped an arm around her, putting a hand on Theo's shoulder and guiding them to the side of the house. His brother seemed upset by something. "What's up?"

"In all the excitement over your engagement tonight, I almost hate to give you some other news."

Breeana eyed Theo. He was still battered and bruised, but there was a flash of heat in his dark eyes. "What's happened?"

"You remember at the lake when I told you about Sarah Davidson's murder? Well, I just found out Mel Salera, the slime ball who mysteriously inherited the Davidson estate, is one Melena Salera. A woman. Doc Finley just called me with the news.

"The woman responded to my voice mails by going to Silver Lake on her own and planting herself on Sarah's property. Doc told her I was away—taking care of some other business. I'm heading back there tonight to go a round, or two, with her."

"No way, Theo," Sully said. "It takes a hell of a lot of nerve for her to show up and take over. She must be in an all-fired hurry to collect on Sarah's estate."

"I kid you not, and apparently, she is one gorgeous piece of work for a cold-blooded killer. I'm going to enjoy making her life a living hell while we nail her for Sarah's murder. Let me know when you get those autopsy results, bro, and then we can start building a case."

"Will do, but be careful, Theo. Remember your stint with JTF2? Some of the world's most deadly assassins are women, beautiful ones. They will kill as ruthlessly as men, without warning, or conscience."

"Hey, I hear you."

"And Theo? Remember something else," Breeana said. "Maybe she isn't guilty."

"We all know there isn't much chance of that." Theo sighed, kissed her on the cheek, and took his brother's hand in a firm grip. "Take care of your lady and future son, man. I'm jealous as hell, but I couldn't be happier for you. What you two have will last a lifetime. I can feel it."

"Thanks for everything." Sully reeled him in for a back-slapping hug. "I mean it. Without you, I might have lost them both."

"Just let me know when those wedding bells are slated to jingle. If I remember correctly, I offered to be the flower girl."

"Right, you did." Sully winked at the mountain of a man who was almost his mirror image. "You'll look stunning in a dress, but you might want to wax your legs."

After so much unhappiness and uncertainty, the sound of their laughter was music to Breeana's ears. She hugged her future brother-in-law before wrapping herself in Sully's solid embrace. They strolled hand-in-hand with Theo to his rental car, the dogs loping along behind them.

Rainey had been laid to rest in a quiet ceremony that morning, and although Breeana would miss her and Miranda, at least she was coming to terms with her grief. She cried a little less every day and remembered the good times they had shared a whole lot more.

She had Cody back and the love of the man standing beside her to see her through.

Yes, life was as it should be.

In Mallard Bay.

THANK YOU FOR READING this book. I hope you enjoyed it but even if you didn't, please take a few moments to go back online where you purchased it and leave an honest review. Authors absolutely depend on reviews to know how readers feel about their books and series. Thank you, it's appreciated.

For a free book, please hop over to my website at **https://www.kallielane.com**

A word about the author...

This is me in a nutshell. I was raised in Montreal and still have a home there, although most of my thriller and suspense novels come alive in my writing den, at a small cottage I love in the mountains. I guess I've always been a country girl at heart.

My constant companions these days are a Rottweiler, an American Bully, and a cat rescue. I'm widowed and have two adult sons who, I'm sure, worry about what trouble I'm getting into on a daily basis. Case in point; I've managed to break a few bones and dislocate others over the last few years when 'playing' with my dogs. While they are advanced obedience trained and a pleasure to have, I sometimes roughhouse with them a little too much. I also enjoy taking the boat out in the wee hours of the morning to see the stars and the night sky at the cottage. But, yes, I always have my cell phone handy. I'm sure if I didn't answer, someone would call 9-1-1.

I worked in the pharmaceutical and biotech industries for several years, and now I can finally enjoy writing as my real job, which I've dreamt about doing since I was a teenager. Wowzers! How lucky can a girl be? My spare time is shared with family and friends, including writer friends, and I work out to keep myself in shape, rather than dog wrestling! I'm an avid reader and spend more time with a book or tablet in my hands than watching television. Oh, I also like to travel, whether it's for business or pleasure, but I'm mostly found at the keyboard fulfilling my passion for writing.

I love to hear from readers, so please drop me an email at kallie_lane@ymail.com and I promise I'll message back. Lastly, I hope you enjoyed what you read. I would love it if you would leave a review where you purchased this book. It matters to me (and all authors) how you feel about our stories. Wishing you the very best!

To learn more about Kallie, visit her website at **https://www.kallielane.com** or follow her on Facebook at **http://www.facebook.com/KallieLaneAuthor**

Here's a sneak peek at book 2 in the Shadow Soldiers Suspense series, available wherever you purchased book 1...

Dark Abandon
Chapter 1

Silver Lake

Melena Salera downshifted on the curve of serpentine road, revving the RPMs to clear the top of the next rise. She shifted smoothly into fourth gear, after cresting the peak, and opened up the big V8 on the straightaway. The vintage '76 Firebird roared along the winding ribbon of asphalt, the upbeat tempo of *Higher Love* cranking through the speakers. Melena joined in and belted out the chorus. She tapped the rhythm on the steering wheel until a movement in her peripheral vision caught her attention. She slammed on the brakes with both feet. A deer gamboled across the highway as the Firebird screeched to a shuddering halt.

Clenching her teeth, she swallowed the lump in her throat that might have been her breakfast burrito while the deer trotted for cover on the opposite bank of road. Too late, Melena remembered those deer crossing signs she had ignored for the last several miles and breathed a huge sigh of relief. The deer had escaped unharmed. Fingers still clutching the steering wheel, she started off again, this time at a sedate pace with the radio switched off.

She wrapped her scattered thoughts around the reason for making this trip into the wilderness. Well, perhaps not quite the wilderness, but she was a city girl and anything outside the burbs was like the boondocks to her.

Her return flight to Montreal had touched down from Chicago that morning. As a sales trainer for a leading pharmaceutical company with branches in both the U.S. and Canada, Melena travelled back and forth regularly.

Based on the urgent nature of the messages left on her answering machine, she had retrieved her car from airport parking, used GPS to get directions, and, with her usual impulsiveness, sped the hundred and thirty kilometers into the Laurentian mountain region. A sign for Silver Lake glinted in the sun and she angled into the turn. It wouldn't be long now before she came face-to-face with the owner of that smooth-as-cognac voice. Although, were she honest with herself, the lawyer had sounded surly when he demanded she meet him at Silver Lake. Even so, his voice had been full-bodied and rich, a voice capable of stirring any woman's fantasies.

Oh, right, Mel. He is probably five feet tall, is bald as a billiard ball and weighs over three hundred pounds. When are you going to get it through your head? Knights in shining armor are only found in romance novels.

By the time she pulled up to the boat docks, the road had dead-ended at the water. Where was she supposed to meet the lawyer? Noting a white-clapboard building, a general store with gas pumps and a phone booth out front, she parked her ride. A bell tinkled when she opened the door to the store.

An older man, pear-shaped, dressed in tan shorts and a T-shirt with a fishing hat perched on his head, chatted with the reed-thin woman behind the counter. Melena nodded at them then headed for the row of fridges at the back of the store. Her sandals scraped the linoleum as their voices followed her up the narrow aisle.

"Doc, is there any news yet on the funeral service for Sarah Davidson?"

"Nothing yet, Stella. Theo hasn't had a chance to iron out the details. He charged out of here a few days ago to deal with an emergency in Mallard Bay. He should be back tomorrow at the latest."

"I hope so. The women's auxiliary needs to prepare the food and set everything up for the luncheon," Stella grumbled.

Melena processed that bit of news. *Theo? Could he be the lawyer, Theo Sauvage, who contacted me?* She had raced here to meet him and he wasn't even available.

Doc's voice continued as she stopped at a rack loaded with chips to the left of the cash register, pretending to look while she eavesdropped. "Theo told me he needs to speak with a friend of Sarah's, a man named Mel Salera before he can arrange for her burial."

Melena swallowed a gasp. She didn't know anyone named Sarah. *Why would the lawyer need to contact me about the woman's funeral arrangements? And why does he think I'm a man?*

"I don't know anything more than that." Doc rubbed his chin as though deep in thought. He pushed back the brim of his fishing hat to run a hand over his thinning hair. "Either way, the funeral will be held in the next few days. Theo is not going to drag it out longer than necessary. He loved Sarah like a grandmother."

"We all loved her, Doc," Stella said, a sad note in her voice. "It's hard to believe she's gone."

Her mind reeling, Melena abandoned the chips rack, paid for the soda, and left the store with the couple still deep in conversation. Her curiosity was peaked. *What's this all about?* Even if the lawyer wasn't available, she should at least talk to the locals to find out what was going on. Jogging down the stairs, she headed for the waterfront while formulating a plan.

Oomph! She ploughed into a wall of solid muscle. Strong fingers snaked her wrists as the man's gaze raked her body with chilling insolence, his mouth forming a sneer as he catalogued her diminutive size, spiky hair and icy stare.

He dressed to impress. Designer labels galore. Gold chains hung around his neck with enough karats to pay Melena's grocery bill for a year. His dark hair was tied at the nape with a strip of leather. Not unpleasant to look at, but repulsive all the same.

It was obvious that he liked to control. He also liked to inflict pain, judging by his grip on her wrists. *A sleaze with money.* The harder she tried to break his hold, the harder he held on. *Damn him.*

She glanced around, hoping to catch someone's attention since she couldn't reach the cell phone in her pocket. Not that calling 9-1-1 would do any good. There probably wasn't a police station for miles.

Cripes, no-one on the docks was near enough to see she was in trouble. Short of screeching her head off, she was on her own with this thug. And pride wouldn't allow her to scream. Not yet, anyway.

"You know," he challenged, pulling her harder against him, "a woman could get hurt throwing herself at the wrong man."

"Really? Not if the man in question gets slammed in his cul-de-sac," she snapped, shoving her leg between his thighs. "You have five seconds to release me before I knee your junk to hell and back. One...two...three..."

Anger flashed in his eyes. He didn't let go. She wouldn't back down, praying he wouldn't notice her trembling as she tensed her leg muscles to deliver the promised blow.

"Bitch." He released her on the count of five then cocked a thumb and index finger in her direction. "I owe you one."

"Jerk." Melena got her feet moving, skirted around him, and headed for the docks. His glare burned a hole between her shoulder blades as she hustled toward the safety of families loading provisions into their boats. She forced herself to relax and put the idiot out of her mind. By the time Doc meandered down to the lake a short time later, she had herself under control. She fell into step beside him.

"I heard you talking at the store. I'm Melena Salera, the person Theo Sauvage is trying to contact. He's obviously not here, and I don't know where to find him. Can you help me out?"

Pulling up short, Doc set down his gas can and eyeballed her with an arctic blast. *Why the chilling stare?* She struggled to hold her ground and wait him out. A moment later and his bitter expression morphed into a grin. *What in heaven's name is the matter with him?*

"Theo will be back tomorrow morning at the latest," he said. "He booked a room for you at the local B & B on the off chance you showed up. You'll be mighty comfortable there."

"I don't know..." Melena yearned to sleep in her own bed tonight. This seemed like a wild goose chase. Still, she was exhausted, too tired to move really, much less drive back to Montreal. Besides, the thought of coming all this way for nothing rankled. Her bulging shoulder bag bumped against her hip as she tugged it higher, reminding her of its contents, everything from passport, keys and wallet to a change of clothes, toothbrush and cosmetics.

She never travelled without overnight amenities in her purse when she checked her luggage on a flight. Everything she needed to spend the night was right there, so why not bunk in and wait it out? "All right, I'll stay, but I can only stay one night. If the lawyer doesn't show tomorrow, I'm headed home."

"Can't ask for more than that, little lady." Doc did a little jig, picked up the gas can again and hustled for the docks, snagging her elbow and dragging her along. "Come on. Let me gas up my boat and I'll take you to the Home Sweet Home B & B."

Yikes! Is the man harmless or insane?

Muttering under her breath, she asked herself, "Should I go with him?"

Fool that she was...she went.

Maybe not her smartest or smoothest move. Her nose crinkled in disgust. It was possible no one at the B & B would know anything about Theo's reason for summoning her to the lake. Still, Melena intended to investigate and see if she could discover why the lawyer had insisted on meeting her. Pumping Doc for information ended up being a colossal waste of time. His lips were sealed shut on the subject. She settled instead for the rush of wind on her face, sunshine reflecting off foam-green waves, and the vista of rustic cottages dotting the mountainous shoreline as they travelled down the lake.

According to Doc, the bed and breakfast was on a private island leading into the last bay. A half hour later, he pulled up alongside a boathouse, threw the fishing boat into neutral, and leaned over the side to grab hold of the pier. Melena jumped for the dock while he stretched a hand up to her with keys dangling from his fingers.

"What's this?" she asked, reaching for the ring full of old skeleton keys.

"The keys to the castle, my lady," he said, pushing away from shore before she could drop back onto the boat. "Follow the path through the trees and you'll come to a house. The big brass key is the one for the front door."

"Hold up a minute!" Panic set in with the realization Doc had pulled a fast one. "What happened to my reservation at the B & B? I want to go there. I'm not staying here by myself."

"Hells fire, there is no B & B. Didn't want to tell you before 'cause I knew you'd take off without talking to Theo. But you'll be real comfortable at Sarah's house. Plus, if Theo is delayed until tomorrow, I'll come back and check up on you. Meantime, quit your whining and get a move on. The fridge is full and you can make yourself at home." Doc reached down to adjust something on the boat. "Oh, before I forget, if you see Doodlebug, you be sure to feed him. He gets ornery when he's hungry. Actually, you should leave a door open for him, in case he gets the urge to come on home."

"Did you say doodlebug?" Doc said nothing, staring at her as if she was whining again, and waited her out. "Okay, I'll bite. What's a doodlebug?"

"Well, now," Doc harrumphed. "Doodlebug is Sarah's lap dog. He headed into the bush the night of the *accident,* and he hasn't been seen since."

"Uh-huh." Melena glared at him then eyed the distance between the boat and the dock, wondering if she could make it. Six feet was a little too much for her to jump. The old coot knew how to throw a sucker punch. "Well, since you're stranding me here, I'll make sure I feed him...if I see him."

Melena loved animals and felt instant compassion for the poor little creature. How many nights had he been alone in the woods? Besides, he'd be welcome company for her.

"Now that everything's settled, I'll contact Theo in Mallard Bay and let him know you've arrived. He'll be right anxious to make your acquaintance."

Doc backed away and threw his boat into a forward thrust, Melena gawking as he rammed his hat down on his head, gunned the engine, and tore out of the bay. "Good luck, Mata Hari. You're going to need it."

She threw her hands up in frustration while mulling over his parting words. He obviously guessed she intended to snoop around since he'd brought her here. Why else would he refer to her as a famous female spy?

Undeterred, she hiked the path through thick forest until Sarah's house popped into view on a terraced clearing with its rough-hewn logs, natural shellac with forest-green trim and matching tin roof. Window boxes overflowed with red geraniums and white begonias. Hummingbirds flitted to bright red feeders hanging beneath the porch eaves. Melena climbed the stairs onto a wide-planked porch and inhaled a deep breath of pine fragrance.

Her conscience prickled for a few seconds. Her self-appointed role of investigator weighed her down. Her actions were an invasion of the dead woman's privacy. Still, she'd been dumped here by Doc and had nowhere else to go. She might as well do what she came to do.

The key turned smoothly in its lock. Remembering the missing dog, Melena braced the door open with her handbag before she entered the house. A sigh of pleasure escaped as she took in her surroundings. Sunlight streaming through skylights reflected burnished log walls and gleaming hardwood floors. Floor-to-ceiling windows stood on either side of a massive fieldstone fireplace, a flock of intricately carved geese poised to take flight from its mantle.

Overstuffed furnishings in bold primary colors scattered the living space. A footstool here, an occasional table there, with potted plants and trailing greenery perched on every available surface. Antique bookcases, low and rambling, held everything from the classics to contemporary suspense and historical romance novels.

The smell pervading the cabin was a pleasant blend of wood smoke, scented lamp oil, and lemon polish. A screened sundeck opened the far side of the room to rattan furniture and the outdoors. She loved the house. An oasis in a hectic world, and she suspected it reflected Sarah Davidson's easy-going lifestyle.

Melena's sense of right and wrong nudged her again for invading the dead woman's space. Her throat tightened with guilt. She sauntered to the kitchen and the fridge, hoping to find a bottle of wine to drown her scruples. No such luck. Bottled water would have to do.

Drink your water, Mel, then go find something interesting to read, and mind your own business. The lawyer will be here soon enough to toss you out on your keister.

A growl came from somewhere behind her. She froze then turned slowly toward the sound. One quick look and her legs almost folded. The largest wolf she had ever seen slinked toward her from the same doorway she had walked through a minute ago. He stared at her through flame-gold eyes, his gaze never leaving her face.

Melena had no doubt—Doodlebug had come home to roost. Except, he wasn't a pint-sized lap dog, and he wasn't happy to find a stranger in his dead mistress's kitchen. The wolf's head lowered as his ears flattened. His lips curled back to expose sharp, fanged teeth. A desperate glance told her she would never make it to the door before the animal tore her to pieces.

Eyes wide, her only defense was to mouth a silent prayer. The wolf's hackles rose. She stopped praying when he lunged toward her. A terrified giggle bubbled up as she realized she had been set up by a cunning old fox.

Touché, Doc. I'm a dead woman because of you.

An instant later, the wolf sent her crashing to the floor.